# is it
# actually
# love
### for
# Lexie
# Byrne?
### (aged 42¹/₄)

# is it
# actually
# love

*for*

# Lexie
# Byrne?

(aged 42$^{1}/_{4}$)

## Caroline Grace-Cassidy

**Black&White**

**Black&White**

First published in the UK in 2023
This edition first published in the UK in 2024 by
Black & White Publishing Ltd
Nautical House, 104 Commercial Street, Edinburgh, EH6 6NF

A division of Bonnier Books UK
4th Floor, Victoria House, Bloomsbury Square, London, WC1B 4DA
Owned by Bonnier Books
Sveavägen 56, Stockholm, Sweden

A CIP catalogue record for this book is available from the British Library.

ISBN: 978 1 78530 634 1

1 3 5 7 9 10 8 6 4 2

Typeset by Data Connection
Printed and bound in Great Britain by Clays Ltd, Elcograf S.p.A.

www.blackandwhitepublishing.com

*Sandymount Strand.*
*The Squawk Of The Seagulls.*
*The Shelly Banks.*

*For Noeleen Grace.*
*17th December 1946 – 9th May 2024.*

*Forever loved and missed mam,*
*live on, elsewhere, in here.*

# PART 1

# 1

*"At Christmas, you tell the truth."*

Mark, *Love Actually*

SHANE MACGOWAN AND KIRSTY MACCOLL trade Christmas insults from the speaker above as I set down my tray, collapse into the plastic seat and shake out my napkin.

"I'm so hungry," I say, "I could eat a cow between two bread vans."

Annemarie releases the bulging lid of her see-through plastic salad bowl and a garden of greenery explodes. I half expect David Attenborough to pop his head out.

"Ahh shite, forgot the yogurt." She slides her chair back and totters off on her wedges, back towards the food court.

Although I appear to be contentedly slobbering over my bagel, mature cheddar and red onion crisps with hot chocolate, I'm actually extremely on edge. Shoving the tray to the edge of the table, I wipe my sweating palms off one another. Just relax, Lexie, I tell myself, take a slow breath in.

Here's reason one.

You know when things just aren't right between you and your bestie? When eye contact is uneasy and those normally comfortable silences are crammed with nonsensical chit-chat? When it just feels fake? Well welcome to my world. We're behaving like this because something horrendous happened to Annemarie but she's decided to sweep it under the carpet and turn a blind eye to it. We've been trying to move past it regardless but it's awkward and our friendship has become a charade. Between you and me I'm about sixty seconds away from bursting point. It's not helping that I'm hormonally hangry and feeling like Baby in *Dirty Dancing* (my favourite movie of all time) in that scene in the rehearsal space at Kellerman's where she combusts and gives Johnny Castle a piece of her mind.

I'm internalising this frustration very well, by the way, but I made my decision. I'm calling Annemarie out on it this lunch-time! I have to speak my mind. It's actually keeping me awake at night – well that and my six-month-old baby – and a full night's sleep to me at this stage is more appealing than a two-week sun holiday in the Sicilian *White Lotus* hotel. Sliding off my black-rimmed reading glasses, I fold the handles down, place them in my hard case and snap it shut.

"Can you not close that any quieter? It's like a gun blast every time," she berates me, sitting back down elegantly with her millions of live cultures. Luckily for her, I've this carb fest to occupy my mouth . . . for now. I can demolish my lunch in record time. Jackie, my old colleague and trusted friend, used to get great craic out of timing me. What can I say? I'm a woman who likes her food. Jackie's settled in New York City now, carving out an acclaimed acting career. I tell you what, I could so do with her no-nonsense advice right now! Thankfully, she'll be home next summer for a play in Dublin's Abbey Theatre, and I can't wait. But first. Food!

"Hellooooo lover. It's time to get intimate." I turn on my sexy, raspy voice, speaking directly to the bagel, clamp it with both hands. "Let's get this Christmas party started!" I raise it up in front of my mouth, tilt my head and take a generous, welcome bite before the onion and sage stuffing falls out.

"Mmmmmmmmmmmmm." I roll my baby blues and groan loudly at its salty deliciousness.

"You haven't just walked in on George Clooney in the shower, Lexie! I can see the whites of your eyes." Annemarie snorts, her miniature flashing Christmas tree earrings on spirals bobbing up and down.

"Mmmmmmmmmmmmmm! Om nom nom nom!" I shimmy my sturdy shoulders, fold one generous thigh over the other and swing my leg freely. Groaning with extra exaggeration but inside wondering how she's going to react to what I have to say after I devour this? The bells are ringing out for Christmas day above me as I catch a glimpse of Rachel and Polly, rounding the cash desks. I focus my attention on them, turning sideways in my seat. The desks are magnificently decorated, draped in emerald green and ruby-red tinsel, inset with twinkling fairy lights. Miniature Poinsettia plants perch on top of each till, their bracts all contrasting colours under the fluorescent lighting. It's quite the contrast this quiet, understated Silverside shopping centre perfection, compared to the overwrought shoppers this Friday lunchtime, less than a week before Christmas.

"Why have you turned away from me? That was a joke, but oh-kayyyyy, whatever, Period Pam," she murmurs, raking up her grassy-grains while my carnivorous tastebuds explode. At least Jackie used to participate in lunch, which by definition is "a meal eaten in the middle of the day". Not the garden of goodness followed by the splodge of gloopy-gloop with pine nuts and unpronounceable-seeds that Annemarie's consuming. Don't even get me started on the time she bought me a jar of Kimchi and my apartment stank like sewers on a hot day for a week!

"I'm popping the Primrose so don't give me that!" I manage to respond through my half-full mouth despite the anxiety I can feel getting revved up to flood my veins.

"How'rya Lexie." I look up. "Just wanted to wish you a fab Christmas, chicken." It's Rachel, part of our domestic team. She propels her wide, furry, blue brush past me, then does a very impressive twirl with the lengthy handle, her partner Polly traipsing slowly behind.

"Same to you, Rach. Nice date." I snigger, pointing to her brush. She holds the tip of the handle, throws her head back dramatically and follows it with a low backward leg kick á la Maureen O' Hara.

"She's a supermodel, walks for Stella McCartney. Her and Kate Moss used to hang out, go everywhere together before she got *clean*." She spins the brush upside down, struts across the floor with her hips swinging high, bobbing the brush up and down, making it look freakily like it's walking on its own.

This strikes me as so funny that I hoot. It's the release of anxious energy I need. In fact I laugh so much I'm in danger of choking on my bagel. I pat my neck and swallow. "Come're, did you manage to get accommodation in Galway for Christmas?" Dabbing my mouth with my recycled napkin I take a gulp of hot chocolate to wash it down.

"Not yet but we're on cancellation lists for a few fancy hotels, with spas. I need me a sauna and jacuzzi, ya know? Heat up these intermittent fasting bones. We'll get a room, chicken. If there's one thing I'm sure of in this life it's that people's plans are always cancelled last minute. Me granny always used to say the devil fools with the best laid plans."

"Ain't that the truth." I receive that with a stiff nod. That quote literally sums up my life this last year: so many cancelled plans with my man. "Going to take a trip along the coast on your mopeds?" The longer I keep Rachel talking, the less anxious I'm becoming about confronting Annemarie.

"Hell, no. There'll be feck all trekking along the Wild Atlantic Way for us in sub-zero conditions, just chillaxing. I'm not getting off my fat hole for three whole days and I cannot wait." She sticks out her tongue as I see a flash of silver from her stud piercing then she spins the brush back around.

"You don't have a fat hole," I tell her, tensing my own curvaceous backside in the hard chair.

"No, that's coz of the intermittent fasting but I've earned one! I bloody better have one by next week coz all I'm planning to do is to stuff it, morning, noon and night! Galway mussels in spicy tomato sauce and creamy Guinness, Rachel's comin' to get ya'! Better leg it, chicken, nearly our lunch hour." And off she moves, pushing the brush in front of her, leaning on the handle in a zigzag line.

Polly, who also works on the domestic team, shakes her head after her girlfriend. Her bottle of antiseptic in hand, she whispers loudly, "Don't know how she thinks we can afford this winter hotel break. She's freezing everything – her face, her eggs. And I'm freezing my ass off coz she won't let me put the heating on in our place with these crazy cost of living bills!"

She rolls her eyes that are shaded by thick, fluttery fake lashes and squirts the liquid up into the air, waving her cloth at the chemical particles. "Better do some work I suppose." Annemarie coughs with exaggeration, fanning her hand in front of her face. Let's just say Polly isn't cut out to be a Domestic Goddess. I burst out laughing again and it feels almost therapeutic. This is not me. Normally I'm the glass-half-full-fun-loving-Lexie-Byrne, especially around the holidays, but I've a lot on my Christmas plate right now, I'm unsettled.

"Enjoy, have a lovely Christmas you two." I grin up at Polly and turn back in my seat.

A lot on my plate – that's putting it mildly. You see, apart from reason one I mentioned, this Annemarie fake-friendship-fiasco, I forgot to mention reason two. My fiancé's ex-wife is getting married in the Cotswolds next week, and he's the best man! I know, right? Urgh. The thought makes my stomach lurch. I've to suffer two whole nights in her snide company. First world problems, but God forgive me, she's an evil wagon. Oh, she's cunning, though! She plays a very bitchy, passive-aggressive game with me, but when Adam's around she appears sweet as day and just a little naïve. She's a lot of things alright but naïve she is not! Lifting a couple of crisps off my plate, I crunch down on them. So yeah, to say I'm dreading this wedding would be the understatement of the year. I'd rather go on a double date to a vegan restaurant with Hannibal Lecter and Buffalo Bill! And I can't vent to her sitting opposite me about it, as I usually do, because we aren't sharing anything meaningful anymore. One of us has to fix this and it's looking like it has to be me.

Okay, here goes I think.

But just as I open my mouth, she speaks.

8

"I need to tell you something, Lexie." She closes the plastic lid on her salad with finality, reaches down, pulls her notebook up out of her bag.

"What?" I sit forward. Maybe this is it? Maybe she's going to break the ice.

"I'm going to roast our turkey on Christmas Eve instead of Christmas morning."

I sink into my chair like a deflated balloon. See what I mean? Utter drivel. Oh, please allow me to introduce you to the top-scoring player in our game of charades. Looking ten years younger than her forty-four years. Barely a wrinkle in sight on that porcelain skin. Rosehip oil she maintains. And filtered water. Twice yearly IPLs. The only person in the entire world who can rock a navy polyester work uniform and make it look funky. And she's the only person I know who actually pinches her cheeks instead of using blusher. It's my best friend of over ten years, Annemarie Rafter.

"That's riveting information." I stare at her sickeningly nause-ating motherhood notebook. Narrowing my eyes, I peer closer at the grey and white, glossy, hardback:

*For All The Things My Arms Have Held The Best By Far Is You.* A picture of a woman (read: girl) in cut-off white short-shorts with a newborn baby in her arms, on a sandy beach. No black rings under her eyes, no vomit or leaking breastmilk on her spotless, tight T-shirt. No bloodstained shorts after only giving birth six hours ago, by the look of the baby.

"Oh what a tangled web we weave . . ." I mutter but loud enough for her to hear. Nothing prepared me for those first few months of new motherhood. I mean, surely there should be an extreme boot camp or something where they torture you with sleep deprivation and worry?

9

"What?" she asks, flicks her eyes up at me, using her thumb to click her pen.

"Nothing." I clamp my bagel again as she juts her narrow chin purposefully (chin: singular) and busies herself flicking to a new page, folding it back, starts to write.

*Journaling*, she calls it.

*Boring*, I call it.

"Thank God you had the notebook with you! Imagine?" I put both hands to each side of my head and do that head-exploding action. Taking another delicious bite, I rest the remaining half on the plate.

I don't care about her new Turkey Plan but I do care about my new "Fix-Our-Friendship Plan", so I can concentrate on my "Tell-My-Fiancé-I'm-Not-Moving-To-The-Cotswolds-To-Live-With-Him Plan". So many plans, Lexie, I hear you say – I told you I had a full Christmas plate, didn't I?

You've no idea of the stress, because I hate plans! Most especially the latter, to give Adam (that's my spectacular fiancé by the way) the news he's not expecting to hear. However, I'm hoping I can leave this talk until after Martha (that's his evil ex-wife by the way), celebrates her nuptials next week. Get that out of the way first. One trauma at a time.

Fishing out a small pink marshmallow from my drink, I pop it in my mouth and suck on its sweetness. Did I mention the guy Martha is marrying, Dominic, just happens to be Adam's oldest friend? I think it's all utterly bizarre and deeply creepy, but Adam just says, "That's life in a small rural village for you." Be careful what you wish for, let me tell you! That picturesque rural village, nestled in the outer reaches, boasting that open fire, cosy pub warmth and welcome, is laughing up its un-perfect sleeve!

But Martha will *hopefully* be another man's problem soon. Sing halleluiah! I cross my fingers on both hands under the table. After what happened over there with her and Adam's younger sister in the summer, a move to the Cotswolds is never going to happen.

I need him to uproot himself from his life and move to Dublin, to be with me and our daughter, Frances. But things are complicated. Adam has another daughter with his ex: Freya, who is sixteen (and sensational by the way!), and they share equal custody. Obviously I'd never dream of asking him to leave while Freya's still in school. But she is waiting on a letter. A letter that could literally solve all our problems! A letter that could change my life!

My love-sick heart heaves at the thought of this conversation, because Adam Cooper is such a good man, such a kind man, such a devoted man, (such a ride!) and I hate myself that I'm about to inflict more pressure on him (and his ridiness!). I'm hopelessly, head over heels, *Normal-People*-Has-Nothing-On-Me, in love with him but I need him here. I know this sounds silly but my teenage self found her dream. Adam really is my Johnny Castle. He's everything I've wanted in a man since I saw Patrick play Johnny in *Dirty Dancing* at my friend's sixteenth birthday. I was huddled in the back row of the cinema, an overweight, acne-ridden, introverted, insecure teenager, who'd never had a Valentine's card slipped in her bag all through my mixed-school years, like the other girls did – and thought *oh wow* when Johnny walked into shot. I sat bolt upright in my seat. It was truly an *aha* moment in my life. That soulful, grinding, evocative music inspired and invigorated me, and I left the cinema that day, foxtrotting my way to the bus stop in my stonewashed double denim, Reebok high-tops, questionable shag hairstyle and train-track braces, thinking for the first time in my young life that I didn't need to be the best looking, the thinnest, the tallest, the funniest girl in the world, to meet my prince.

It didn't last.

I grew up.

I found out the hard way that pure passion and that meeting of minds was not easy to find. And as I grappled through my life as a singleton, I forgot I ever thought a Johnny Castle existed. But he does. And now I'm engaged to him! Adam looks at me the way Johnny looked at Baby, and that's all I ever wanted. I still pinch myself when I think about how we met. Talk about sliding doors. He was in Dublin on a wet and wild St Patrick's night and he hit me with a door outside the Brazen Head. In typical romantic story-book fashion, I did not want to go out that night. I dragged myself off the couch, moaning to Garfield my old cat about, "Why won't people just leave me alone?" I planned to show my face for Jackie's leaving do, have one glass of wine, go home, crawl into bed with a takeaway until, boom! he hit me with that solid oak. I toppled over, legs in the air, well-worn-off-colour-once-black-then-brownish Spanx on show (yup, I still have them!), the embarrassing contents of my messy bag rolling down Lower Bridge Street towards Usher's Quay. But our eyes connected and my life was changed in that split second, almost three years ago now.

"Well tonight thank God it's them instead of you? I mean how un-Christian is that? Disgraceful. And from the mouth of our very own Bono." Annemarie *tut-tut-tuts*.

"Quick. Write it down. Stick it in a bottle." I lean across and tip the page on her open notebook. "Sure maybe Bob Geldof will find it one day washed up, see your complaint and apologise to you for all the hundreds of millions he's made for famine relief in Ethiopia."

"Har-de-har," is all she says, no expression, completely dead-pan, still scribbling.

God, isn't she a bag of laughs lately? This communication problem with her is only making me miss Adam more – he'd find a way to cheer me up now. Not that he's perfect, obviously! Ain't no such thing, right? I reach for my bagel, take another warm bite. In fact, our biggest problem, and it took me a while to identify this, is that Adam Cooper is a people pleaser. Adam wants to please *everybody, all of the time.* He's pulled in so many directions and something has to give. *Ba-boom-ba-boom-ba-boom* all of a sudden my heart starts to flutter faster. And there she is at full stretch. Auntie Anxiety! She's a new, unwelcome guest to my worried-that-something's-going-to-go-terribly-wrong-on-edge-mildly-sweaty-feeling-stressed-more-than-a-little-bit-para-nioid-waking-up-four-times-a-night-brain-working-overtime symptoms. Always out of the blue. I swallow, breathe. It fades off. I hate it, it's like an articulated truck drives into your stomach, and the driver jumps out and starts to punch you in the heart.

"I'm sitting here just thinking about ham." She's playing a good game of "thoughtful", raps the pen off the table. "Will I do a Christmas ham too? You love ham, don't you? That's a ham bagel, right? H.A.M. Ham?"

I dab my mouth, stare at her. "Are you actually serious?"

"Shank or butt?" She flicks the Christmas tree earrings and they bob, the spirals twisting and turning the colours like a kaleidoscope.

I twitch my nose. "I couldn't give a shit about ham, Anne-marie, and I definitely don't want to spend my lunchbreak talking about ham. *Ham* I making myself clear?" I lean across again and pluck the pen from her hand, then place it gently on the table.

"Something better to talk about?" She picks it back up but refrains from tapping it.

"God, no, your conversation is riveting thus far." This is my cue. Time is ticking and I have to confront her.

She slides the pen into the little black elasticated holder. "Gonna watch *Home Alone* tonight with Ben," she says with no connection whatsoever to our conversation. "Keep the change, ya filthy animal." She curls her glossy top lip and does a remarkably good impression.

"Merry Christmas, little fella, we know you're in there and that you're all alone." I can't help myself, we love to quote *Home Alone*. She raises her spoon in acknowledgement, then turns the bowl in her hands anticlockwise, concentrates on scraping the remains off the sides like she's in *The Hunger Games*.

*Just let her finish her lunch*, I think, biting into the remaining bagel. Where was I? Oh yes, anyway, back to Adam and my "plan". I honestly thought we could live a modern-day lifestyle. Do it our way. Make it work long distance. So confident was I, that I told him so after a few drinks.

"Let's throw out the old-fashioned manifesto of how a serious relationship can be mastered. Let's do this long distance, our way!" I'd hiccupped.

"Let's do this Ouuurrrr Waaaaay!" he'd sung out in delight, put his two hands on either side of my face, gently probed my lips apart with his tongue and kissed me passionately.

"Our way" turned into Adam remaining at Rosehill Cottage, his beautiful, listed home in the leafy Cotswolds, taking care of

Freya and working as an A&E trauma nurse during the week. Then at weekends, flying over to stay with us when Freya goes to Martha (who lives a hop, skip and a jump directly across the road from Adam, you starting to get the picture?).

But it's not working out. So Adam has suggested the most sensible option. Me to leave Dublin, quit my job here in Silverside and move in with him, and I might have considered a move very seriously if it wasn't for one thing.

His family.

Hear me out on this. They aren't all evil, but the pendulum swings massively in favour of the evil ones.

Adam's family, the Coopers, are beyond demanding, and Martha (even though she is an ex, is still a huge part of the family) would be in my face every day. As it is she's constantly scuppering our weekend plans. Despite her upcoming wedding, she's still in love with Adam. She never got over him divorcing her, and she's using this up-coming wedding to Dominic as a way to get him back. I've no doubt she's watching *The Graduate* on repeat and visualising Adam as Dustin Hoffman, banging on the glass to win her back. It's a tight-knit village and I just can't fit in there. I'm also struggling doing it all on my own and I'm lonely. I underestimated royally how much work single, working mothers have to do. It's exhausting and I fear I'm getting a little bitter about the one-sided workload.

"Jesus, hello?" Annemarie waves her spoon in front of my face.

"Don't call me Jesus." I wag a finger at her.

"You're miles away, sorry you think I'm so dull, but you tell me if there's anything as tasty as a sneaky late night hot-toasted-turkey-sambo . . ."

"Oh you're not still on about . . ."

". . . with a glass of mulled wine, especially the night before Christmas . . ." She dips her wide, green eyes, ". . . when all through the house not a creature was stirring, not even a . . ." She tilts her head, waves her long-handled spoon as a conductor might swing her baton.

"Mouse." I sigh loudly, rub my eyes.

"Top of the class!" She grins.

"Ahhh shit! I've done it again!" I lick my finger, run it underneath. She's made me smudge my eyes. I'm a paler shade of fair-skinned so I'm an every-day, cat-winged, dark liquid-liner user. Took me years to perfect my technique, but I can do it now in seconds, if only I could stop rubbing at them.

"Mouse. Exactly. Speaking of mice – was reading this book to Ben last night, *Mousey Mouse's Most Mucky Misadventure*. Did you know they eat broccoli, cucumber and beetroot? I just thought they ate cheese?"

"You do know they don't really wear clogs or go *clip-clippidy-clop* on the stairs?" I sigh again.

"That's different but when do you see a picture of a mouse without cheese? They go hand in hand, right? Well, apparently not." She drums her nails on the table.

"Fascinating." I fake a massive yawn, tap my fingers lightly on my top lip.

"It's organic, by the way, from the Farmacy, already rolled and boned and ready to pop in a hot oven." Stops drumming.

"The mouse?"

"The turkey."

"Oh."

But that's it. The push I need. It's the mouse that broke the turkey's back. I manoeuvre my plate to one side, place my elbows on the table and lean my chin in my cupped hands.

'Annemarie?" I say, determined to speak my mind and address the elephant in our friendship.

Forget the mouse and the turkey.

It's Trunk Time.

# 2

*"Tell her that you love her. You've got nothing to lose and
you'll always regret it if you don't."*

Daniel, *Love Actually*

"YOU KNOW HOW MUCH I LOVE YOU." I hold eye contact with
her, hoping it will defuse the tension.

"I love you too." She blinks rapidly.

"So why are we just talking nonsense?"

"Whaddya mean?" She knows darn well.

"I mean, listen . . . I'm sure your turkey delighted in its
fantastic, roaming, outdoor life, wore Crocs, studied applied
gobble-gobble with the farmer's wife, but we need to . . ."

"Let's go!" She jerks, the table rocks and my elbows fall off
the table. "I wanna stick my head into the crèche on our way
back. Finish up. Time's up." She reaches down for her oversized
orange tote.

I gather myself. "Ain't that the truth." I gently bang my forehead with my palm. She necks her glass of iced water. I eyeball
her steadily and she knows what a Lexie Byrne eyeball means.
I mean business. I open my mouth.

"Do you not think it's time we—"

"Think I'll leave all the trimmings until after we open the presents on Christmas morning, though. Might even make a couple of cheeky Mimosas," she interrupts again. Her bag on her legs, she joins her index finger and thumb, and kisses them.

"You know we need to talk abo—"

"Onion and thyme stuffing, sprouts, goose fat potatoes, roasted parsnips, my homemade thick oxtail gravy . . . Sound good to you?" She deflects with the skill of a toddler. "You'll need comfort food after your not-so-best-friend's wedding!" She snorts, reaching across for her iPhone that's on the table and tipping it awake. She always rests her phone in the middle of the table, propped up against some condiment or vase or something else. Ever since her son, Ben, was born three years ago. Always contactable, 24/7. She's the most committed mother I know, in every single way. Dare I say sometimes it's just too much? Those invisible blades whizz above her head. She squints, reads something, throws her free hand in the air.

"Oh for fu— Ben's present still hasn't been shipped! Why'd I risk it? Should have bought it months ago when I saw it in Ashmore's Toys. You told me not to!"

I clutch my head. "It was March. A little premature for Christmas shopping, I thought, and you wanted me to store it in my matchbox apartment for ten months! Now can we . . ." I try again.

"Just a second." Her nails *click-clack* on the keys.

"Uh-huh," is all I grunt. This banal-just-say-anything-to-fill-the-silence-bullshit conversation has been like this between us ever since I found out that Tom, her husband, cheated on her. He slept with Groovy Gail, his part-time bookkeeper and part-time lover, it appears, and horrifically, poor Annemarie caught them in the act. Can you imagine ever trying to get that image out of your head? I shudder.

But get this, she blamed *herself* for his cheating, citing her post-natal depression and non-existent sex drive as applicable reasons for his infidelity. I was dumbfounded and struggled to hide it.

*"He had to get it someplace! A man has needs, Lexie!"* is what she actually said to me.

*"Have you had a lobotomy?"* I yelled back at her.

"Right! That's sent to the complaints department." She dusts her hands off one another.

I just sit back in the chair and shake my head slowly at her.

"Come on." She stretches her arms above her head.

"I'm not finished talking to you, I—"

"Lemme just get rid of this, one sec." I'm fighting a losing battle. Like a Duracell Bunny she jumps up again, rushes over to dump her plastic in the recycling bin.

*Don't let this moment pass,* I chant in my head as I watch her chat to Eoin from the Smoothie Bar. The aforementioned but not appropriately nicknamed Groovy Gail (groovy girls don't do that!) had DM'ed her on Instagram apologising over and over the very same night she caught them in the act, swearing it was a once-off. I'd tried my best to dissuade Annemarie from scrolling through her grid but I'd failed. GG was a part-time lots of things. Yoga teacher, bookkeeper, beekeeper, marriage wrecker and (you couldn't you make it up) marriage celebrant! Okay, I'm not blaming the woman, she wasn't the one who was married with a young son, but in fairness she knew *he* was! He was her boss and she knew Annemarie well, she'd left various comments on Tom's page under pictures of a newborn baby Ben in Cotswolds General Hospital, and she'd deposited a dozen love heart and baby bottle emojis in other Ben-related comment sections. I made Annemarie block her after that but I felt a queasiness in the pit of my stomach and I haven't been able to look at Tom since.

I continue watching my best friend in the entire world as she sashays back towards me. She's been through a lot. An awful lot. Is still going through a lot. And I miss being there for her.

But I just can't fathom how she's forgiven Tom. I really can't.

"There she is. The mustard expert herself. Remember your pregnancy mustard cravings? Borderline obsessive," I say but more gently when she sits back down. We don't work weekends and I have to get this off my chest now, before Friday runs away, we break for Christmas and I head to the Cotswolds for Martha Cooper's upcoming black-tie nuptials (yes, she kept Adam's name post-divorce). I could care less about her stupid fake wedding but not about her keeping his surname. I do care about that. Is that pathetic?

By my very nature I avoid confrontation, I'm the opposite of argumentative, except when it comes to Annemarie. We've had our fair share of humdingers over the last ten years.

"Alright, enough, why am I always the one who has to cave first?" I implore.

"*Cave*? I'm sure I don't know what you're talking about?" Her eyes dip and she shifts her bag, knowing well what's coming.

"Annemarie, come on! Enough of your nonsensical babble, what's going on with us? Talk to me. Properly. We are being horrible and fake and I hate it." At last, I finally blurt it out. I crumple my napkin and throw it down on the tray.

21

"What are you saying?" She cocks her ear at me and rolls her impossibly toned shoulders hidden beneath the baggy uniform shirt.

"Someone has to say something. I'm here! Me. Lexie." I pat my chest. "Why aren't you talking to me? I'm worried about you." I lower my voice now to a whisper. "And be truthful, please? What are you afraid of?" I stretch my hand across the table, the cuff of my white shirt catching an earlier drop of spilled hot chocolate.

"Oh, Oprah, hey gurl, didn't know you were in Dublin!" She clicks her fingers, tries to defer and abruptly pulls her hands back, before I can make contact. I feel my face immediately burn.

"What?" She eyes up my reddener, sees my discomfort.

"Nothing," I spit. "Fine, don't say I didn't try." I push back my chair, fish behind me for the thick strap of my vintage brown leather satchel bag.

"Alright-alright-hang-on-hang-on!" She rushes and I drop the strap, the bag sways, its brass clasps click clacking off the metal leg of the chair. "I thought you were messing with me?"

"No. I'm deadly serious." I lick my dry lips, looking away from her.

"I am talking to you. Mouth. Moving. Words coming out." She rotates her index finger in front of her mouth, knocks over the salt and pepper grinder. We're both terribly on edge, I recognise. So I pull my seat back in, lean across. I do love her dearly, I've just told her that. This is protective mode she's in – and I get that, but I also have to break it down. We used to tell each other everything, and I mean *everything*. We have been one another's sounding board for years. And I feel like a part of me is missing. I don't feel like *me* without *her*.

"But you aren't talking to me, we're *pretending* to talk but it's not us. This. Is. Fake." I jab my finger at her and back to myself, my finger embedded in the loose knot of my red-and-yellow striped tie. She looks over her shoulder around the busy food hall, does a double take.

"We're not us? Who are we then? Coz if we have the choice, I'll take Jennifer Aniston, in her Brad Pitt era, with her real golden LA suntan and extra-long beachy bleached hair, thanking you very much." She giggles and slaps the table lightly.

"Forget it, I give up." Irritated, I run my thumb under the elasticated waistband on my navy work skirt. Even my bra feels too tight, my hormonally inflated C-cups constrained and bulging after that carb-fest.

She stares at me. "Are you hungover?"

"No. Are you?" I stare right back.

"I – I never drink during the week."

She knows well I know this is a total lie. The white sizzling tablets at the bottom of her glass of water behind our desk on one too many mornings of late. But I know this woman better than she knows herself sometimes and this is not something I'm bringing up this side of Christmas. She's hiding so much.

I digress.

"The fact is this." I purse my lips together.

"You're a jammy bitch because your lips are natural but look done?" she tries as an exit strategy.

"I – I . . . I miss you Annemarie." I feel my cheeks burn even brighter. "I miss *us* . . . how we used to be . . . a lot."

"Oh. I see," is all she says, and my heart rate speeds up immediately; I'm more than a little angry at her weak reaction. I was expecting a mushier response to my declaration, an "oh Lexie, I miss us so much too" at the very least.

I pick some lint balls off my thick furry insulated tights. "That's it? That's all you have to say?"

23

"What is that supposed to mean?" She narrows those piercing green eyes. "Are you implying that *I'm* to blame? That *I'm* the problem here?" She proffers her dainty hand behind her ear; multiple rings adorn her cobalt blue shellacked fingers.

"That's exactly what I'm implying." I stand firm.

"Wow." She removes her hand and drops it to her lap.

Then:

Silence.

We're in a stand-off.

We both pretend to be distracted by the shoppers who swarm inches from our table like sharks. Trays full of hot food or steaming cappuccinos with mince pies and freshly whipped cream, eagerly waiting to pounce if either of us dares to make a move. The glass dome roof rattles with the hailstones dashing from the skies. Snow is forecast and I've been doing a novena for it in the hope that all flights are grounded and I can skip this wedding nightmare. Annemarie leans far back on her seat, the two front legs dangerously wavering off the ground, and dramatically looks left to right.

She speaks first:

"Well hello, Pot! Kettle's over here!" She pokes a finger at me. "Looking for you here, pet!" Her eyes flash, but mischievously. A look I've missed. "You wanna talk? Okay then, let's talk, starting with your life, your relationship!"

"What about it?" I ask just as her bloody phone beeps loudly.

"Hang on!" She drops the chair back down, rummages in her bag on the floor. Setting the grinder upright, I scoop the spilled salt into my hand and toss it over my left shoulder. She pulls out her phone, panic drawing across her face in case it's the crèche.

"Phew. It's not the crèche."

24

See?

"One sec." I watch her bang out another message on her phone, her thumbs a blur. "It's Amazon Help coming back to me."

My life? My relationship? With Adam? What's she going to say about him? I conjure him up. Just his physical presence tugs at my heartstrings. Over six feet tall, broad shoulders, strong jaw, overgrown dark messy hair. I sigh, picturing those deep brown eyes beneath the spiky dark lashes that lovingly lust after lil' ole me. The silver feather chain his grandfather left him, tight around his neck, his staple, well-worn leather jacket, and the thick dark stubble he tries to keep at bay but always fails at. Our relationship is great – the sparks are still flying for us, even if things are tough sometimes.

"Done! It's on the way." She drops her phone back in her tote and I snap out of my daydream. As she bends her thin frame over the table, her unruly red curls tumble around her shoulders. I see suddenly her perfect skin is actually pasty and dry in patches and her eyes have grey circles underneath. I'm tired now too. The adrenalin oozes out of me. This was not the Lexie-Byrne-Annemarie-Rafter-Best-Friend-Reunion-Tiny-Tim-God-Bless-Us-Every-One-Christmas-Soppy-Love-In I'd hoped for. Now I just want to get through this afternoon, pick up my daughter from crèche and collect Adam from Dublin airport tonight. We'll stick dinner in the microwave, bathe Frances, shower her in kisses, put her down together and then I just want to curl up in the safety of his arms. Netflix and chill. Melt into him, inhale his manliness and unbutton his shirt and tear . . .

She jolts me back.

"You're still all coming to me for Stephen's Day?" she asks, again out of context.

25

"We are, if that's still okay?" I have been looking forward to her cooking and her company, but not to seeing Tom.

"And you'll be okay around Tom?" She knows me too well.

"Oh. It's so long since you mentioned his name I wasn't sure if he was still called Tom?" I widen my eyes, mockingly.

"Last time I checked." Her tone is sarcastic.

"Of course," I bare-face lie.

"Good." She retreats, slightly.

"So what about my relationship? Adam?" I'm not letting her off with this, I want to hear what she has to say about him before we go any further.

"Yeah, Adam. Still under the impression that you and Frances are going to move to the Cotswolds in the New Year?" She raises both bushy eyebrows up high.

"He is, but we're not." I run my fingers through those fluffy hairs at the nape of my neck that appeared after childbirth and are impossible to pin up. I don't like where this is going. I can read her tone only too well.

"Oh? I didn't know you'd made the definite decision?" She sits up straight.

"Well we haven't exactly been sharing much." I know I sound defensive, but I can't help it. Why has this turned on me and my relationship, I'm wondering? I should have kept my mouth shut.

"Told you this long-distance thing would never work once you had a baby, didn't I? But would you listen? Ah no, you were all hippy-dippy with that 'we're doing it our way' nonsense." She forces a laugh.

"It does work," I insist.

Abruptly, she stops laughing. "Doesn't sound like it."

"It's just not ideal." I open my glasses case, slide my glasses back out and really close the case as loudly as I can.

"Bloody hell, Lexie!" she grumbles.

"I have to close it," I reply, childishly, and slide my glasses on.

"He'd miss his family terribly, you know he loves that cosy village life so much. I don't think I've ever met a man as committed to his family and village life as Adam. I can't understand why you don't give it a try?"

"You know why!" I glare at her, use my middle finger to push my glasses up my nose.

"Are you giving me the finger?"

"No," I lie.

"You're gonna let those bitches ruin . . ."

"Fuck's sake Annemarie!" I yell, baffled by her antipathy. "Why are you trying to make me feel bad about him leaving the Cotswolds? Like I don't have tons of anxiety about it already!" The truck driver leaps out of his van, pulling on his boxing gloves.

"Calm down, Lexie."

I flinch. She looks around, checking to see if other people have noticed my outburst. If they have, they don't care; they just want our table.

My cheeks have deepened to such a burning crimson now they are uncomfortable. There I was trying to get our friendship back, being open and nice, and she's poking at all my sorest spots when I'm trying to help her.

"Don't get snotty with me." She pushes her chair back, which scrapes off the granite tiles, stands up and thrusts her hands into her skirt pockets.

"Don't annoy me then." I stay seated, glaring up at her.

"Lexie." She clears her throat. "You're the one who's just asked for us to talk honestly! Did you not hear yourself? The first honest thing out of my mouth, you clearly don't like, so you plan to storm off like a big Lexie baby! You only want to hear what you want to hear. Your relationship is far from perfect too. Grow up." She tucks her chair back in under the table.

"You're obsessed with pointing out the negatives of mine and Adam's living arrangements!" If I stand up we will be face to face and I don't want that.

"Me? Obsessed? Um, you're the one who's obsessed . . . with Tom's indiscretion . . ."

But Praise the Lord! She's going there . . . at last.

"Infidelity," I clarify.

"See? You won't let up!" Her face turns to thunder and I can tell she's instantly sorry she's brought it up. I re-strategise hastily.

Lowering my voice, I look up at her. "I will let up. I *have* let up! I simply don't agree that we never mention it again and sweep it all under the carpet. Because that's unhealthy and we've never done that before. That's bullshit. I know you better than anyone, and I know you're hurt inside, because I would be – cheating is a shit thing to do to someone, but I'm here, that's all, I'm here to listen. So you can rant. You cannot pretend it never happened. A problem shared has always been our motto!" I search her face for a reaction.

"What's the point in dwelling on it?" She grits her teeth. "Yes. It happened. It was a once-off. I've moved on. In case it slipped your mind, we have a son to bring up and a hefty mortgage to pay for the next twenty years, so." She pulls her hand out of her pocket and winds her hair tightly around her thumb, which immediately tells me she's uneasy.

28

"Fine." I clutch my bag tighter on my knees. "I just needed to . . ."

"I shared it with you! I told you what had happened. But I don't believe in whining about my problems all the time, I believe in getting on with shit." Her voice cracks.

"Convenient." I simply don't believe her.

"Tom had a one-night stand. I had a choice: leave him with no place to go and me not in a great place or able to support Ben solely . . . or . . . forgive him, let it go and get on with it. Life isn't *Dirty Dancing,* Lexie, sometimes Baby just has to sit in the corner, watch her sister's musical act, accept her fate, applaud and suck it up!"

"I know . . ." I swallow a lump forming in my throat.

"Not much of a choice, eh?"

"You always had – have me."

She places both hands on the table and bends over, inches from my nose, her curls shielding her face on either side like heavy curtains. "Listen to yourself. I can't move me and Ben in with you Lexie, to your one-bed apartment, and I know you don't want to hear this but you might not be living in Ireland next year. Let me do me, okay?"

"I *will* be living here!" I make a fist and bang the table, and the grinder falls again.

She picks it up and waves it at me. "You do know you need to pull on your big-girl pants because the answer to all *your* problems is for you and Frances to move to the Cotswolds, you must see that?" Replacing the grinder, she tucks her hair behind her ear. "Adam's got a beautiful home, a big space, all that land around it, it's an idyllic village, it's . . ."

29

"It's never gonna happen, Annemarie! You of all people, having met them all, know I can't live there with his family. You know what I overheard Martha and Deb say about mc in the toilet at the Moritz Hotel. Why do you keep saying this?" I'm incredulous now. She knows the torturous week I spent there in early summer with them all, his demanding younger sister Deb and his ex-wife were both hateful to me, despite their brilliance at hiding their two-facedness around Adam, like a pair of bitchy Meryl Streeps!

"Tell you what, Lexie? You don't ask my advice and I won't ask yours – how does that sound?" Her Christmas tree earrings sway manically now. "Do something about it! Stand up to Martha, the silly cow! Deb is just her sidekick!"

"Let's just go," I say. This is not going to end well if we don't drop it now.

"You don't really want to talk . . . about *you* anyway." She flicks her hair dramatically.

"Maybe not, but I'm desperately trying to figure out if we can save our friendship!" I drop the bomb.

*That* changes everything.

Her face falls.

I wait.

"Alright, let me say this and it's the last time I'm talking about it. Yes, it was humiliating when Tom cheated. I felt nauseated seeing them naked tangled up together." Her green eyes go a shade darker. "But we – I mean, I – I really wasn't . . . What I mean is, I'm totally fine, I swear, you have to believe me. I'm not upset. It wasn't that much of a shock." She smiles at me.

"I'm sorry, Annemarie, but that's a lie. You're not totally fine." This is utterly pointless.

"I really am, Lexie." She looks down at me.

"No, you're lying, but the last thing I want to do is make this even worse, so you win. I'll never mention it again. All I want is to get our friendship back on track . . . I need you and you need me. That's the truth. I'm lost without you properly in my life . . . I'm—"

Suddenly she grabs the back of her chair and turns it with a deafening scrape on the tiles. People stare as she plonks down. Her shoulders drop.

"I'm lost without you too." Her lip trembles. "I miss you so much. I know you've the best intentions and you're only looking out for me, it's just . . ." She darts over her shoulder again, lowers her voice, crooks her finger for me to lean in even closer.

"Just what?" I do lean closer, my voice tentative.

Her voice is so low she's almost whispering. "I swear I'm not lying to you, I just do not know how to tell you this . . ."

# 3

*"This is Christmas. The season of perpetual hope."*

Kate McCallister, *Home Alone*

"WHAT? SPEAK UP! I can barely hear you!" I'm shrill with interest as I almost chop myself in half I'm so far across the table. "You don't know how to tell me what?" I demand, my blood pumping.

"To tell you . . . about . . . Tom . . ." She trails off.

Her voice is so small, her mouth barely forming the word. I do a disgracefully bad job of hiding my interest as I leap up and drag my chair over beside hers.

"Look! Table! There! Quickly! That woman is leaving! The tall blonde one! Go, Beth, Go!" a woman's voice hollers. A small girl with swinging ponytails skids on the tiles and, faster than a greyhound, throws herself across our table, sending the unfortunate grinder flying once again.

"We're not finished just yet, pet, sorry. Won't be a minute." I smile at her cute, freckled face despite the despair clamping my chest, but my smile sours as she bares her teeth, glares at me and growls.

"Down, girl," Annemarie says as her mother approaches with two hot dogs in hand, ketchup and mustard dripping over the sides, down her hands, like a dissolving Spanish flag.

"Don't stand up if you're not vacating the table!" she scolds us. "Come on now, not during lunch hour a few days before Christmas. We've been hovering over there for the last fifteen minutes watching that man read his rag-bag paper over his empty, crusty coffee cup. Now look what you did! He's after standing up! He's rolling up his paper! He's tucking it under his arm! For the love of God! Run, Beth! Run!" she roars at the child.

I squint as the little girl takes off again and I see the man leave just as Rachel and Polly, now on their break, take his table with two huge Geraghty Burgers and chunky chips.

*Shoulda got the burger and chips,* the little people who live in my brain scold me. "Sorry," I mutter, grimacing as she *tut-tuts*, then moves off to a frustrated Beth, licking her own wrists free of condiments.

I whirl back to my best friend. "Go on. What? Tell me? About Tom?" I wheeze just as the announcer bell chimes three times. Annemarie raises her finger to make me pause.

I wait for the three dings at the end of the announcement.

"Go on? Spit it out." I hit her bony shoulder as I urge again. We're side by side now. I can smell the coconut leave-in conditioner her curls inhabit.

"Are you ready for this?" She bites her bottom lip.

"*Yes,*" I implore.

"I haven't had sex with Tom in over ten months," she says flatly then a flush roars up from her neck.

"W-what? Oh . . . OH!" I gasp, catch my breath. My jaw drops before I hastily close my mouth while my brain people get out their calculators and do the maths.

33

That's a *long* time.

"And I don't care," she reveals with a curl of her lip.

"That's a very long time." What do I say to this? My brain is working overtime but coming up with nothing.

"Yeah, couldn't care less." And for the first time in ages a look of relief passes across her face. Like a first confession.

"Really?" I whisper, desperate to hide the shock I know is graffitied all over my face.

"Honestly." Her eyes are wide as saucers as she delivers this news.

"I – I . . ." I trail off, bewildered, useless in the moment, her words spinning me into a stunned silence.

A shrug of her shoulders. "Zero interest in sex."

Slowly I say, "But why?"

"You tell me?"

"Oh, Annemarie." My hand covers my mouth. I had no idea things were *this* bad.

"God help him, he tries, all the time – well, not all the time now, thank God, but he used to."

"I'm not following, what happened . . ." I'm struggling to understand what this means exactly as I stare at her.

"I just can't do it. Sex. I can't do it anymore. I don't like it. I don't want it. Simple as." A wry smile curls again.

"Is it . . . a . . . woman's issue? Like a . . . post-birth issue?" I try.

The wry smile dies. "Lexie, it's nothing physical. It's *emotional*. I flinch if Tom touches me. I have zero sex drive. Zero desire for *him*. Or anyone. I wanna curl up in a ball when he tries to be intimate – no, you wanted honesty, actually I wanna scream when he tries to touch me . . . I fall asleep on the couch at night

34

because I dread the thought of getting into bed beside him. Oh, I had excuses for ages, all through the pregnancy and after the birth, but when Ben was six months Tom wanted sex again . . . and I did not. I tried and tried, it was horrendous. It made my skin crawl. So we don't . . . anymore. I can't," she fades off, obviously embarrassed.

"Fucking hell," I exclaim through my fingers before removing my hand. "Oh! I know what this is – it's because of Groovy Ga— sorry . . . because of Gail? Right? You can't get the two of them out of your mind, that's perfectly natural. What you saw was pretty distressing!"

"No. Not at all. Quite the opposite. I just told you. This isn't a new thing, it's well before that happened. Levelling with you? I feel sorry for him that he's married to me. He deserves so much better. At the very least he deserves a real wife, a real relationship, not this farce. That's why I told you he had needs. He had to get it someplace." She sounds so matter of fact it's scary.

"W-what? That's not true? It can't be that bad?" My voice is wheedling.

"It is. Listen to me. This is all profoundly humiliating so just listen."

"I *am* listening. God, I'm glued to your every word. But . . . I – I saw you guys at the hospital, in the Cotswolds, when Ben was born – the love between you both, it was clear as day." And it was, it really was. I saw it with my own two eyes. Annemarie and Tom were so in love.

"You're right, in that moment I loved him more than I ever thought possible." Her voice is faint. "The thing is, I still love him, but . . . just not in *that* way. Not in the way he needs me to anyway. Look it's all very confusing for me, never mind for you. I'm all over the place." She screws her eyes shut.

I'm trying to think of any way I can make her feel better here, but I'm clutching at straws.

"I tried to pretend but that's all I was doing – pretending. And I've had enough of pretending. Life's too short. If I'm being really honest with myself I've never been a very sexual person." Her shoulders hunch as she says all this way too quickly.

"What are you saying, it's over?"

I shake my head, replaying all the times I've been out with her and Tom in my mind. Surely I would have noticed *something*?

"I don't know," she says with the tiniest little flicker in her eye, barely visible at all.

Poor Annemarie, this is truly awful. Devastating, actually.

"Can we finish this conversation another time? Nothing whatsoever is going to change between mine and Tom's relationship this side of the New Year, I can promise you that. Don't mind what Rachel says, I *can* plan for that. It truly would take a Christmas miracle for me and Tom to sort this out!" she murmurs now. "And you know me, I don't believe in miracles!"

"Ben?" I offer hopefully.

"Ben. Yes, Ben was a miracle, that's true," she says calmly.

"You two look finished?" A girl, dressed as an elf, shakes her bell-ended red-and-white candy cane oversized hat at us.

"No," we both answer at the same time. We are definitely not finished – Annemarie needs my help now more than ever.

Huffing, the elf jingles away to the rhythm of Chris Rea's "Driving Home For Christmas".

"You know it wasn't until I saw you and Adam together that I fully realised something was really wrong, I didn't have those feelings for Tom. Why didn't I have those feelings?"

We exchange what I can only describe as a stricken look.

"But, that night, the night he was unfaithful, you'd bought that red sexy underwear, wore it under a trench coat and went to his workplace on Howth Head? That's incredibly sexy!"

"I'd been researching, reading articles on a sexless marriage and . . . spicing things up . . . It was worth a try. I'd also downed two Chardonnays and it shouldn't have to be like that."

"So are you sleeping separately now?" I put my hand on hers, and this time she doesn't pull it away. It's cold and her knuckles are like the top of a knitting needle.

"Not officially. He's been begging me for us to go and talk to someone, see a marriage therapist. Or a marriage counsellor, whatever they're called."

We just let that hang. I wait. Squeeze her hand in mine.

"Some nights I tell him I'll be up soon, in the hope I can try to be intimate. But then I think about the act and I physically shudder." And she physically shudders in front of my very eyes. "I can't. It's visceral. My whole body tenses up. So I open a bottle of wine instead, watch *The Real Housewives of Beverly Hills* re-runs, admire the desire Lisa Vanderpump still has for old Ken, drink a glass, sometime two, and fall asleep on the couch, wake up with a headache."

"Oh, Annemarie." I try to warm her hand with mine. "I'm so glad you're telling me this, because . . ."

"Because hopefully you won't talk about your staggering sex life so much and make me feel even worse!" She laughs but it's caught in her throat.

"I won't." I snigger because that's the kind of nervous energy I expend when I'm in pure shock.

*No, you're not in shock,* the little voice in my head says. I am! Or am I? Have I just not been paying attention? Call myself a friend?

"Don't laugh."

"I'm not," I say apologetically.

She squeezes my hand back. Like me, Annemarie is an only child; but unlike me, her parents had no time for her, both selfish, narcissistic personalities, two failed musicians who got divorced and moved to the States, and she never sees them. She'd moved out when she was seventeen and got a job in Silverside, where she's been ever since. Annemarie has always been fiercely independent. She was accepted and brought into our little family in her early thirties when I first met her.

"It's so passionate Lexie, your relationship, it's . . ." Her lip trembles.

"It's unusual Annemarie, it's still bonkers to me how I . . ." I do not want her to compare her relationship to mine and if I have been throwing shade on her marriage I need to apologise profusely.

"Do not explain!" She almost facepalms me.

"I'm really sorry . . ."

"Do NOT apologise! I'd secretly hoped the insatiable lust you have for each other would've faded after an eight-days-overdue, ten-pounder Frances . . . A vaginal delivery with forceps, suction cap, episiotomy and fifteen paper stitches . . ." She tries another joke but her lip still quivers. "I'm a shit friend to admit that."

"No. It makes you human and I totally get it, and I'm sorry. But please speak to someone, a professional, Tom's right. Surely it's worth that much? Surely it's worth fighting for?" I say emphatically.

"Maybe. We'll see." She composes herself. "But now you see that I'm not some silly walkover, right? I do feel sorry for Tom and I have to take some responsibility for what he did, whether you like it or not. I pushed him away. I reneged on the marriage deal." She checks her Fitbit.

I bite my tongue. I still don't agree with her. I don't think in any capacity that Tom should have cheated on her, despite these circumstances, but I force a small encouraging smile.

"Alright," I say.

"We're late, it's nearly twenty past and August will combust!"

I feel so bad for her. For them both.

She pulls a bottle of water from her bag, twists the cap and drains it. "It's stupefying that after three years you'll be tearing that well-worn leather jacket off Adam's back tonight as soon as Frances is sound asleep." The plastic crackles in her hand.

And kissing the face off him, unbuttoning his shirt, reefing the brown leather belt out through the silver buckle on his jeans, rolling his jeans over his hips . . . Flutters. I pinch myself.

"We need to talk more about all this, though," I tell her seriously. "After Christmas? Go out into town, just the two of us, like we used to. That's why this has all happened between us? We don't have the time or the freedom to really talk. Bar talk, it's the best."

"We put the world to rights so many time in the Brazen Head over the years, didn't we?"

"Totally."

"We talked and talked, about every little thing going on in our lives. I do miss that."

"How about dinner and drinks soon, in some brand new trendy bar that makes us feel old? Where we can judge the outfits or lack of on the young and the wrinkle-free? I feel terrible leaving after this conversation and—"

"I'm a big girl. I'm fine, honestly. I'll figure it out." Casually, she waves her hand.

"I'm so relieved you've confided in me."

"Me too. I've been wanting to tell you for months but I didn't want to rain on your love parade and you've been . . . well, so very busy. Let's go." She gives me a weak smile.

"I'll be more respectful, I promise. I'll keep my bedroom antics to myself in future." I pull my cross-body leather bag on.

"Just don't rub it in my face."

We hold eye contact, and despite the horrors of what she's just told me about her failing marriage, we both scream laughing, clutch our stomachs and double over. This is what I've missed so much! Our shared sense of humour. When we've pulled our immature selves together, I pant, just to keep this lightness in the mood a little longer. "Back to my poor pelvic floor, I'm bursting for a wee." I wipe my eyes and I hug her tight.

"Let's go." I release her, slide back my chair, bang it into the chair close behind me.

"Are you leaving, ladies?" an American accent asks Annemarie, desperation in her voice.

"I'm so sorry," I tell the old lady in a grey gaberdine bent over her soup; some has spilled over onto the white plate the deep bowl rests on.

"Don't worry, pet," she says as Annemarie hands over our table, stacks the tray and brings it up to the drop-off, her spindly legs teetering in her strappy wedges.

I turn back to the older lady because she immediately reminds me of my other old friend and the third reason for my anxiety: Máiréad Farrell. My beloved friend.

Máiréad Farrell is – *was*, Lexie, I correct my inner thoughts, and my heart plummets. She *was* one of the residents at Sir Patrick

Dun's Nursing Home, where I volunteer every weekend. I get an almighty knot in my stomach when I think of Máiréad and the promise I made to her on her deathbed. Inspired by her, I took my good self off to New York and earned a qualification in Gerontological Nursing thanks to a sum of money she kindly left me. I completed a six-month course at NYU – while pregnant with Frances. I had an incredible time in the Big Apple, living with Jackie and going to school there and taking it all in; the sounds, the smells, the chaos, the multi-cultural life the city breathes. But it poses yet another issue with Adam not living here. I can't take up a job I desperately want because I get free childcare with my job here, and right now, financially it makes more sense. I'd be working a forty-hour week just to pay the crèche fees if I worked in geriatrics my first year, so I'm still just volunteering at Sir Patrick Dun's at weekends . . . for now. Until I sort out my future with Adam.

Eh-hem.

Máiréad was not only a resident but my dear friend, and I loved her so. She was a strong, independent woman, but life had slapped her with a big bowl of lemons. No lemonade to be had. Not a fizzy bubble to be seen in her long and lonely, eighty-something years. She had no one else in the world. She used to push her old gingham squeaky shopping-trolley-on-wheels around Silverside, from the minute we opened our doors until security turfed her out as the last shutter came down. I'd made it my business to be kind to her and give her my time.

*"If I didn't come here, I'd never see the face of one,"* she'd tell me, living as she did, in a run-down council house; it saved on her heating bills. That was, until they evicted her, to build a high-tech IT development. Oh, they had offered to rehouse her in County Leitrim, but to a true Dub like Máiréad, it may as well have been Outer Mongolia. She would sit upstairs in Geraghty's,

all day, every day, hunched over a single pot of tea, watching the world go by. At times she'd thought she was invisible, she'd told me. She died holding my hand, but just before she passed, she confided in me that she'd had a baby when she was eighteen. Kathleen, she'd called her, before she was ripped from her arms at birth, in a mother-and-baby home in Tuam, County Galway. She gave me her engagement ring from her beloved Jim, from a marriage that was never allowed to happen. I'd made her an absolute promise, that I would find her long-lost daughter and return the ring her birth father had bought for her birth mother in 1947. Theirs had been a forbidden love: Máiréad, a young, uneducated office cleaner and Frank a well-educated, wealthy English Navy Captain's son.

"D'ya know how I can tell it's gonna snow out? Take a look at these, pet." The old lady lifts her less than steady hands out in front of me. Her fingers look arthritic, bent across one another. "The cold kills the joints." She tries to wiggle her fingers but they barely move.

I give her my warmest smile. "Ow, they look sore? It is Baltic out there, isn't it? Soup's a great choice, eat up while it's hot."

I rummage down into my bag for my phone. So now you see, apart from calling Annemarie out on our game of charades and my plan to tell Adam I ain't moving across the pond, there is yet another game I am playing. This one is a game of life or death as far as I'm concerned. It's a horrendously nerve-wracking, impatient waiting game at this stage.

I'm frantically awaiting a return message from Máiréad Farrell's long-lost daughter, Kathleen.

And I think I can keep my promise.

I think I've finally found her!

# 4

*"If you aren't gonna use your heart, then what's the difference if it gets broken?"*

Kevin McCallister, *Home Alone 2*

"**A**RGH, YOU DIDN'T!" I hiss under my breath, pulling my empty hand up out of my satchel, patting my skirt pockets frantically. I've left my phone charging behind Information again and me expecting Kathleen to text me back! Peri-Peri strikes again!

This new perimenopause brain is no friend of mine lately. I'm in a brain fog of sweaty forgetfulness half the time despite the winter frost. I can't tell you the amount of times I lose my phone, keys, diary, forget the milk and bread, leave stuff out of Frances's nappy bag like ... nappies! My GP has also warned me about "the last kick of a dying horse" and to take no chances on unprotected sex. The perimenopause is truly mind-blowing.

The search for Kathleen has been going on for nine and a half months now. Every spare moment at night, researching, googling, wading through old Galway newspapers online, heart-breaking mother-and-baby home horror stories, archives in the local library but I came up with nothing. Then I came upon an ancestral heritage site called My Hopeful Heritage, I paid for the yearly membership and I found Kathleen by her date of birth and location of birth! Eventually it's all paid off . . . kind of.

I just need her to agree to meet me. I messaged her two weeks ago but she still hasn't messaged back after our initial connection, and I don't know why. The ball's firmly in her court but I'm determined not to give up hope. It will literally break my heart if I'm never able to return Máiréad's engagement ring and fulfil my promise. It's also a very valuable ring! I took it to a jeweller's, Jewels & Gems, in the Cotswolds in June with Adam, the same shop he bought my engagement ring from.

"Where did you get this?" the old man in the shop had asked, his eye stuck to the small hole in his circular magnifier, examining the ring.

"An old friend," I'd told him.

"It's antique Victorian, eighteen carat, yellow gold platinum, old Euro diamond engagement ring, very nice piece. Insured?" He'd twirled the magnifier in his hand.

"Um, no?" I'd made a face at Adam.

"Should we?" Adam had looked at me, his spiky lashes throwing little shadows on his handsome face. He'd draped his strong arm over my bare shoulder in my strappy sundress, as the Cotswold sunshine had blasted through the small Georgian-barred shop window and it seemed like all the rings encased behind well-polished glass were sparkling stars.

I made a mental note to insure the ring as soon as possible.

"Well, I'd value it at somewhere in and around . . . twenty-five thousand pounds." He'd looked up at us.

"Woah!" Adam shrieked, dropping his car keys on the floor.

"Whatttttt?" We'd bent at the same time to pick them up and bashed heads. "Oh wow, that's about twenty-eight thousand euro! I have to find Kathleen!" I'd held onto Adam's arm so hard, he'd flinched.

"I'd advise you go get it insured immediately. Don't leave it on your to-do list; so many people do." He'd polished up the ring for us with a shammy before we'd left the shop.

"Maybe she doesn't want to be found?" I can still hear Barbara, my own mother, in my head now. This was what she'd said about Kathleen not getting back when we talked on the phone last Sunday. Me in Sir Patrick Dun's setting up the bingo and chocolate shortbread biscuits Annemarie made for the residents, and Mam in her sunny, Bougainvillea-scented villa in Nerja, Spain.

"Don't be harassing the poor kid, dear." As always with my mother, a pan could be heard sizzling in the background.

"Kid? Mam, Kathleen's in her sixties!" I'd yelled, laying each larger print card out on the tables with a rubber number stamper on top.

"Lexie, we're all kids when it comes to our parents. Speaking of kids, I miss my baby."

"Hardly a baby." I'd chuckled.

"You're my baby. And Frances. I'll be over to see you soon, *very* soon – the moment just needs to present itself to me, dear. The universe will let me know when that is. I know it's hard for you to travel on your own with all the unnecessary paraphernalia you young mothers weigh yourselves down with. God knows how we all survived in the seventies and eighties! We didn't have child seats or high-tech prams with James Bond safety devices, we sat you on our knees in the car, there were no helmets or seat belts,

45

we had you under our arms when travelling with a few bottles of formula, a cotton nappy and a large safety pin, and away we went. I gave you the top off a bottle as a soother!"

"Sounds terrifying," I'd envied.

"But you're our only child and I do not want to miss out on our only granddaughter. I'm assuming you won't try again, at your age? What was it your gynaecologist had you down as again? A geriatric pregnancy, wasn't it? Can't wait to pick up that little doll and peck her to death."

"That's disturbing . . ." I'd smiled as the residents started to shuffle in.

"Kiss her all over then." There was the *click, click, click* of another gas hob being ignited.

"Better."

"Now my paella's bubbling over, I ran out of saffron . . ." She prattles on about her dish that is hundreds of miles away and I can't taste, then pauses as I hear sloshing and slurping sounds. Thanks, Mam. "Your father is at his boxing class again, came home with a black eye last week! We're really embracing this winter season of our lives, this twilight, it's time for a glass of sangria, I skip the siestas! Too much energy!" And just like that she'd hung up.

Great chat, Mam.

*"God rest ye merry gentlemennnnnnnnnnnnnnn . . ."* the Silverside Christmas Carollers start up on the floor beneath us, as they bellow harmoniously and melodically echoing loudly all over the vast, high-ceilinged centre.

"Let's go. Only a few hours left and we're free for five whole days." Annemarie tugs my bent elbow, links me and everything feels better. More normal. A problem shared and all that. We make our way through the heaving Christmas crowds, past more rows and rows of Poinsettias, spraying a blanket of deep red all over the centre.

"Answer me this. You told me you found your Johnny Castle?" she says.

"I did."

"What do you suppose happened to Baby and Johnny after he dragged her out of that corner, danced with her, raised her high above his head and kissed her?"

"They lived happily ever after?" I unlink her, do that famous Baby strut down the five granite steps, holding onto the handrail, rolling my hearty hips and throwing my head back. Annemarie roars with laughter and follows me down.

"You really think so?" she questions. "Happily ever after?"

"I do." I'm still catching my breath.

"So you think Johnny was happy to let Baby go work in the peace corps, change the world? While he stayed in a small town in America, working as a labourer or whatever it was he did?"

"His Uncle Paul got him into the union!" I say. "House Painters and Plasters number 179."

"So Johnny would've had Baby's back? Spurred her on to greatness?"

"I – I think he would have, yeah."

"I'm not so sure, Baby." A more than impressive Johnny Castle impression. "Maybe *Dirty Dancing* gave us all false hopes."

"Or maybe it showed us how to be strong women!" I extend my right arm, drop my left fist into the crook and raise it upright as we get caught in a large group of tourists in "Springdale, Ohio Irish Christmas Charity Boat Run" luminous T-shirts, all swinging Carrolls Irish Gifts bags. We wrangle our way through them.

"True love is a real thing," I tell her, settling my bag.

"But is *everlasting* love a real thing?" she asks.

"I suppose I'll soon find out."

We squeeze past the swirling queue of exhausted-looking grandparents for Santa's Grotto, cut through the smoothie bar, wave at Eoin, the manager, round the record store, a brief reprieve from the Christmas carollers as Taylor Swift blasts out at us with her moody but excellent advice and I can't help walking in time to the beat, as we shake it off towards the lifts.

"I'll see you at the desk, going up to the bathroom," I tell her unfolding my bag over my head.

"I need to go too."

"One of us should get back to August!"

"Oh well." Annemarie stabs at the circular button. Shoppers push past us, laden down with bags. Trolleys belching with rolls of glittery wrapping paper, Christmas puddings, selection boxes, tins of biscuits and colourful Christmas crackers. Toys piled higher than people can physically hold on to. Carols continue to ring out around the centre, this one celebrating a newborn king. I'm seeing Adam tonight and nothing can stop the excitement in my heart, I'm simply not in control of that.

The lift stops and allows people to burst out, leaving us blissfully alone in a calm bubble. I hope I didn't force her confession, that was never my intention.

"Sorry if I pushed you into . . ." I start.

"Please don't say sorry. That word." She blocks her ears. "If I have to hear Tom apologise one more time for what happened, I'll scream. I can't tell him it's okay anymore. He just keeps saying, sorry, sorry, sorry all the time. He *posts* cards to me that say SORRY, he texts me SORRY. He emails me SORRY. One morning he even spelled the word out with Rice Krispies on the kitchen table! Admitting it to you was the first time I've said it out loud. I shocked myself a little. I need space to clear my head, once Christmas is over I will . . ."

My brain winces as I consider all this.

"I really need to take these bastard wedges off." She reaches down, rubs her skinny ankle.

"Wear flats." I raise a foot to demonstrate how comfortable I am.

"I'm not an animal," she scorns.

Then we stare at one another, unspoken words but at last a comfortable silence. When the lift doors part, we step out together towards the toilets.

"At least we cleared the air," I tell her as I put my shoulder to the stiff door of the ladies toilets and push it open.

"More than Polly's done in here – jeez, the stink! That girl doesn't know how to spell hygiene." She holds her nose as I twist myself behind the toilet door and slide the lock across.

With that job done I'm relieved but hyper aware now it's just a few more hours until I'm with Adam again and the butterflies in my stomach begin to bash. It's always the same symptoms when I'm about to see him. It feels a little like heartburn, then those butterflies start to dance. They do an Irish jig and swing each other round, bouncing and cheering and generally having the craic for themselves in my stomach. That's the intensity of my passion for Adam Cooper. But now I'm second-guessing my plan. How will he take my news? Is Annemarie right? Is the practical solution to move to Rosehill? Am I making a huge mistake?

# 5

*"Just remember, the true spirit of Christmas lies in your heart."*

Santa, *The Polar Express*

WHEN I COME OUT OF THE CUBICLE, Annemarie's standing at the sink, whistling "Jingle Bells", tip tapping her wedge and brushing her unruly curls up into a neat bun.

"I'm starting to second-guess myself . . . Am I—" I blurt, but before I can finish she butts in.

"I was being a bitch. Of course I want you to talk to me about Adam, okay? I was being . . . well, a jealous cow and just not very nice! You of all people don't deserve that." She zips open her tote that's resting between the sinks.

"You weren't being a bitch, I get it. One hundred per cent. And just to add, well . . ." I shout over the clamorous hand dryer and it stops mid-*whoosh*. "I'm finding the long distance single-mother stuff difficult. It's really hard," I admit.

"It is. It is." She nods like a bobbing car-head, holds up a miniature lipstick. Annemarie's a sucker for the travel-size stuff.

"In fairness he is trying his utmost to be here as much as humanly possible, it's not his fault, it's . . ."

". . . *your* fault?" She furrows an eyebrow, pulls the lid off her lippy and concentrates on twisting the colour up high.

"No, you know what I mean. He tries to please everyone," I say honestly.

"Including himself." She sucks in her lips to dry them, and they make a smacking sound.

"You still think he has the best of both worlds?" Uh-oh. What have I started? I feel an Adam ambush coming on; she's always thought Adam has it easy.

There is a pause as another woman walks into the ladies, laden down with bags.

"I didn't say that . . . Don't worry, I'm not going there," Annemarie says quietly, waving the lipstick when the woman has entered her cubicle.

"You didn't have to." I shrug.

"I will say that he can't leave his teenage daughter to move over here and that you've known that from day one." She rounds her lips. If they ever needed a stand-in for Nicole Kidman, they need look no further than Annemarie.

"Well not right now he can't, we're still waiting on this bloody letter! I'm praying Freya gets a yes, for her and for me – so I can minimise any Martha contact, is that selfish?"

"No, not at all . . ."

We look at one another in the reflection of the glass. Annemarie leans in closer and rounds out a bright shade of red. "Brazen Hussy," she says, smacking her lips.

"Who, Martha?" I gasp. It's not like Annemarie to be such a name-caller and she's dropped a few already today. Martha really gets on her last nerve.

"It's the name of my lipstick." She pushes her tongue into her cheek, snaps the lid on with a click and smirks. Maybe she *does* think the name applies to a certain person, though. "And lastly for today, I don't think you're actually aware of this, but you honestly haven't been around for me. You've been so distracted." She's very matter of fact as she removes a small tin, opens it and pulls out several bobbie pins.

I'm gobsmacked. "That's not fair, how can you say that? Back that up, please." I turn and perch my bum on the edge of the countertop, looking at her.

"Not just with Adam, Lexie, you've been so preoccupied with finding Máiréad's daughter, it's borderline obsession. All your spare time is gone with this search. Every time I called you it was, 'I'm online here searching, can you call me back?' Always distracted, always googling."

"I didn't realise I was being so abrupt with you." But now I vividly recall a phone call where I cut her off mid-sentence and hung up as the email from Kathleen pinged in. I feel terrible. All she had going on with Tom and I just wasn't there, she's right!

"It's just I don't think us drifting apart has been all my fault. Wanted to get that off my chest too. It's done now. Clean sheet. New page?"

I nod, push myself off the damp counter and finish drying off my hands on my skirt. Annemarie holds three long brown bobby pins between her clenched teeth, takes her time sliding each one of them into her bun and securing them tightly as my mind flashes back.

*

Annemarie was planning a surprise for Tom and needed me to take Ben overnight. That was all she'd told me on text. I'd just returned from that painful week in the Cotswolds where Martha and Deb were nothing but demeaning and sarcastic around me and I'd been privy to that most hurtful and eye-opening conversation.

"Don't make me ever go back there," I'd moaned to Annemarie as we shared a pizza and Oreo milkshakes in town on the terrace of Lisa's Trattoria with the kids, that sunny evening. After dessert she'd thrown a rucksack over her back and asked me to help her shop for the "surprise occasion" in She Loves Secrets, a discreet lingerie store off South William Street. She emerged from the changing room dressed in a beige trench coat.

"What the hell are you wearing, Inspector?" I'd asked and she'd pulled me back in with her and opened the coat to reveal a sexy, red lace teddy suit, satin pink trim and suspenders underneath, tags still hanging off.

"Oh! I SEE!" I'd gasped then we'd howled laughing afterwards in the car as I'd spun her over to the seaside town of Howth, where Tom worked, Ben and Frances strapped in the back. Tom had told Annemarie he would be stocktaking all his fishing supplies, from rods to feeder lines, until all hours, so he'd just crash on the sofabed they had in the back stockroom. I'd left her at the end of the pier, giggled at her inelegant tottering and taken the kids back to mine for a mushed banana on toast tea for all three of us.

But when she arrived she'd found the steel door off the latch. She'd recounted the incident to me as though she was a witness in the stand. A very calm, detailed, yet traumatic recollection:

"I pushed the steel door and it swung open freely. I should have guessed something was amiss right then as Tom's paranoid about locking that door. The cats get in and eat the tackle. I tiptoed on the ball of my foot through the shop, to the open door of the stockroom. Surprise! I stepped in, my hands pulling apart the seams of the unbelted trench coat. Then my eyes seemed to take a lifetime to register what was moving in front of me. It was Tom.

53

Wriggling on the sofabed. Naked. That odd tan line of his ancient beach shorts the first thing I'd noticed. 'Shit!' he said. I dropped the coat. I don't know why. I stayed true to my plan for some reason, but it was only as the coat hit the sawdust and Tom moved that I saw her. Gail. Stark naked, legs akimbo, beneath him. Tom leaped up, covered his fishing tackle, if you will, with Ben's sleepy-sleep pillow and kept shouting, 'Oh no no no, oh shit,' over and over. Still I stood there in my stupid skimpies, frozen. I mean it was plain to see what was happening but my brain just wouldn't compute. It was like it was stuck in first gear, revving and revving trying to get up a steep hill. 'It's the first time,' he said. 'It's never happened before. Tell her,' he kept yelling at Gail, 'tell her.' I was rooted to the spot as he kept begging for my forgiveness. Gail and myself stared at each other. Her butt-naked, me in a pathetic barely there outfit. Even in that moment I thought, who has a stomach that flat? 'I'm so sorry,' was all she said. Still my brain would not function. I watched Gail crawl on all fours across the sawdust. She grabbed her bag under a load of empty beer bottles. 'Jesus Christ, Tom,' she roared at him and ran out the backdoor, completely naked. I heard an engine turn over and she sped off in her car. He started to cry – huge, racking sobs – he fell to his knees, the sawdust scattered all around him and the beer bottles rolled. I'm not sure how long I stood there for, watching him fall apart, but I eventually picked up my coat, pulled my arms through, found the belt, tied it tight, kicked off the shoes and walked away."

*

"I said, new page?" Annemarie's hand is still outstretched.

"New page it is!" I agree, clasping her hand in mine. "Didn't know how insensitive and unavailable I've been and you're absolutely right, I've been preoccupied trying to do right by Máiréad." I have been obsessed, I can't help it.

"Ah, you're in love and you're the most kind-hearted person I have ever known." She pops her items back into her tote. "Why don't you and Frances come over to me at seven? Tom's in Kinsale. I can defrost a veggie lasagne, make sweet potato fries? We can curl up on the couch and chat? Sip a glass of Noir? Stick on some nineties hits? You could get a cab home? Or even better stay the night?" She looks up at me, her wide eyes hopeful.

"I'm collecting Adam from the airport at eight." I grimace. *Shit*, I think. *Of all the nights she offers.*

"Oh, of course, I forgot." She steps back, and instantly I try to dissolve that distance threatening us again.

"Sorry." I tense.

"No, don't be silly, don't mind me, I'm a hot perimenopausal mess lately."

"Aren't we all, sister."

She clacks the tin of hair accessories shut, and we finally leave as I heave open the door.

We pass the jolly Christmas carollers, midway through a rendition of "Mistletoe and Wine", and suddenly I'm guiltier about our strained friendship now than I was earlier! That backfired. I hadn't realised how distracted I've been, not just with Adam but with finding Máiréad's daughter. I need to do better for Anne-marie. There I was, parking all the blame on her shoulders – well, well, well, Lexie, seems you aren't the brilliant friend you make yourself out to be after all.

Well that's about to change!

# 6

*"It's all humbug, I tell you."*

Ebenezer Scrooge, *A Christmas Carol*

"SPEAKING OF MISTLETOE AND WINE," I mutter under my breath, "not long to go now." The butterflies are still stomping out the Riverdance and I'm counting down the hours until I can hold him, picturing the pricier-than-normal bottle of white chilling on its back in the fridge for us. When the big hand hits wine and the little hand hits o' clock! Pop! My mother tells me wine o' clock is not a good saying, it's very harmful.

"Hundreds of women drinking bottles and bottles of wine at twelve o' clock in the afternoon, according to the reports I've read!" Barbara had chastised me recently.

"That seems pretty far-fetched to me?" I'd responded, telling her I see more than my fair share of women than most people every day in a shopping centre at twelve o' clock, and most of them seem to be running from pillar to post, working, grocery shopping, collecting kids from crèche or school, planning lunches and dinners, dropping to gymnastics, picking up from soccer, buying birthday gifts for parties, arranging playdays, dentist appointments, teacher's meetings . . . I've yet to see any woman, that I know anyway, with her feet up, glugging a Chardonnay, at twelve in the afternoon. Of course Mam told me not to be facetious. I wasn't.

Anyway, I digress. I'll make it up to Annemarie after Christmas, make her my number-one priority. But I can't change my plans for the next few days. And I've been so looking forward to this evening, before the madness commences. Just me and Adam. Alone time. To accompany our wine I bought ready-made seafood risottos and toffee melt-in-the-middle puddings. I almost broke into the fridge last night but stopped myself, attacking a selection box instead. My stomach rumbles at the memory of that murdered Curly Wurly. Isn't that bizarre, I've just stuffed my face?

"About bleedin' time too! Thank God! I thought yiz were never comin' back! It's bleedin' bedlam here. Christmas shoppers are all off their heads!" August, my colleague-slash-boss, pulls off her lopsided flashing Santa hat, her short damp hair stuck to her head, pulls open her bag. "I hate Christmas! What's wrong wit' people? The shops only close for one day! Twenty-four hours – 1,440 minutes, or 86,400 seconds! I watch *The Chase* on repeat, I know these facts! A woman just lost her mind in front of me because her visa card won't work. Said her whole family are gonna starve to death. I'll see yiz on the other side. I'm havin' a smoke, goin home to bed, an' orderin' a Nandos . . . for two!" she pants, comically.

"Sorry, the queue for the ladies was off the charts. Some big tourist group from Ohio," I lie to her.

"Oh yeah, I saw dem!" she acknowledges with a full-rotation roll of her eyes.

A clever, well-planted lie.

"Askin' me where they could buy Aran sweaters and confused as to why none of us were wearing them. I told them that Aran sweaters were only invented so us Irish could recognise the tourists!" Grandiosely, she waves her unlit cigarette in the air.

"Where's Lisa?" Annemarie casts around the desk.

"Horrific period pains, she had to go home to her bed and hot-water bottle."

I pick up the ever-ringing phone, every light flashing red at me with customers on hold. The carollers are dinging and donging merrily on a high. I've often wished those red lights could be yellow, a much more mellow colour; the red has my blood pressure going through the glass roof.

"Good afternoon, Silverside Shopping Centre, it's Lexie speaking, how may I help you?" I cradle the phone under my ear, trying to pull my long Santa hat on over my fat bun.

"Well helloooo there, Lexie Speaking."

The voice.

My knees literally weaken.

It's him.

"Adam! Hiiiiii!" My hand clutches the receiver tighter, presses it into my ear. "Why are you ringing the work line?"

"I couldn't get you on your mobile?" His *voice* still actually turns me on, it's insane!

"Oh shit, sorry, we were up in Geraghty's having lunch, just realised I forgot it." I spin around to see its fully charged light twinkling at me.

"Er, Lexie . . ." He clears his throat.

Oh.

I slap my head with the palm of my hand. If I had a penny for every *Er, Lexie.*

"Yup?" I bite my bottom lip, but my teeth slide off the Vaseline I've applied. I turn, face the oval mirror above our coat racks. I look myself in my eye, shake my head. The happy smile slides off my face in front of my very eyes.

"I'm not going to make it tonight . . ." The words get lodged in his throat as the end of the sentence fades away.

"That's fine." I bite the lip, watch the red turn to white. Settle my Santa hat in place. Lick my finger several times and run it under my smudged eye, clear the mess.

"I am gonna get over to help you! I swear! But it's going to be lunchtime tomorrow, I'm afraid . . ." He falters.

I pull two tendrils of blonde hair down from my bun, curl them on my index finger.

"You there?"

"Yup."

"Something's come up . . ." I can hear the torture in his voice, already I know he's tried to make this call for an hour but he's in knots about letting us down.

"That's grand, Adam, no worries." I breathe heavy on the mirror and I disappear.

"What's that sound?"

"Nothing." I slowly reappear, but I still look miserably disappointed.

A grumble of noise sounds as the overhead lights in the centre power on. The dim daylight outside is fading fast on this late wintery, December afternoon, like my dreams for tonight. I'm so tired of asking "why?", so I don't. It will be to do with Martha changing plans again, of that I'm sure. I'm not going to mention the money he wastes on changing flights anymore either, even though I feel so bad for yet another financial hit for him. He can scarcely afford it too, working as hard as he does as an A&E nurse.

"I'm really sorry, Lexie." He clears his throat again.

"It's grand, honestly."

I hear the rattle of his keys.

"Martha got the date wrong for Freya's Dublin Horse Show qualifier, it wasn't this morning, it's tomorrow morning, in Chipping Campden! She's terribly sorry about the mix-up." He sighs, turns the key and his engine purrs to life. I can just picture him in his well-worn leather jacket sitting in his trusty Volvo. His dark, messy hair falling over his eyes as he leans over the steering wheel talking to me on speaker. His long legs reaching for the pedals.

*Sorry my arse,* I think. But say: "Well that's a bummer." I wipe the streaky mirror with the palm of my hand, then curl the cord around my finger. The diamond in my engagement ring flashes at me under the bright industrial lights. Also the symbol of my distant dreams, it seems to say.

"Why she traded her Jeep in for that Mini I'll never know. She totally wasn't thinking about me needing her to help me out pulling the horse box."

Yeah, right.

"You know Freya's desperately trying to qualify for the RDS in Dublin next August, it will really help her to get that place on the course builders course." I can tell he's just run his hand down his thick stubble by the warble in his voice.

"I know," I say sympathetically.

"Sorry." His voice sounds tired now.

"So you said." I have to lean forward to let Annemarie squeeze past me, the area behind our information desk is anything but spacious. At any given time we have at least ten lost bags, a dozen jackets, hats, scarfs, phones, keys, dozens of credit cards all under our counter.

"I'll make it up to you. How's my beautiful baby girl, how's Frances?" he jabbers on, as an indicator *click-clock, click-clock, click-clocks*.

"She's fine, still a bit sniffly but she's up in the crèche. They're all full of the sniffles in there." I try to sound grand. I'm anything but.

"Everyone's so excited to see her next week! I'd say she'll get more gifts than a Kardashian. Mum's been to the Woolgate Centre three times this week." His indicator continues to click, then stops.

"That's so kind." I try to be upbeat but inside I'm flattened because I know darn well Martha has done this on purpose, deliberately given Adam the wrong day. I used to think I was imagining the worst of her, but now she's so transparent. Well, to me anyway. I just really wish Adam would see that too. But she hides it so well in front of him.

"I love you, so much, both of you." I can just visualise him cruising along towards Great Yew, one elbow resting on the open window despite the bitter weather. His usual driving habit he isn't even aware of, pulling at the tight chain around his neck, the silver feather swaying on his tanned bare skin as he watches the road and his wing mirror way more often that most drivers I know. Involuntarily, my shoulders shiver. I've been known to stare at how his feet change the pedals, how he moves the gear stick. I know, I'm a lost cause.

"Lexie!" Annemarie pushes past me again, dragging open the top drawer where we keep the gift cards. "I need some help here!" She pulls out a new pile, rips off the blue rubber band with a snap and shakes her hand where it's snapped back on her.

"You're not too mad at me?" he shouts now over the gushing wind flooding in.

"There's, like, twenty stressed people in a queue here, I have to go," I say.

"Are you very disappointed about tonight?"

"No, I fully understand, Adam." I know I sound flippant and I don't mean to.

"You didn't go to any trouble, I hope?"

"No." If I had a penny. A storm of hormonal tears threaten.

"You really are the best. FaceTime me when you guys are back tonight? I'll be back at Rosehill soon." The wind is chopping up his words.

"Will do." I swallow all emotion.

"See you tomorrow, can't wait. I know I'll only be in Dublin for one night, but we'll make the most of it and we can still all travel back together as planned. Oh! Just quickly! Did you get your dress for the wedding?"

I release a slow breath. "Not yet."

"Lexie! Seriously?" Annemarie shakes her cobalt shellacs at me.

"Lexie! The wedding's in a few days. Get shopping," Adam directs me, laughing.

"Lexie! Get off the phone and do some work!" A man's deep voice. No clue who's shouted that at me. My head spins.

I hate shopping. "I will."

"I know you hate shopping."

"It's fine. Since I don't have to drive out to the airport later and it's late night here, I'll collect Frances and go down to Threads. They'll have something that will do me."

"It's black tie, remember." He uses his nurse-to-patient voice now.

"Lexie! Get off the phone!" Annemarie yells at me now.

"Gotta go." I hang up, turn to face Annemarie, her cheeks flushed. "About that veggie lasagne in the freezer and sweet potato fries . . . will there be garlic bread?" As hard as I try there is a definite wobble in my voice.

She looks up from stamping a use-by-date on the gift card. "Adam's not coming?"

"He is. But it'll be tomorrow."

We share a tremulous smile.

"Garlic bread, red wine, maybe we can stick on *Fight Club* after the nineties hits, ogle Brad's six-pack?" She shimmies her shoulders and I'm grateful that's she biting her tongue.

I nod. ". . . and you'll open the cheese board just for me?"

"Ohhh . . . I dunno about that!" She validates the card with the requested amount, adjusts her Santa hat that is far too big for her small head, and wishes her customer a very merry Christmas.

"Please." I clasp my hands prayer-like under my chin, so the tips of my fingers get lost in the under flesh.

Annemarie won the Big Red Silverside Shopping Centre Christmas Raffle. We salivated over the prize. Those mouth-watering cheeses ensconced in the clear cellophane for the last three weeks, the prize on display, teasing us on our counter. It was bursting with Cheddar, feta, Edam, Manchego, Gouda, Danish blue, Stilton, Gorgonzola and my personal favourite, Brie. Expensive Pinot Noirs from the Valley of all Valleys no doubt. Jars of chutneys and crackers that looked so slim we wondered if they would be strong enough to hold a chunk of cheese.

"I don't think so, I'm saving it."

"What are you saving it for?" I demanded to know.

"Christmas."

"It *is* Christmas!" I said politely but firmly.

63

"Excuse me? It's Lexie, am I right? Do you actually work here or are you on work experience? Adult TY work experience perhaps?" A rotund man in clear-rimmed glasses clutching a folded-over McDonald's brown bag that is starting to exhibit sweat patches roars at us, I recognise him now by his paper tucked under his arm as the crusty coffee cup man from earlier.

"I – I work here," I stupidly give him an answer, pull at the crest on my jacket as proof.

"Then kindly gossip on your own time. I asked this one with the red hair for a fifty-euro voucher for Mrs Hughes next door – she minds Barry, the dog, during the day – how long does it bloody take? My curly fries will be soggy! Move it!"

"Well I see the Christmas spirit is alive and well," I hiss under my breath but smile sweetly. "Apologies sir, I'll get that for you right away." A twirl of my hoop, a squeeze of the white bobble on my hat and I burst into action. The rest of the afternoon is non-stop, hundreds of vouchers are sold, multiple coats are lost, hundreds of lotto tickets are purchased, dozens of car park tickets are lost, three children are lost and found, and reports of stolen wallets and phones all filed. By the time we make our way up to the crèche at six o' clock, I'm shattered and starving yet again.

"See you later, good luck with the dress, I'll get supper prepared." Annemarie zips up her high-neck, furry white coat as she settles Ben's chequered hat and ties the drawstring under his chin.

"Supper? Where have you moved to, Downton Abbey?" I'm still more than shocked (and a little grateful) she hasn't said anything more about Adam cancelling again. It's been a huge bone of contention these last three years, his cancelling of plans; she must really want this get-together later very badly.

"Ha." She takes Ben by the hand. I reach over and tickle my lovely godson under his chin.

"Will Auntie Lelly bring her tools later?" I pretend to bang the world's tiniest hammer.

"Tools Lelly! Yes! Plurse!" He giggles, his nose running, trying to look up at me through the wool covering half his beautiful light blue eyes.

My tools are usually a small brown paper bag of chocolate ones, mini saws and hammers, that I get from Pick Your Mix on Level three.

"Now, not too many tools, okay Auntie *Lex-ie*?" Annemarie frowns, over-pronouncing my name to correct Ben.

"You can never have too many tools, isn't that right, Ben?"

"Toooools!" He stamps his foot in his tiny Timberland boots. "Yes, Lelly!"

His mother frowns. "Yes, you absolutely can have too many. By the way, you are more than welcome to rifle through my wardrobe later for the wedding, I told you that already?" She holds his hand tightly and heads for the glass sliding door.

"Annemarie, there is nothing more depressing than opening your ultra-tidy, colour-coordinated, winter-summer-separated wardrobe and looking at your beautiful, vintage dresses and jumpsuits knowing I can't even get my head through the neck-line, never mind over my hips!" I've had enough trauma for one day I think.

"She ate all her tea, didn't ya princess?" Honour, one of the childminders, approaches me, my daughter in her arms, wiping her mouth with a water wipe. Frances sees me and her eyes light up. Dressed in her pink dungarees, matching polo neck and white tights and patent leather shoes, she raises her arms out to me and I reach for her, hug her so tightly I'm practically inhaling her.

"Hel-loooo my darling! Oh I missed you today! Yes I did." I blow a raspberry into the warm folds of skin on her neck and she sniffles but gurgles with delight. I never knew I could love this hard. This fiercely. She has my sharp features but Adam's dark hair and big brown eyes. She grabs a tuft of my blonde waves that spill over my shoulders, recently released from the constraints of my bun. It's her favourite thing to do.

"Your buggy is the last one in there, Lexie," Honour tells me, pulling open the storage room door and rolling it over towards me as I try to undo Frances's painful grip.

"Good girl, let Mammy's hair go, I'm spending far too much money on post-baby regrowth shampoo and conditioner for this to keep happening. You're scalping me, love." I wince. Make no mistake, a six-month-old can hurt a grown woman. A clump of hair falls to the floor as I slip Frances in and tuck her bag and duffel coat under the buggy. I pick up my murdered hair, stamp on the pedal and drop it into the nappy bin.

"Thanks, Honour. Have a brilliant Christmas," I tell her and press a twenty-euro note into her hand. Annemarie and myself had already gone halves on a box of luxury chocolates and three bottles of Baileys for the crèche staff last week.

"Ahh thanks a million, Lexie, you really don't have to. You got us stuff already," Honour says, delighted.

"I do! I don't know what we'd do without you, you babysit for me too." I owe them far more than some booze, chocolates and a crumpled twenty!

Honour crouches down, gently rubs the lobes on Frances's ears the ways she likes. "Well, it's easy having this one to look after, isn't it, Frances? Not to mention the sight for sore eyes when her daddy arrives on occasion to pick her up." She rises and gives me an over-pronounced wink. "That man could kill a woman."

"Don't I know it." I chuckle.

"I mean, who can look that sexy in a baseball cap, pair of faded jeans and a grey sweatshirt?" She seems to be genuinely confused. "If ya don't mind me saying, Lexie," she adds quickly.

"Not at all. I agree with you," I tell her matter-of-factly.

"You back on Stephen's Day?" Honour asks me with her big black book in hand.

"No, back on the twenty-seventh," I tell her. She writes that down and I give her a last wave before pushing Frances out.

You know, I still feel odd pushing a buggy, like I'm someone else. It's still hard for me to believe I'm a mammy. Maybe because I just never expected to be one. Nor did I desperately want to be one. I was never sure one way or the other. Or maybe it's because a mammy in the park assumed I was Frances's granny last week! In fairness to me, that morning I'd had two hours' sleep with Frances's two back teeth breaking through all night and her roaring the place down, the poor pet. I'd pushed her like a zombie to the Krazy Kidz Kafé in desperate need for the strongest coffee I could ingest and a fat bacon roll smothered in ketchup. I'd almost cried (read: I did cry a little bit) when it was closed. A yellow sticky note on the window said, "Closed due to staff shortage!" – oh and I'd forgotten to take my Ugg slippers off. My bad.

"We're going shopping, pet." I check she's strapped in carefully, kiss her again and push her out onto the escalator, gravity gripping the small wheels, all the way down to Threads. Frances loves the hustle and bustle of the centre, she sits back and people

67

watches, happier still when I buy her a baby cone with hundreds and thousands sprinkles, her chubby legs swinging in her patent shoes and her face covered in white deliciousness. She's her mother's daughter alright.

"What to wear to your fiancé's ex-wife's wedding to his best friend?" I slag myself, leaning over the handles of the buggy to set the cone upright again in her tiny hand. I stop outside Threads, stare at the mannequins. The one good thing about this Irish-owned family boutique is that the mannequins come in all shapes and sizes. It's the way I like to shop. I tend to look at a mannequin around my size and buy the entire outfit it's wearing. Top to toe.

"The black dress in the window?" I say as I approach the sales girl inside. She's up a small stepladder in a skintight denim catsuit and sky-high platform boots. I admire the bravery!

"The V-neck wrap, hun?" She totters down in the boots. How, I ask myself, does she not topple over?

"Yes, please."

"What size, hun?" She sashays toward the back of the boutique despite the obvious weight of those platforms weighing her body down. I push Frances in front of me, following her.

"I dunno. I don't do sizes, can you just hand me out a few to try on?"

She turns, and if she had the ability to frown, I think that's what she would be doing. Her face is focused on Frances. "D'ya wanna get rid of that ice cream, hun, it's all over her little lap?"

"Oh sh— sorry." I bend for the baby bag, zip it open, but I've no wipes in it.

She circles me, her prey. I pull out a clean nappy, wipe the mess and fold the remainder of the mushed-up cone into it.

"I'd say you're about a size . . ."

"No!" I holler and she stumbles back as Frances laughs loudly. "I don't want to know what size the world pins on me! I haven't had weighing scales in my home for ten years now."

She pats the air with the palm of her hand. "Christ on a bike! Ya scared the shite outta me. Sorry little one. Fine."

She looks me up and down, circles me once more, then yanks out three dresses from the tightly packed, long gold rail before handing me a colossal key with the number three in rubber swinging off it. I hand her the nappy and she grimaces.

"Lovely. Thanks." She clomps away.

"Thank you!" I call after her and shove Frances into the largest changing room, pull the ill-fitting drape across the rings. She warbles to herself as I wrangle out of my uniform and pull the first one off the hanger.

"It's black tie," I mimic Martha, unkindly. "That means a full-length dress, Lexie," she'd thrown after me, sarcastically. I can see her pinched expression, her dewy skin, her sleek, black bob with feathered bangs, in her perfectly skintight, cream, ribbed summer dress and Birkenstocks as she begrudgingly invited me to her wedding in the summer.

"Sorry, your daddy is fabulous," I tell Frances, who's chewing her pink sleeve now, drool skating down her chin, "but your half-sister's mother is a wagon. Now, let the Changing Games begin." The material on the dress is Lycra and the first one gets stuck on my head. Frances starts to cry. I can't blame her; me bent over like this must be a terrifying sight!

"It's okay, baby, Mammy's in here. Help!" But no matter how hard I wriggle and push and pull, I'm stuck. Not for the first time, I have to call the assistant, who, after a struggle and loss of more of my precious post-baby hair, frees me from the dress.

69

"Maybe this one, hun?" she pants, leaning against the mirror, before she hands me another and exits the dressing room.

"Any chance you have 'Pretty Woman' on Spotify?" I call after her and then burst out laughing as the opening bars ring out through the speaker above me. I picture Julia Roberts dancing away as she tried on that famous brown polka-dot dress.

I grin as I turn to admire my reflection in the mirror: the black dress hugs me in all the right places, pinching me in at the waist, good on my bust but it stops just at my calves, more three-quarter length than full length.

"You don't tell me what to wear, Martha." I pull my phone out and snap a picture of myself and send to Adam with the caption: *Will this do?*

A beep back immediately.

*"Stunning! Now all I'm thinking is how to get it off you!!"* Sweating face emoji.

"Right, Daddy's happy. Let's go to Auntie Annemarie's and you can play with Ben, and we'll have something homemade and healthy to eat. In fact, we might even have a sleepover!" I rub my nose gently off hers, then pull back the curtain.

Humming the tune to my favourite Julia Roberts film, I push Frances with one hand, the dress draped over my other arm, towards the till.

# 7

*"If you're worried and you can't sleep, count your blessings instead of sheep."*

Captain Bob Wallace, *White Christmas*

"ONLY FOR YOU." Annemarie hands me a slim cracker with the biggest lump of Brie I've ever seen clinging on for dear life.

"And a very merry Christmas to me!" My jaw drops, tongue hanging out.

"And this." She takes her other hand from behind her back, exposing a crystal wine glass swimming half-full with red wine.

"It truly is a Christmas miracle!" I beam, throwing my free hand out wide before I accept the glass.

"Gimme, gimme." She manoeuvres me out of the way to reverse the buggy. "There she is! There's my little goddaughter. There's my Franny." She uses that odd voice she puts on with her tongue placed between her back teeth.

"Please stop calling her Franny," I implore.

"But it's so cute."

"I'll start calling Ben, Benny."

"There's my Frances." She doesn't miss a beat as she pushes Frances into her beautifully designed living room.

"Oh come to Mama." Leaning against the hall door, I sniff the Brie. "Wow. Life ain't so bad, Lexie. Count your blessings, dear!"

I hear Barbara, my mother, in my head as I take a huge bite, rolling my eyes, the creamy French cheese smooth yet tangy, and as it goes down I appreciate the slightly acidic aftertaste.

"Oh, you got something to wear?" Annemarie returns with Frances's things and my Threads bag after storing the folded buggy away.

I swallow my soft cheese fully. "I did."

"What did you get? Do they do full-length in there, black tie stuff?"

"Kinda." I open my mouth to take another bite.

"Show me?" She swings the bag at me. I jump back.

"I'll show you later. When I recover from the clean swipe of a hundred and fifty euros I don't have to spend on a bloody dress." I bite into the cracker again, take the tiniest sip of the wine to wash it down as Ben toddles out of the playroom in his red and green dinosaur pyjamas towards me.

"Lelly! Tools! Lelly! Tooolllssssss!"

Annemarie glares at me as I mouth "sorry". I hand her my glass as I pull the little brown paper bag from my coat pocket.

"I'll put the dress bag on the door handle just in case you forget it later," she tells me.

I won't mention maybe sleeping over yet in case I change my mind. I need to see how Frances goes as she pushes herself out in the walker Annemarie keeps for her now that Ben has outgrown it. Frances loves it: where most kids use their legs to get around,

Frances has a unique way of using her arms to grip onto things for leverage to launch her around. She flies around the house that way, Annemarie's wooden floor making it all the more fun.

Annemarie rounds us all up. "Everyone inside, I've the heating on and dinner's in the oven."

I follow her thin frame into the brilliant white room, chewing greedily, and inhaling the food smells, then flop onto her leather sofa in their open-plan living-kitchen-diner. Annemarie has one of those block islands I love and a kitchen she actually cooks in.

"Smells amazing in here." I sniff the air like a bloodhound as she hands me back my glass.

"All made last week, did a huge batch cook Sunday morning so just had to take them out of the freezer. I made Tom take a few for his trip." Annemarie sits beside me, in her tight workout gear, makeup free, her hair in a wet, twisted topknot. She turns, settles her back against the arm rest and drapes her weightless legs over mine.

"I haven't been over in so long," I acknowledge, taking in her festive, tastefully decorated room but feeling bittersweet with what I know now about her and Tom. Beautiful glass angel decorations with a splattering of red ribbon twirl from her mantelpiece. A white tree draped with green tinsel and golden lights that twinkle on and off in the window, and what looks like literally a hundred beautifully wrapped gifts in colourful paper and black strings beneath.

"Any news from Kathleen, I meant to ask?"

"Nothing," I reply with a fat lip.

"When I said today you were obsessed with finding her, I didn't mean for it to sound quite so disrespectful," she says sheepishly.

73

"Oh don't worry, we said a lot today, I can't remember half of it now." I tip my head, nodding the matter away; it's done now. "But no, no message."

"Can't believe she still hasn't made contact. I'm assuming you didn't tell her that you found out Máiréad's ring is worth a fortune?"

"Well, I was rather hoping she wanted to find out who her mother was, to be honest. I only mentioned the ring as an afterthought."

"You know what I mean."

"I really thought I'd found her—"

"You did find her!"

"I know, but you can only really be found if you want to be, and maybe my mam is right, maybe she doesn't want to be found."

"Máiréad would have been so proud of you, you've worked tirelessly to find her daughter."

Ben pushes a squealing Frances past us.

"Broom! Broom!" he yells.

"Careful," Annemarie throws.

"Faster!" I joke as Annemarie tilts her head at me.

"Seriously?"

"Just messing!" I grab her knee with my cupped fingers, right on that spot no one can take, and she jumps, laughs and slaps my hand away.

"I nearly spilled my wine!" She wavers her glass out wide. We sit in comfortable silence for the first time in months, sipping our drinks as we watch the backdrop she has stationed on her mounted plasma TV. It's a Christmas scene. An open log fire crackles loudly, with a garland around the fireplace decorated in twinkling lights and red berries.

"This is very therapeutic." I swirl my drink, listen to the crackling of fake burning logs.

"Hmmm. Isn't it?" she throws back. But I can tell she's distracted and probably wants to talk about Tom again, so I wait, patiently.

"Lexie?"

"Yeah?"

"I really meant one thing I said earlier," she says hurriedly.

"What's that?" I ask.

"We need to be more social," she blurts. "You and me! Annemarie Rafter and Lexie Byrne."

"Oh." I was expecting more to do with Tom. I turn my head to look at her. "We will, I promised you." Crunch. I watch her watch me, as I catch the last of the cracker crumbs in my cupped hand.

"But when?" She swings her legs down, sits up straight, looks over at Ben and Frances. "Because you're right, we do need to prioritise this. Our friendship. Us. We don't spend enough time together anymore. I felt like a different woman tonight cooking dinner, like I had my ally back, ya know? I need to find a babysitter, someone I trust—"

"I'm not sure the FBI have a babysitting service." I scratch my chin in jest.

"Funny. Am I a helicopter parent? No! Don't answer that. I can't help it. I waited so long for Ben, he's the only one I'll ever have and he's my entire world."

"Quick! Grab the notebook, write that down in case you forget."

"Don't mock me," she implores.

"I'm not . . . I get it," I tell her gently. After all those rounds and rounds of IVF in five different countries, Ben's unexpected and terrifying arrival in a hotel room, a month early – dramatic doesn't even come close. But she's also been there for me every step of the way with Frances, all those terrifying early weeks, and I'll never forget her kindness to me during my breastfeeding trauma. The Motherfucking Mastitis. The fear of failing. She made me leave the Breast is Best brainwashing group and helped me pick the right formula. Slept over and did the nighttime feeds to let me get a full night's sleep when I was borderline delirious.

"I mean it, I want to start living again. Ben's getting older now and, like I said, I want us to put us first for a change."

"I know. Me too." I say, smiling at her. I'm not able to shrug off that memory of her kindness post-birth, and I hate the fact that I haven't thought about that in such a long time.

"You might squeeze out another one?"

"Um, No! I'm nearly forty-three. That train has left the station and I don't want more children anyway. I mean, can I say that? Does that make me a bad mummy type?"

"Of course not. Even if I could have got pregnant again, Tom didn't want another one. Every opportunity Tom gets, he tells me how much I changed after Ben's birth, and of course I changed—" She stops herself, swirls her wine and avoids eye contact. "But I don't want to talk about Tom tonight! I want to talk about Lexie and Annemarie."

"I'm all ears." I flick my lobe.

"Lexarie?" she suggests.

"No." I shoot it down immediately.

She drapes her legs over me again. "I want us to put us first for a while, until we get back on track? Properly?"

"Hundred per cent." I raise my glass.

76

"I don't need Tom . . . or any man, once I have you," she smiles, shyly.

"You'll always have me, that's a given. I was just thinking about how kind you were to me when I failed at the aul boob feeding." I kick off my flats.

"You didn't fail at anything!" Her green eyes flash at me.

"No, I know, I know," I say, crossing my feet. I *know* that, but it's still hard to feel totally okay about it.

"That's what friends are for. Helping you to count your blessings," she says with a grin.

"You're right and I want to be the best friend I can be, that's why I think you shouldn't shut down the idea of couples therapy. I mean it's worth a shot for . . ."

". . . for Ben," she jumps in.

"No! I absolutely did not mean that! Happy parents, happy child, regardless of them being together or not," I tell her forcefully.

"I agree." We take a moment watching our beloved children. Ben pushes Frances round and round the room. I laugh at her smiling face, crimson big red cheeks, a runny nose and free-flowing drool.

"I dunno, don't think even good old Dr Ruth could fix my marriage to Tom . . ."

"I'm pretty sure she's dead, so that would be her greatest sexual healing ever!"

"She's alive, she's ninety-four." A click of her fingers.

I'm about to ask how she knows that, but I refrain.

"Marriage is tough," I add.

"How would you know?"

77

"I saw divorce," I reply matter-of-factly.

"She should have married Aidan anyway." She shakes her topknot.

"That was a different show."

"Can't believe Big just died liked that."

"Men!" I throw my hands up in the air. She cackles.

"Carrie Bradshaw went after what she wanted all the same . . ."

". . . just like Baby Houseman; risked it all for her Johnny," I say.

"I took no risks on romance, played it as safe as a woman can." She lowers her voice.

"It shouldn't be about risk . . . It should be about . . ." I search for the right word.

"Go on?" she urges me.

I click my fingers. "Connection," I blurt.

"That's what you and Adam have is it? Connection?" She crosses one bare foot over the other. I briefly marvel at the perfection of her feet, her toes all perfectly aligned, the right shape and size and her matching cobalt shellacked pretty toenails. My feet never see the light of day. I respect them too much to do that to them.

"Totally. We're like magnets. We just want to connect all the time, it's so hard to explain and most of the time I can't understand it myself, but it's certainly not about risk. It's just so easy. We want the same things."

Ben pushes Frances past us again. Every time I see her, I drown in her beauty; it's true what they say, you never know how much you can love someone until you have a child.

"Fwanny, fas'taw!" he yells. "Fas'taaawwwwwwww!"

"Slowly, Ben." Annemarie leans across and steadies him by the arm. "Any therapist is gonna side with Tom on the

you-know-who-in-our-bed situation, the huge bone of contention before the lack of S.E.X and adultery, that is." She nods
at Ben, who is now brushing Frances's hair with a spoon. "No,
Ben, leave Frances's hair. Put the spoon back, good boy," she
tells him firmly as he rubs his eyes.

"Gwizzley Beaw, Mammy?" Ben pulls at Annemarie's tracksuit
bottoms. "Can we have Gwizzley?"

"You don't know that," I try feebly as Annemarie swings her
legs off me and lifts her bum. She pulls the remote control from
under her, switches the Christmas fire scene to Netflix, and no
sooner has the colourful cartoon popped up of *Grizzley Bear and
The Lemmings* than Ben and Frances look up transfixed, instantly
hypnotised.

"I'd tell any therapist that I'm the one who had to get up ten
times a night when he cried in his own room, not Tom!" She
drains her glass, holding it up high as the last dribble slides down
painfully slowly.

"Want a refill?" I ask.

"Absolutely, but I'll get it. Fresh Parmesan on the lasagne?"

I nod emphatically, hanging my tongue out.

"It's almost ready," she giggles.

"I'm sure that's a familiar cry from most women though, right?
The baby in the bed dilemma?" I call after her as she grabs an
oven glove. "I mean, Frances ends up in my bed most nights too."

"Oh no doubt about it. How is it men don't seem to hear crying
babies in the middle of the night?" Steam engulfs her, but she
deftly wafts it away. The aroma of her lasagne is mouth-watering.
Frances laughs hysterically at the TV, unaware of our troubles.

"Not all men." I wag a finger, lick my still slightly cheesy
fingers. "Bring me back a wipe, will you?"

She refills her glass, but only halfway, then tilts the bottle to me by way of invitation. I shake my head again.

"You sure? It'll go to waste, this is all I can have with Tom away."

"I'm sure." I'm starting to feel tired.

She returns, hands me a wipe, sits beside me again and I clean my hands, all ready for my main course.

"I was a disappointment to him," she suddenly whispers, pulling her knees up into her.

"No." I sit up and hold her knees with both my hands. "You weren't . . . You aren't!" I correct myself into the right tense.

"Ah I was, and him to me, if I'm brutally honest. We married so fast, we barely knew each other, you said so yourself at the time, remember? More Mr Right Now than Mr Right. There was a connection, though, plus we had both just turned forty. I've no doubt in hindsight our ages definitely pushed us together."

"You were forty, not eighty-five." I rock her knees back and forward as if I might shake some sense into her.

The timer sounds in the kitchen, and before she can respond, she removes my hands from her knees, gets up and pads away on her spotless oak floorboards, back to the oven. The aroma of bubbling cheese permeates the air. I put my glass down, get up, lift Frances out of the walker and into my arms, and follow Annemarie.

"Can I help?" I ask as I take a seat on the high stool at the island. Frances wastes no time in clumping my hair in her little torturing hand.

"Set the table? Will Frances have a bit if I blend it?" She puts the steaming lasagne in the middle of the island and wedges a silver ladle slice in the middle, then the garlic bread and sweet potato fries arrive in two huge bowls and she flicks off the oven.

"I'll try her, I've a pineapple yogurt and rice cakes if not. I assure you she won't starve. My mother tells me I didn't eat a fruit or vegetable till I left home! Look at me now? Malnourished is not a word you'd use to describe me, right?" I do a little twerk. She laughs heartily – too heartily – then brings all the food over to the marble-topped dining table.

"Alright, it's not as sexy holding a baby, I get that." With one hand I tug open her top drawer and grab the cutlery.

"You know what?" She walks back, spins around, drops the oven glove on the counter as I rub the base of my back. "Let's do it! The night out. With you. In town."

Frances wriggles in my grip. When Annemarie holds her arms out, Frances bounds to her. I set the knives and forks on the marble.

"Hundred per cent! I'm in, just name the date and I'm all yours! Honour's always up to babysit for me outside of the crèche, she only lives in the old red bricks with her mam and granny, five minutes from my block."

"There's a girl I know on my road put a flyer in my door for babysitting. Let's party like it's nineteen ninety-nine!" she says giddily.

"That's more like my old Annemarie!" I bend low to pull out two plates and baby bowls, then shut the cupboard with a flirty swing of my backside. "I really *do* want to go out-out for a bop! And a mojito!" I tell her doing a little light step back and forward, shaking my hips.

"Okay then! Let's do it! Tomorrow night! You and me, whaddya say? The Brazen Head, just like old times! How about it, Lexie?" Her eyes dance, her skin flushes, her breath pumping out. An excited Annemarie, it's been so long.

But my head spins.

Adam will be here tomorrow night! I haven't seen him in two weeks and we'll be suffocated by his family and friends for the next few days. She's obviously either forgotten or wants me to go out with her anyway. My best-laid plans for the romantic risotto, melt-in-the-mouth desserts, expensive wine and his hot, naked body slip away as I find myself saying:

"Brilliant! We're on!" Plaster the smile on. I owe her so much.

"Thank you, Lexie. Yay!" She reaches for my hand. "That's what I should have said to you earlier by the way, at lunch." She lets go, plops Frances into the highchair, clicks the two over-the-shoulder straps in place, then slings her arm around my waist. "You're my best friend. I appreciate you so much. What would I do without you?"

"God only knows." I wink.

"I don't deserve you but I'm going to be better. Watch out, Lexie Byrne, coz Annemarie Rafter is back!"

# 8

*"Shakespeare said, 'Journeys end in lovers meeting.'*
*What an extraordinary thought."*

Iris Simpkins, *The Holiday*

I'M STILL IN MY SHORT, RED, FLUFFY DRESSING GOWN, having just settled Frances for her Saturday morning nap when I hear his key rattling in my front door.

"Oh man. He's here," I utter as my heart lurches the same way it always does; the butterflies vault over one another as they bash out the Riverdance. This is ridiculous, I do know that. To be perfectly honest, I wish I could manage the physical attraction better. I know it's clouding other issues, but I can't help myself. When I told Annemarie it was about our *connection*, I could easily have said *obsession*, but I didn't.

"Breathe, Lexie," I whisper as the door closes quietly, no rattle of the small pane of glass. He's always considerate about Frances. I inhale deeply; maybe this time seeing him will feel more normal. Just like any normal couple after three years of being together.

Typical.

Regular.

Accustomed.

His footsteps get nearer on the wooden hallway floor.

Nearer still.

The kitchen door opens agonisingly slowly.

And there he is.

In all his drop-dead-sexy ways.

"There she is." He leaves his khaki canvas bag on the floor, throws his arms out and drops them down by his sides.

Nope. It's still the same. My palms start to sweat, my eyes delight and my pulse positively races.

"There he is." I beam, tug the hair tie from my hair and shake out my newly washed waves. Thank God I was liberal with the cocoa butter and body spritz after my shower.

"How are you?" He unzips the well-worn leather, eases his strong arms out from the sleeves, the silver zips rattle as he drapes it neatly over the arm of the couch. His presence makes every part of me flutter. Every time I see him it's like the first time.

"I'm good . . . now." I grin like a soppy teenager as I take in his still lingering summer-tanned skin.

"She napping?" He nods his head to the bedroom, his dark hair falling over one eye.

"Just gone down five minutes ago. I wasn't expecting you so early?"

"Got to Birmingham airport as early as I could and a seat came up on the earlier flight that was full." He pushes his hair back with a flick of his long fingers. "So here I am."

"Gimme one sec." I dart past him into my bedroom as quietly as humanly possible, so I don't wake Frances, and I unloop my belt, throw off my robe and pull on my loose-fitting jeans and sleeveless white T. I shove my feet into my apartment-only flip-flops before I dart back out.

"Came in as quietly as I could." He grins at me. I stand nervously, sliding my foot in and out of my flip-flops.

"She's out for the count," I tell him. He nods, tucks one side of his loose, grey V-neck T-shirt into his black jeans and the action draws my eye to his leather belt and silver buckle. That bloody belt buckle should be ashamed of the thoughts it instils in my head.

"Can't wait to give her a cuddle, I've missed her so much. Two weeks is just thirteen days too long, I know, I know." He adjusts the feather, pulling it to the centre of the chain. He's over six foot tall and very broad, so every time he's beside me he makes me feel petite at five foot seven, which I really am not.

"Coffee?" I ask.

"In a minute."

It always takes us five minutes to adjust. The butterflies are tiring, their legs slowing, they crawl into their beds, close their tiny eyes. We hold eye contact for far too long. Neither of us blinks.

"Look at you, Lexie Byrne." He strides closer to me now, his arms swinging by his sides. His masculine musky scent floating under my hungry nostrils.

"I'd rather not . . ." I only half joke, stepping forward to meet him. Inches apart.

I look up into those chestnut eyes of his, crowded laughter lines that crease and dance when he smiles as he does now. I've died in these eyes on numerous occasions.

"I'd rather look at you, sir." I try a laugh as he settles his hands on my hips and pulls me in even closer to him. I raise my arms and drape them around his neck. In this moment, once again, I'm overwhelmed that this is my fiancé. *This* man. The sexy, good, kind, intelligent, worldly, funny, loyal man . . . loves *me*.

"I love you," he says softly.

See!

"Lucky me," I groan at him.

"God, I've missed you." Every part of my body wants him as he bends his head and his cold lips meet mine, our lips part. I'm lost in his mouth, I love the subtle itch of his thick, dark stubble and the firm press of his soft lips. He tastes of mint chewing gum and that smell of strong, masculine cologne erupts. I run my hands through his hair and he groans heavy in my mouth.

Chemistry.

I've googled it. *"The complex emotional or psychological interaction between people."*

"How long?" We part and he nods to the bedroom again.

"At least half an hour." I bite my bottom lip, hard. Let's put the action into this interaction.

Desire washes over his face. His eyes cloud. He gently pulls at the top button on my jeans, which pops open easily, and slides the zip down. My jeans fall to the ground and hurriedly I step out of them. It's always this way with us.

Burning passion.

Before I know it, he's lifting me in his arms. I'm no feather, so this turns me on even more. We kiss again, harder this time. Breathless. My smooth legs wrap tightly around him. My flip-flops fall to the floor. Our hearts pumping against one another. Finally, I pull away, gasping for air.

"Jesus, woman, you'll kill me one day," he groans as he pecks my neck and, still carrying me, lays me softly on the couch, my legs hanging over the end. I watch him as he unbuttons his own shirt, my eyes glued to every pop of every button exposing the dark hairs on his chest, his taut stomach.

"That all ya got?" I try to joke and regulate my breathing.

The brown leather belt makes a swooshing noise through the silver buckle and his jeans fall, and he lowers himself, carefully, down on top of me.

"God, you're so gorgeous, I love you so much," he moans in my ear as he nuzzles my collarbone.

I arch my back for him. "I missed you so badly," I whisper breathlessly, dragging my nails down his back.

"I've been dreaming of you every single night all week." A feathery touch on my shoulder blades; his fingers finding the clasp on my bra and easing it open. He drops it to the floor. His head falls to taste my skin and I arch higher. I twist his hair as my senses erupt. His hand moves down my side, his fingers gently caressing the skin on my stomach, his lips press down harder. I arch higher.

*DIIINNNGGGGGGGG!*

The doorbell shrills out.

"What the—" He jerks up.

"Do. Not. Move." I twist his hair.

"Ow. Lexie, that hurt!" he cries, not so masculine now.

"Sorry." Genteel I am not.

"Ohhhh! Lex-ieeeee. Lexie Mary Byrne!"

A muffled voice. I cock an ear. He moans audibly now, in frustration, as my phone rings out on the kitchen table, voice activating. The name:

MY MOTHER. MY MOTHER. MY MOTHER.

"What on—" I stop myself – no, even this can't be allowed to ruin the passion, so I pull him back into me. I don't know what this chemical attraction is but I know I'm powerless to it. We kiss again, harder, our tongues exploring one another's mouths hungrily, his hands finding that spot on the nape of my neck, that gentle massage that sends me wild, and I rotate my neck for more. His touch is so light I wonder if I'm imagining it.

"Oh. Adam." I arch again, drag my legs up.

*DINNNNNNGGGGGG! DOOOOONNNNGGGGGG!* The bell is held for far longer and shatters the moment. And now Frances starts to cry.

"Noooooo," I cry along with her as Adam pushes himself off me with the palms of his hands, his brow is sweaty and he's panting, his bare chest rising and falling, his hair over his eyes.

"Who the hell? Who's that?" I roll off the couch rather inelegantly and topple onto the carpet, reach for my jeans.

*D I I I I I I N N N N N N N N G G G G G G G ! !*
*DOOOOOOONNNNNNNNNNNNNNGGGG!!*

Frances roars at the top of her lungs now as I do up my jeans and slide my flip-flops back on.

Adam's struggling back into his own jeans, hopping on one leg and nearly toppling over. I throw him his T-shirt as I go towards the door dragging my own top on over my red face.

"Coming! Hold on!" I call out. "We're commmmmiiiiiiing!" I catch my reflection in the hall mirror, settle my bird's nest of hair and from the living room I hear Adam laughing – I can't help but laugh at that myself!

I flip-flop down the hallway as Adam slips into our bedroom to comfort our daughter and I pull open the door. My face freezes.

What the actual—?

"Mam!" I shriek as my mother stands on my doorstep, dressed like the abominable snow woman in a white, faux fur, full-length coat and a red trilby hat, holding a small brown canvas suitcase from the 1980s.

"What kept you dear?" She barrels past me, pulling her ancient suitcase behind her.

"Barbara!" Adam says, almost crashing into her with Frances in his arms as he exits the bedroom.

"Adam, hello, son! Don't you look . . . flushed." She spins her head over her shoulder, winks at me. "Hope I didn't disturb anything. There she is! Come to Grammy. I didn't know you'd be here, Adam, I thought Lexie was going to the Cotswolds next week to spend Christmas there with you? Did I get that wrong? No? Not yet? Is it the hat?" She refers to Frances's howling as she removes her hat from her neat, shortly cut silver hair.

"W-what are you doing here, Mam?" I struggle for air as she hands me her trilby.

"Well now, your father broke his nose playing darts in Fitzgerald's bar. He's been boxing for six months with never anything more than a black eye. Juan elbowed him by all accounts. He's such a baby, utterly miserable. He's no fun. Sprawled out on the chaise longue, expecting me to wait on him hand and foot. I said, it's only your nose dear, you can still walk to the fridge! Anyway, he needs a few days to cop on that I'm not his maid, and I want to bond with Frances. I told you on the phone I was coming soon to do that, remember? Just waited for the universe to give me the sign. So here I am. Surprise!" Jazz hands.

"Lovely to see you again, Barbara." Adam has only met my parents a handful of times in three years but they always got along very well. He actually asked my dad for my hand in marriage in Nerja, which I thought was utterly hilarious but also secretly kinda cute.

"You too Adam. Have you been out for a jog?"

"Urm—"

"It's so great to see you!" I jump in, and it IS!

"You won't be seeing me for too long, I'm only here for two nights." Her glasses hang on a pink chain around her neck; she lifts them now and slides them on.

"Um—" I look to Adam.

"We won't be here Sunday, Barbara," he says, pressing his lips in a flat line.

"Where will you be?" she demands.

"We leave tomorrow, we've a wedding rehearsal dinner at home . . ." Adam shifts Frances up in his arms. Her sleepy eyes connect with me. She whimpers, rubbing her tired eyes.

"Is this not home?"

*Pointed, Mother,* I think and change the topic as fast as I can. I've only seen her in Nerja since she left Ireland and I'm always in holiday mode, so it feels a little overwhelming and wonderful to have my mammy in my hallway.

"The wedding's in the Cotswolds, Mam, remember?" I have told her this at least ten times. She just never listens on the phone, she's always multitasking, and at seventy-three years old she's definitely in need of a hearing aid – but she won't hear of it. (Sorry! Pun unintended.)

"What time do you leave at?" I can see the sheer disappointment in her kind eyes. "Serves me right for planning a two-day surprise." She pulls the glasses off again, which sway above her large bosom, and reaches over to tickle Frances under the chin.

"Not till lunchtime," I tell her. "Eh! Hug!"

We embrace tightly. I feel so safe in her arms and breathe in her familiar and comforting scent of Estée Lauder that she has never not worn in my entire life. I step back, feeling odd that I suddenly feel like Little Lex again and I'm in my forties.

"Well, I better make the most of my twenty-four hours with you all then, my dears," she declares. "I'll need to change my flight."

"I can sort that later, Barbara," Adam offers. "I'm well used to changing flights, unfortunately."

"But you're here now." My head rushes to my night with Annemarie: she's got a babysitter for the first time and is getting her hair done in town as we speak, I can't cancel! "And you're coming on a girls night out tonight," I declare.

"Oh you're going out?" Adam says and unintentionally expends a short breath of relief.

"Annemarie – I'll fill you in later."

"How lovely, I'm also catching up with my friend Marina, in town, she's driven up from Wexford, I didn't think I only had one day—"

"That's fine. Coffee?" I say.

"Decaf?"

"No." I shrug unapologetically. "My caffeine addiction doesn't permit."

"Let's pop out then, dear. I flew Ryanair. I need a strong Baileys in a decaf."

# 9

*"The best way to spread Christmas cheer is singing loud for all to hear."*

Buddy, *Elf*

"I. GOT. A. TEXT!" I SHRIEK. "It's truly a Christmas miracle!" I sing the words, clutching my phone tightly and dropping the butter knife with a clatter into the sink. I cannot believe my eyes. "Adam, come quick! You'll never guess what?"

Shoving the triangle of warm toast into my mouth, I chew down rapidly. Frances *goo-goo-gaa-gaas* from the highchair in her red-and-white cotton Santa sleepsuit. Mam headed into town to meet her old work pal, so we had a free afternoon, and as Frances had another quick nap after being so rudely awoken earlier, we made the most of it.

"Aaadddd-aammmmm!" I bang my chest to swallow the buttery doorstep white batch, gasping for air before I explain what's happened. "Máiréad's daughter's just WhatsApped me! Oh holy night is right!" I break into a Kevin Bacon *Footloose* dance move. My arms swinging, legs flailing, left to right, as I dance on the kitchen tiles in my bare feet, in just my white, lace

92

bra and matching lace full brief knickers. I lose my breath quickly and bend over. A gurgle of laughter from Frances as I rise and tickle her under her chins.

"We're never getting on Ireland's Fittest Family, pet." I pant heavily, sucking in a deep breath. "Adddd—" I stop as a half-naked, dripping wet Adam, strides into the living room.

Oh so yummy.

No, not the hot buttery toast.

The man.

"W-what? What is it?" Immediately he fixes those dark eyes of his on our baby daughter, checks she's alright. "Jesus Christ, Lexie, with all the hollering I thought Frances was choking or something!"

"No, she's fine . . . but I'm not, just look at this!"

I thrust my phone inches from his face. He steps back, pulling a towel from over his bare shoulders, and his bicep curls. Those same biceps that just half an hour ago held me so tightly I thought I might break.

"What's it say?" Roughly he rubs the towel through his hair, the strong sinew of muscle distracting me momentarily.

"She's not Kathleen – I mean, she is Kathleen, but she's called Winifred Emit now. I just got this text! She's finally made contact with me and now I have her phone number, so I don't have to rely on a DM on the Heritage site!"

I drop my jaw as far as it will allow and stare hard at the look of confusion on his chiselled features. I pull myself together; now is not the time to ogle this perfect piece of man. "Kathleen. Máiréad's daughter. Is now Winifred Emit!" I'm bouncing in place, wrestling my waves into a low ponytail before remembering I've just blow-dried it for my night out.

93

For a very intelligent trauma nurse, sometimes his listening skills are laughable. I have no patience.

"Keep up." I shake my head, flatten my fringe. "Winifred is just the woman I've been trying to trace for almost a year?"

Still I wait.

"Oh wow! How amazing. Well done! Where is she? In what part of the world I mean?" He continues to towel dry his mop of hair, grinning at me.

"In . . ." I drum roll my fingertips off the countertop, ". . . Ireland!"

"Feck off?" His new favourite phrase. And pronounced in his English accent always sounds to me like:

"I will not, you fe-eh-hek off." I drop into the kitchen chair and immediately text Winifred back asking when I can meet her, feeling thrilled with myself. I finish the text and hit send.

He plants his cold lips on mine. My shoulders shiver and all of a sudden nerves swamp me. I'm about to hit him with a big problem after Christmas. How is he going to react?

"You're amazing. I knew you'd find her, Detective Inspector Byrne." He makes a circle with his index finger and thumb, and looks through it. Then he pulls me even closer; his body's still damp. Adam isn't one of those gym robot types who roams the plains, but he runs, often, and is in super shape. I should take a leaf out of his book; well, I did go to yoga three times this year, but that's as much as I could fit in, and there was a terrible smell of feet.

"New clothes?" He cups my bottom.

"You can see them?" I squeak, tilting my face to his.

"Why, they are the most beautiful clothes I've ever seen!"

I run my hands down my bare legs. "Made from the finest silks known to man."

"Thank him from me, won't you." He makes a hungry sound.

I really do spend too much time in leggings: there's literally a seam mark embedded down the side of my leg. "Speaking of the Emperor's new clothes, I better go get some on."

"Any toast left over?" He looks hopefully over my shoulder.

I lick my fingers. "Come on, man, you know me better than that?"

In my bedroom the air hangs heavy with the lingering scent of Adam. Of us. I drag the mirrored door across my overflowing wardrobe and pick my outfit off the hanger for later on tonight. New jeans my mother actually sent me from Spain for my Christmas present, don't ask me how, but she has a knack of picking jeans out for me and I intend to team them with a crisp, white, man's dress shirt and heels. I lay them out on my bed. Adam sings "War Is Over" to Frances in the kitchen. He still seems very happy with my curves if this morning's performance was anything to go by. Our love making was, as always, thrilling.

"Frances is ready when you are," he calls out. "I'll get dressed when you're finished in there."

"Two secs," I return.

We're going to take Frances to the park, and I love these days, when it's just the three of us, our little family. Adam was more than happy, encouraging even, for me to have a night out tonight despite him only arriving this morning – no doubt the alternative of being left alone with my mother was a part of it! I giggle to myself. I pull on my T-shirt, leggings and a thick fleece grey hoodie, and tie up my runners. Quick mirror check. I never really lost the (don't make me say it) "baby weight" because I detest that term and no, my body didn't "bounce back", I mean I'm not a kangaroo, am I? And apart from growing a human being, I ate what I wanted and walked as much as I could. I've accepted the trade with open arms. A bit of an overhang in exchange for my precious daughter? Hell yes! Deal! Forty brought me so many positives, self-appreciation being the main one. No longer do I force that critical eye upon myself, inspect or criticise my body in the mirror. Never do I try to squeeze into old clothes; if they don't fit, they go to charity.

"Leave your case on the bed! And I'll do Frances's bag when you're out tonight," Adam calls again.

"Hers is all packed, under my dressing table!" I call back. "I bought her new clothes for the wedding. Cost me a small fortune!"

"Ah you've got enough to do, I would have done that. I'll have them all by the door when you come home later, do not fall over them!"

"Are you implying I'm a sloppy drunk? Don't answer that," I shout back as I eye up the black dress from Threads and the tan, strappy heels on top of my case.

"If the shoe fits," he jokes and I laugh as I exit the bedroom.

"It never fits at the end of a night out, that's half the falling-over problem! Sore feet! Bastard heels!" I unplug the Christmas tree and turn off the flickering reindeer.

I let him go get dressed. He's changed Frances into her warm suit and duffel coat, and I pull my thick padded coat on.

"Oh Lexie, while we're out – we need to talk about finalising the date for your moving plans to the Cotswolds," he says, striding into the room still pulling on his leather jacket. He zips it up with a whoosh as at the same time my stomach drops.

# 10

*"Come out to the coast, we'll get together, have a few laughs."*

John McClane, *Die Hard*

I'M POSITIVELY SEETHING as the sharp December air hits my breath the second we step outside the communal front door of my block.

"Holy moly, that's a chill alright." Adam rubs his hands together and pulls up the collar on his jacket as I bend and tuck the wool blanket high up under Frances's chin. We walk on, in silence, out the gates and he stops.

"The park? Which way again?" And I see he hates himself for forgetting.

"Left," I say, trying to appear casual but the simplicity of what I do with Frances on a daily basis being unknown to him hits me.

It's a fifteen-minute walk to my local park and I catch our reflections in the coffee house window as we stroll past. We look like any regular family. But we're not. I pull my hood up against the biting wind as Adam pushes the buggy and Frances kicks her yellow Winnie the Pooh wellies. I'm seething because after he said that about finalising my moving plans, he threw the tea towel into the washing machine and just stared up at me awaiting my response.

"I mean unfortunately we don't have time now to get into the finer details of the move with your mother here but I was just thinking in the shower, maybe we can iron out a few details before she gets back from her lunch? Book flights at least so that we have an actual date?"

I'd looped the scarf around my neck. His free hand slid to the cradle of my back.

"I was hoping tonight we'd really talk logistics about you and Frances finally moving out of here but there's too much going on."

Just like that.

Just like I hadn't been about to say the same thing, in reverse.

He got there first.

And he's right, I can't risk my mother getting wind of a row, I do not want her to worry, so I bit my cheeks even though my heart felt like it had just been smashed.

"You're right, we really do need to talk. But let's have our walk first? Can we talk on the way back, I just want to enjoy the three of us being out together?"

"Should I be worried?" His brow had creased.

"Worried? No." I'd busied myself strapping Frances in.

"You okay?" A shift of the silver feather.

"Grand."

And we'd left.

"Why is it that I'm getting the feeling you're stressed, Lexie? I just want to be with you both, all the time, that's all. I think you want the same?" he says now as we stop at the crossing and wait for the green man to flicker.

"I do." Oh God, this is going to be a bloody nightmare of a conversation on the way back. I only hope Mam is still out when we get home so we can digest it all. Because I'm out tonight, so we won't get to finish this chat properly until after the wedding. The noise of the crossing pierces and an old bus belches black smoke as we cross the busy road quickly and head down into the soft-surface circular playground. I flop onto the bench and watch him gently ease Frances down the slide. The clouds hang low, and even though I have this life-changing conversation to have with Adam, all I can really think about right now is Máiréad's daughter. I pull my phone out. Still no reply to my "when can we meet?" question. My heart lurches for Máiréad. I'm so close to seeing the child she never knew. Life is so unfair sometimes. How I wish she was still alive. A robin red breast swoops down and perches on the arm of the bench. A shiver starts at my feet and runs up the nape of my spine.

"Will we grab pastries in Leontia's bakery on the way back, do us for lunch?" Adam's voice pulls me back to the moment, and the bird takes flight. Every woman in the park tears themselves away from their iPhone and oat lattes.

"Sure." I nod. Shivering against the cold, as he joyfully pushes Frances in the baby swing. Its movement back and forward is like the ticking of a clock in my head. The big conversation to come. I'm not moving to the Cotswolds, I can barely face the next few days I have to spend there. The anxiety it's causing me is so unhealthy. I made up my mind sitting in Greggs in Birmingham airport, tears smarting in my eyes, feeding Frances her bottle on the way home from that disastrous summer holiday that Adam was totally oblivious to.

*

"Oh? You still here? I thought you went home last night?" Martha jabbed a finger at me as I relaxed in the Chill Out Bar at the Moritz Hotel, the beautiful evening I'd been enjoying with Adam immediately ebbing away.

"No, still here, myself and Frances leave tomorrow." I held my fork aloft, fat strings of thick tomatoey linguine hanging on for dear life.

"What are you doing here?" Adam barely looked up, seemingly unperturbed by her presence, tearing a triangle of pepperoni pizza from his plate and leaning back in his seat as the cheese stretched.

"The village committee summer drinks are out on the patio." She almost lost her chin, so far did she tuck her head. "You remember that Adam, right?" Nothing moved on her face.

"Oh. Shit." Adam sat forward and dropped the pizza, scratching his dark stubble, dressed in a tight white T-shirt and jeans.

"Why are you eating? The barbecue's at six." She checked a watch that wasn't on her wrist.

My linguine slowly fell like my stomach.

"I didn't get an invite?" He looked over his shoulder as if someone may be standing there with one.

"You sent the invites, dummy!" Martha smiled at him, folding her arms. Her hands dropped like two limp fish. Her royal blue, V-neck dress fell to just above the knee, her white shoes so high and pointed they should probably need a licence. She clamped a matching blue clutch tightly under her arm.

"Where's your baby?" She turned to me, her smile vanished.

"Frances," Adam filled in for her. He'd laughed; he just didn't get her little snide ways and passive digs.

"I'm awful with baby names, Adam knows, forgive me." She pushed her way into the booth beside Adam and crossed her legs so they stuck out the side rather than under the table. They were tanned and slender, and I was immediately reminded of the earlier breadsticks I'd devoured dipped in pesto in Adam's parents' house.

"Oh, what an *enormous* bowl of pasta, looks scrumptious," she said, batting her long eyelashes at me, her makeup barely there and flawless.

"Would you like to try some?" I offered politely with a smile.

"Oh gosh no! I don't do carbs. When do you remember me last eating carbs, Ads, probably at our wedding! Adam insisted on mini spaghetti carbonaras as the late supper offering before the silent disco. People still talk about that food; the chef is gone from here now, more's the pity, this one is fond of the stodge." Her mouth turned down as she leaned over and looked down into my bowl.

"Sorry, I'm confused, I didn't send any invites?" Adam picked up his beer tankard by the handle and swirled it calmly. I knew he wanted her to leave so we could enjoy our last evening together, but as aways he was too polite.

"Well, no, you didn't *personally* send them, but I did on your behalf because you are the Treasurer and you were over at hers so I knew you'd forget. You know it's this date every year."

"I – I forgot, it's not the most important thing on my mind." He picked off a pepperoni piece with his free hand, popped it in his mouth. "But thank you." *The pleaser of people strikes again,* I thought impatiently.

"Don't worry, you're here anyway." Her hair had grown out of its bob since I saw her last: sleek and shiny, bouncing above her shoulder blades. Tiny and toned to perfection. I dropped the fork into the bowl, feeling like Big Bird opposite her. I had been starving as we'd been in Adam's parents' house all day, and as lovely as Heather and Jeffrey were, lunch was, in Heather's words, "nibbly bits"; in my words, "just breadsticks".

"Excuse me, Gracie." Martha waved the waitress down, and to my horror she'd ordered herself a glass of pink champagne.

"Is everything alright with the food, Lexie?" Gracie asked me, scribbling on her pad. I'd met her here at Deb's engagement party and we got on really well. Think it was probably the generous tip I'd left her.

"Yes, just . . ." I looked down at my hands; they felt huge. Why was it Martha made me feel so ungainly and insecure?

"Eat up Lexie," Adam kindly edged my bowl back in front of me, "it's your favourite, you've been talking about it since we left my folks."

But I was so uncomfortable as Martha's slim flute of bubbles arrived and rested in her delicate hand as I tried to shovel the pasta into my mouth. I could hear myself chewing: to me I sounded like a cow chomping on grass, and I was starting to sweat. The truck driver was opening the door, ready to start a punch-up with my heart.

"It's so lovely that you're still here, Lexie, I keep saying to Adam he should ask you over more. We love seeing you! I know what it's like to be alone with a baby . . . Well, Adam's always across the road, but you know what I mean."

"Freya is hardly a baby," he said, laughing.

"Well, she's our baby." She took a dainty sip. "Are you struggling with all that amount of food?" she directed at me as I placed my fork and spoon across the bowl and threw my napkin on top.

"I'm just full," I told her, dabbing my mouth clean with my soft napkin. "It's difficult with work to be over here a lot, and I volunteer at weekends in a nursing home when Adam's able to take Frances for a few hours for me."

"Ah isn't that sweet." It sounded positively bitter in her mouth, though.

"Well, it's necessary, to be honest. They run on a skeletal staff at weekends, it's not a private nursing home, so unless I go . . ."

"Lexie runs the entertainment for them, and a lot more besides, she's amazing. She fully qualified now too in geriatric care." Adam was utterly oblivious to my awkwardness as he chomped through his pizza.

"Use your napkin, love." Martha unfolded his napkin, handed it to him and the sip of water I'd just taken got caught in my throat. He didn't bat an eye, just took the napkin.

"Unless I provide some entertainment at weekends there is none," I went on, coughing now. "I hope to take up a full-time position in the area as soon as I can . . ."

"Right . . ." She tip-tapped on her phone, her long, acrylic nails making the most irritating sound.

"There you are!" Deb, Adam's sister skipped around the double doors of the Chill Out Bar. "Oh. Lexie! You're still here?" She looked more than disappointed but quickly shook the look off her face.

"I just texted you this second." Martha opened her eyes wide and flicked them in my direction as though I couldn't see her. "Yes, Lexie's still here. Isn't that marvellous?" All for Adam's benefit, of course.

"Marvellous." Deb turned her back on me. "Who's minding Frances?" She directed the words at Adam in a most concerned tone. Did she think I just left my child by herself in the room or what?

"And hello to you too, my dear little sis. We have a hotel sitter upstairs, we're staying here tonight."

"Why?" she asked, scrunching up her nose.

I wanted to tell her to mind her own bloody business!

"Why? Because we wanted to. It's nearer the airport in the morning and I wanted to treat Lexie to a quiet, romantic dinner, but that's not happening is it?" He pushed his plate away now too, swept his eyes up at the pair of them and side-eyed the door.

"Isn't Lexie's dress beautiful Deb?" Martha said. "It's so . . . comfy looking."

"So comfy," Deb agreed, and although I knew it was a back-handed insult, Adam nodded in agreement.

"Does Barney know there is an extra person now?" Deb asked, staring down at my bowl.

"It doesn't matter, we won't be going," Adam told them, reaching for the half bottle of wine and topping up my glass.

"You have to go! You've never missed a village barbeque." Martha stood up now, her flute empty.

"Tell him, Lexie, tell him he has to go," Deb implored.

"Go . . . of course, go," I said, appetite gone, meal ruined, mood flat.

"I'm not going without you, don't be ridiculous. Look, we'll pop out to say hi, but don't make a fuss about an extra number, we won't be eating. We've just eaten – or tried to at least," Adam added with an irritated *tssk*.

"But promise you will come, Adam?" Deb insisted, purposely not including my name and again it went over Adam's head.

"Lexie, we will hold you personally responsible if the Treasurer of the village committee doesn't show up!" Martha had looked like a small, invisible banana was keeping her fake smile alive.

"Well I wouldn't want that, would I?" I smiled up at them both as they turned and left the bar arm in arm, Martha whispering fitfully in Deb's ear.

*

As if that wasn't awkward enough, much more was to come later that evening when they tore me apart thinking I was out of earshot. A dark cloud passes over and all of a sudden a monsoon of hailstones hits me on the head.

"Ow!" I say, covering my head with my hands as the wind picks up. "Let's go," I call over to Adam as mothers, fathers, grannies, grandads and children scatter from the park, coats over heads. It's deserted in seconds.

"Hang on. I see a cab." He jogs to the gate of the playground, waving his hand in the air, as I get pelted now, running inelegantly with the buggy after him and see the cab swerve in. I clamber in with Frances as Adam folds the buggy into the boot, then himself into the front seat.

"That came outta nowhere, lads," the driver says, Christmas FM blasting as he drives us towards my apartment.

Adam hugs the back of his front seat as he turns around to me.

"I guess our big talk will have to wait. But know this, everyone loves you in the village, all my family think you're great, you do know that? They can't wait to have you there. You're part of our big family now." His smile is so genuine I kinda want to shake him.

Instead I nod vaguely, but I don't believe a word of it because I *know* it's not true. I haven't told him about that conversation I was privy to while Martha and Deb brushed their hair after the excruciating barbeque, where I stood for almost two hours more or less on my own, as Adam kept waving me over but was surrounded by various people. Sure he was having a great time. They think *he's* great. They love *him*.

But that is absolutely not how they feel about me.

# 11

*"Blast this Christmas music! It's joyful and triumphant."*
Grinch, *How the Grinch Stole Christmas*

H E HAS HIS HANDS ON MY ASS. My pulse races. My legs wobble. "Unhand me you beast!" I half-jest, standing in front of my dressing table mirror. I'm less on edge from his comments earlier and glad we couldn't continue chats. Mam texted while we were in the taxi just before Adam jumped out for the pastries saying she was also in a cab home from town.

I slide his hands from my backside, turn around.

"Sorry, I'm a bad man." He rests his head against mine. "You just do things to me."

"Mam will be back any minute." I pull away because he'll ruin my makeup if he starts us off. It's taking me ages to get going-out ready. The process gets longer with every passing year! Where once it was like painting a small wall, now it's like plastering an entire house. My phone beeps again. I move away from Adam, and we both walk back into the living room. Frances is in her playpen in front of the famous pink pig.

"Have to check, it could be Mam, lost or something," I mutter.

He laughs. "She did live in Ireland for sixty-seven years, Lexie, and she's also in a taxi."

"Oh Adam, you've no clue how much Ireland has changed in the last ten years." I focus on my phone, then nearly drop it in shock. "It's her!"

"Your Mum?"

"No, Kathleen! I mean Winifred! She's come back to me. Hold on . . . She's typing. All she knows is what I've told her. The barest details. That I know who her birth mother was and I have her engagement ring to return . . ."

The messages whoosh in.

"Aha. Shit. She's not in Dublin, she lives down west . . ." I read, the phone inches from my nose.

Whoosh!

"Oh! My God! Adam, she is agreeable for me to come and meet her. I can return Máiréad's ring personally." A wave of heat and sheer relief rushes through my body, like a massive surge of adrenaline. I actually feel faint with relief.

"Fantastic news . . . I had every faith in you." He grins and claps his hands.

I bite my bottom lip, staring at him. I'm euphoric.

"Think I'll order myself a prawn dish later when you're out." He turns to rummage in my messy kitchen drawer full of takeaway menus. "I'll no doubt be dragged from pillar to post tomorrow and won't get a chance to eat properly," he grumbles as I continue to stare at him, slightly amazed.

"Eh, hello! Can you believe this?" I wave the phone high above my head. I don't really care what he eats later, this is much more exciting than prawn whatever! I give him a moment before I say, "This is the best news in the world!"

"It sure is." He drags his hand down his stubble, clearly still consumed with the thought of food. "This the best takeaway, right?" He waves a Thai menu at me.

*Does he really not get what this means to me?* I think, but say, "Yes. It's the best. I can't believe she lives here, dunno why I always assumed she was abroad. America or Australia – Canada maybe." *You're finally going to meet her, Lexie,* is all I can think.

"We can go meet her in the summer? The four of us? Once Freya's finished school?" He watches me closely.

God, my head is about to explode.

"Oh no, no, I need to see her sooner than that! I want to meet her as soon as I can. Hold on, hold on . . . I'm hoping for more details here . . . Oh, she's typing again." The bubbles dance up and down like a rollercoaster. I've no idea what she looks like. Her WhatsApp profile is a black horse galloping across golden sand, its mane and tail flying wildly in the wind, nostrils flared.

Whoosh!

My heart drops. I gasp loudly.

"Oh. Shit. She *doesn't* live here, Adam." I'm reading as I tell him.

"Oh." He turns back to face me, grimacing.

Bubbles dance again.

"She's just on holiday . . . I think . . ." I pace around now, frantic with the waiting.

Bubbles dance on and on. I stamp my feet. And on. And on. Finally.

"Oooh. . . Oh! She's a nun," I read, "and has spent her life as a . . . medical missionary. She heads back on . . . Sunday to . . . Malawi! A nun! Bloody hell, what on earth would Máiréad think of that after the way the nuns treated her? She had no time for nuns." I puff out a big breath, clutching my chest. But Winifred would have no idea what the nuns did to her mother, how could she? Still, it's not what I expected.

"Calm down, Lexie, breathe!" He tips some grated cheese from the pink plastic bowl onto Frances's tabletop, lifts her out of the playpen and sits her in, rubbing her tuft of dark hair. "Who is Daddy's baby? Frances is, yes she is, she's my baby." He kisses her head. She reclines from him, her pudgy fingers grasping at the yellow dairy goodness to stuff in her mouth. Again, she is her mother's daughter.

"Are you listening to all this?" I shake the phone, my head reeling.

"Yes, I am, of course I am, maybe you can Zoom or FaceTime and post her the ring?"

I ignore him and watch the bubbles bounce, chewing on my thumbnail.

"And stop biting your nails." He bends and throws the towel he was using earlier into the washing machine, slams the circular door shut.

"I'm not your wife, remember? You can't tell me what to do." Playfully-ish, (read: not really playfully) I stick out my tongue.

"Men can't tell their wives what to do anymore, more's the pity," he jokes, jumping back quickly as I swing at him.

"Not even their ex-wives?" I raise my pencilled-in brows but only half in jest.

His expression changes and he definitely sighs.

"Now, now, don't start." He shoves his hands deep into his jeans pockets. "Martha only has good things to say about you, I swear." He truly believes this, I can tell by his eyes.

And before my head does a 360 degree turn and it turns into an argument, Frances defuses the situation by throwing wet cheese and whimpering. I steady myself, unclick the straps of her highchair and lift her out carefully. We say nothing for a moment – then my phone beeps again. I shift Frances to my left hip.

"Yes!" I lean against the fridge door while Frances pulls tufts of my hair out again. "Okay. Wait! She's passing through Galway tomorrow on the way to see the Moving Statue in Ballinspittle, but for one more day only. She flies out from Cork, she doesn't know when she'll be back!" I look at him, explaining quickly as his thumbs loop the feather into place.

"Shame," says Adam. "Shit timing, Lexie, I'm really sorry. But I'm sure she will travel again soon?"

He looks more relieved than sorry.

"I have to go meet her," I say. "I can't take that risk. God knows when I'll have the opportunity again." I stare at his gormless expression, frustration building inside me – not helped by Frances giving me a new hairdo.

"We can't go to Galway tomorrow, Lexie. We're going home tomorrow!"

I watch the feather dangle and his confused expression. I hate how he just used the word "home" again – it gives me the absolute ick!

"It's not . . . *home* . . . well . . . But I know . . . I mean . . ." I shift Frances onto my right hip, and she grins at me, cheesy drool skating down her chin in two different directions, blobbing onto my shoulder. My hips are well cushioned and she loves it there, her two chubby legs swing madly.

"You know what I mean." He distracts himself with a taller menu, a local Indian, and opens the pages. I think quickly.

"I have to go," I spout before I can really digest the words myself.

"Huh?" Adam drops the menu on the counter, strides towards me, his arms outstretched for our offspring. I unravel my thick fringe from her hand and softly rub my nose off hers, inhaling her as I remove another tuft of blonde from those tiny but lethal hair-removal fingers. I don't know what I did before her. Well, I do: I slept. Had privacy on the toilet. Watched Netflix in bed with takeaway food and Pinot Grigio. Looked eleven years younger!

"Listen to what she's saying here. For one more day only. Then back to Malawi. It has to be tomorrow, Adam." I'm abrupt, but I'm also not sorry about it.

"T-t-tomorrow?" Adam's voice is so high pitched, and his expression looks like he's just seen Elvis.

"As in the day after today, yes. It's Christmas week, Adam, no one knows what actual day it is!" I hand Frances over. He perches on the arm of my couch with her in his arms.

"You know how long I've been waiting for her to get in touch, and the fact that she's here, in Ireland, like, what are the chances . . . ?" I clutch my phone like I might lose her if I loosen my grip.

"But Lexie—"

I do the talk-to-the-hand move. My engagement ring twirls upside down; despite his romantic proposal on one knee in an oh-so-fancy New York restaurant well over a year ago, I've yet to have it resized. Or, you know, even get married.

"There can't be a *but* here. You know I promised Máiréad. This is a sign. I've had a few. I have to go meet her, Adam, I just have to."

Frances whines for me as Adam does what he does best: pulls a pacifier from his jeans pocket and rolls it around the tip of her mouth until she takes it and soothes herself.

"Do you keep one in every pair of bottoms you have?" I'm trying to wean her off it, so it's a bugbear of mine that he keeps shoving it in her mouth. He ignores me. I've realised over the past three years we've been together Adam is very good at that. Not in a rude way so much as in a way to avoid confrontation. He's a very placid man.

And placid is not helping right now.

"It's not possible. There is a BUT, Lexie, a very real but. We won't be in Ireland tomorrow. The rehearsal dinner? The wedding, remember? The flights are booked? Accommodation is prepaid at the Moritz for the two nights, it's past the forty-eight-hour cancellation option." He's slightly breathless now.

I eyeball him, twist my gold hoops round my ears and curl my toes as I think.

How on earth do I tell him this wedding means nothing to me compared to finding Máiréad's daughter and returning her heirloom?

"Dominic's wedding is in two days." His voice calmer, breath aligned, he's gentler now, as he gets up with Frances over his shoulder. "We're out of here tomorrow, there's so much to be done."

"Oh, God. Don't remind me." I drip sarcasm and immediately feel bad, so I force a half-smile in apology.

His dark eyes narrow. "Come on. Please don't be like that." Hurt tumbles out with his words.

I check my watch. "What's keeping Mam? Annemarie will be here soon," I say. "Sorry. You're right. It's Christmas, season of goodwill and all that. It's just—" My brain people are working overtime. Trying to figure out how I can get to meet Winifred tomorrow.

"Christmas traffic," he suggests.

"Huh?"

"That's what's keeping your mother, I'm sure it's hellish getting out of town. How about a glass of wine?" He finds my soft spot. "You're right, it's Christmas, the only time of the year when actual time has no meaning, so let's have a little drink, shall we?" He shifts Frances to his other shoulder, her little eyelids fighting to stay open like butterfly wings.

"Love that idea. Why don't you put her back in her playpen? She'll conk out with the heat of you and be awake all night." I pad over to the fridge. It's rather bare and it makes me a bit sad. Normally in the lead-up to the big day my fridge freezer is bursting to the seams with goodies, wines, cheeses, After Eights, fresh cream, cheesecakes, selection boxes, vol-au-vents, sausage rolls, spring rolls, Toffifee's and all kinds of delicious fattening treats. But we won't return home until late Christmas night and we're going to Annemarie's for St Stephen's Day. I turn to face him, fridge door swinging in my hand.

"Why do you keep calling it *Dominic's* wedding by the way?" I know I should leave it but I can't seem to.

"'Cause it *is*?" he replies.

It really niggles me, I don't know why. Pulling out the bottle of white, I set it on the countertop and yawn. Don't know why I feel so tired, I'd an early night when I got home from Annemarie's last night. I was toying with staying the night but I hadn't enough formula for Frances's bottle left in the tin. I'd dreamt about Adam and, as I unscrew the wine cap I recall the last thing Annemarie asked me when she slammed the taxi boot shut after stowing the buggy for me:

"When the chemistry eventually fades, will you still want Adam as much?" The cold air coming off her breath swirled visibly around her face as she wrapped her arms around herself in just her tracksuit.

"Of course I will! He's the most decent person I know. You look like you're in a smoke machine in a 1980s discotheque. It's freezing, get inside," I'd told her as I settled Frances in the car seat provided then clicked my own belt shut.

"Okay, Dominic and *Marrrrthaaaaa's* wedding is in a few days," Adam says now as he interrupts my reverie, "is that better?"

"No, you were right. Dominic's wedding is fine!" I snort.

I hate the way her name sounds on his lips. I'm not jealous of her. At all. I've tried so hard with her, but she hated me on sight, and after the way she treated me in the summer, I don't trust a single word that comes out of her mouth. Don't get me wrong, I'm delighted she is marrying someone else but more than questioning her intentions. I've already spent days, weeks, months even dissecting this romance since they announced their whirlwind engagement only six days after myself and Adam announced ours, but now I know more. So much more.

He's rocking a gently snoring Frances now, patting her baby-grow-bottom rhythmically. It's not nap time and if I say it again then he'll feel bad, and I never want Adam to feel bad, so I don't. Then he whispers, "I'm going to put her down for a nap."

"Okay-ay." I have to let him parent her too, and he is a brilliant dad, but he's also a part-time one, to Frances, I acknowledge for the umpteenth time this year as I watch him tiptoe out of my living room into my bedroom. I perch my bum on the high stool, my jeans feeling less than comfortable despite the roomy waistband, and I debate having this "prink" (that's a pre-going out drink!) or not. One glass? I'm not really a "prinker", I prefer to start my night in the bar if I'm going out. I'm not one for topping up at home. I'm too much of a lightweight.

"I was saying to Marina, you probably should make the move to the UK, Lexie, for Frances's sake." My mother's voice from behind makes me jump so high, I almost fall off the stool.

"Jesus Christ!" I grab the steel bars under me to steady myself.

"No, Barbara Byrne." She laughs, and I look at her hands, laden with glittery gift bags. Her hair seems freshly blow-dried.

"Did you get your hair done in town?" I'm flabbergasted.

"I did." She twirls, drops the bags and removes her coat. Her mauve linen dress just below the knee is teamed with thick, tan tights and flat, patent leather shoes. Her chunky jewellery rattles.

"How on earth did you manage to get a hair appointment this side of Christmas?" I gasp, in awe.

"Popped into the fanciest salon I could find, tucked away, just off Grafton Street. I asked where my chauffeur could park the limousine and said, 'It's Lady Barbara St Clements for her two o' clock appointment.' The receptionist scoured the book, panicked, asked me to give her a moment and I was escorted to the basin."

"You're unbelievable." I chuckle.

"Thank you, dear." She pats her hair. "Where is he?" she hisses.

"Putting Frances down."

"We talked all about your situation." She's whispering but mouthing every word with great exaggeration. "It makes sense to go live with him. What's keeping you here, Marina asked, and I had to agree." She's going to be like a dog with a bone now. Thanks a lot, Marina!

"My life," I hiss at her.

"Take it with you." She shakes her fresh hair and I can smell that overpriced salon for a second.

I dig my heels in. "I don't want to live there."

"Now don't be stubborn, seriously, get out of this flat and over—"

"It's not a flat, it's an apartment. My apartment." I tilt the bottle at her. I *will* have that prink after all.

She takes a breath. "Whatever you say, just move to the Cotswolds, dear, it's the right thing to do."

"Stop saying that, Mam, and don't you dare say that to Adam. I told you, I don't want to live there!" I get up, take a wine glass from the draining board and shake out the excess water. "You're cutting it fine? Annemarie will be here in a few minutes. Do you want to shower?" I ask her.

"Shower? Goodness, no. A drop of sudsy water in the sink and a sponge is all I need. I don't see any sponges?" She casts around as if a sponge will magically drop from the sky.

"I don't use a sponge."

"Who doesn't use a sponge?" She's mystified.

"Me," I tell her flatly.

"Well, I'll do as I am. I won't stay late, I'm a little tired; so much conversation today. But ravenous. Marina went on and on about some fad diet she's on, so we only had fruit and crackers, I grabbed an M&S egg mayo sandwich on the go after that."

"Wine?" I offer.

"A very small one, dear, thank you. You do need to think about Frances. I thought about you all my life, hence I didn't leave this godforsaken freezing island and hit sunnier climbs until a few years ago." She perches on the other stool, crosses one foot over the other.

I throw the cap in the recycling section of my bin with a little too much force. "Not true."

"Gospel." She makes the sign of the cross with her thumb.

"You travelled with work all the time, Mam," I remind her.

"A fashion buyer has to travel, dear."

"I know, now drop it please. I'm so happy to see you, I don't want it to be anything but fun. Merry Christmas to us." I'm starting to prickle and I don't want to. I'm so happy to have her here, I just want us to enjoy the time. I pour us two generous measures.

"Easy," she protests. "I wasn't going to drink tonight, I need to re-book my flight too." She takes the glass all the same, nearly taking my hand with it.

"Adam said he will do it for you."

"Let me put these gifts in my room? I must have bought half of Benetton for Frances." She takes a generous gulp, makes a sucking noise and nods to the glass. "Nice and sharp."

"Erm, in *my* room, I only have one bedroom, remember?"

"Where am I to sleep?" She looks shocked.

I point to the couch.

"On a sofa?" Her mouth purses like a deflating balloon.

"It's a pull-out bed. Perfectly comfortable, Freya sleeps on it when she's here and she loves it. Adam will make it up for you before we get home. I've left him out clean sheets and a pillowcase. Stick your bags in the hall press for now, just go quietly."

She does what I say for a change and off she goes.

Alone in the kitchen, I enjoy the momentary peace, twirling the glass by the stem. I stick my nose in, then take a small sip. What will Máiréad's daughter look like, I wonder? A nun, of all things. A lump forms in my throat as I recall her dying words, and this time I take a stiff gulp.

"I lost a baby, dem nuns took her away, but I'll never forget her desperate cry or that little pink face, and dem teeny hands, curled up in a tight little ball. I wish I had been allowed to kiss her, wish I coulda held her so I knew what she smelled like, whispered in her ear that her mammy loved her."

I hear Frances cry and Adam singing lowly to her. Something irks me about his reaction to all this news and I feel a little betrayed. He knows how much this means to me. I know he's distracted, but still.

"You're lucky," Mam jolts me as she returns, "your father never changed a nappy in his life." She perches again, picks up her wine.

I am lucky, I know that. I'm also unable to imagine someone ripping my daughter from me as I hear myself promise, in Sir Patrick Dun's, in that white, sterile room to Máiréad, that I would return her engagement ring to her daughter. Her dying wish. I promised her. Somehow I have to keep my promise.

"Never pushed a buggy, never went to a parent–teacher meeting, I did it all." She holds her glass up in a type of victory move. "Women of my generation, we did it all. I washed all your shitty nappies in the kitchen sink."

"Thanks for that. A basin may have been more hygienic." I grimace but smile fondly at her.

"Be thankful for your life, stop moaning," Mam says matter-of-factly.

"I am not moaning!" I protest but she's on a roll again.

"Ah now, dear, be truthful, you've been moaning about this single living situation and this wedding you've to attend for months. Your sparkle has dulled." She swirls the liquid, the stem sitting in between her fingers.

"I thought you forgot about the wedding?" I try to get her off topic. I do not want to think about the bloody wedding, and I'm shocked she was actually paying attention to me on the phone. I've taken many liberties moaning when I assumed she wasn't really listening.

"Oh yeah, I did." She laughs at full volume after only a few sips.

"Shush!" I put my finger over my lip. "Frances is sleeping!"

"That's another thing, all this silence while baby sleeps. Me and your dad would dance around the kitchen to the Beatles' 'Sgt. Pepper's Lonely Hearts Club Band', at full blast, and you never stirred!" She gets up, does a few sidesteps, kicks her leg.

"No wonder I know every word to every Beatles song ever written. You guys brainwashed me." I tiptoe to the front room door, close it quietly, lifting the handle and only releasing when the door firmly closes with a click. I flick on the baby monitor.

"Right. Sit down. I've news." I nudge her towards the couch.

Her eyebrows shoot up. "You're pregnant again! I knew it!"

"No, I'm not and that's . . . insulting," I cry, smoothening down my shirt.

"Oh." Her eyes avoid me as we make our way to the couch.

"I want to explain something to you. You see, although I'm the mother to Adam's second child, I'm still considered an outsider. Adam's picture-perfect village is a tight-knit community, Mam, they all know each other. Even though Adam was divorced three years before he met me, the word on the village grapevine was that everyone thought Adam and Martha, that's the ex . . ."

"Oh I know." She rolls her eyes, which is just how I feel about Martha, coincidentally.

". . . were about to get back together, then he came to Ireland for St Patrick's Day and met me. Let's just say very few of them make me feel like I'm wanted there, his own sister doesn't like me, hence my absolute reluctance to move my life to the Cotswolds. When I'm there I'm anxious and feel like a fish out of water. Is that any clearer?" I face her, hoping for some understanding at last.

*So you better be good for goodness' sake* . . . Adam's voice echoes through the monitor quietly now.

Mam gives an unimpressed huff, holding a cushion on her lap. "They sound just like my golf club in Nerja. The ladies were wary of me because I joined as a single woman – your dad despises golf – and like most women my age who join golf clubs, they thought I was a widow on the hunt."

"How is that even close?" I look at her speculatively.

"Because I was a threat, they thought I might take away one of their rockidy old husbands, just like these Cooper people think you are going to take Adam away."

"I am. I want him to move here," I confess.

"But he has a lovely house in the Cotswolds, dear, you rent a flat in Dublin. Use your head."

"Apartment! And I happen to love my life, Mam." And why shouldn't I? I was happy here before, and I'm still happy here now.

"You love working hard all week in a shopping mall, doing all the stuff for Frances with no partner here all week?" Mam crosses her legs, resting her glass on her cushion with both hands as she gives me a sceptical look.

"Yes! I don't want to be a kept woman, and that's what's going to happen if I move over there. I'll be guiled into staying at home with Frances like Martha did with Freya, I know it."

"Your father and I wanted you to use your qualification you worked so hard for in New York! Adam works in a hospital, he must have lots of contacts in geriatrics? Give it a try, take the leap," she implores.

"It's not that simple, Mam," I tell her. "We've been engaged for over a year but something is stopping us from actually planning a *wedding*. Annemarie says it's the fact Martha announced her wedding as a plot to put ours on hold but I know she's not that clever. Cunning, not clever. Bitchy, not bright. Obsessed and not over him." The words tumble out as Mam digests them.

"Nothing that's worthwhile is ever simple, dear. Think about that. Trust the process. Now let me freshen up." She picks up her wine and with no consideration walks to the door, pulls it open with force and it crashes against the wall. "Oops-a-daisy," is all she mutters.

I re-read Winifred's messages. As I drink, a new message whooshes in. She's apologising that she isn't able to access the internet easily. I put down my wine and reply immediately.

I type back that I could post the ring to her in Malawi but what if it got lost in the post?

As I await the reply I feel sick to my stomach. Imagine it did get lost. Plus, I have this inner need to meet her, like I can't explain it. My gut is telling me I have to go meet her face-to-face. I want to hand over this ring personally like I promised her mother. I want to *see* her face! Tell her what an amazing woman her birth mother was. Tell her all I know about Jim, her father, too. Over tea, not over the phone.

The door opens.

"What was all the noise?" Adam's hair is a mess, and he yawns. "Think I dozed off with her for a minute."

I put the phone down. "Mam's back."

"Ah okay. I was just thinking in there before I drifted, I don't want you to be disappointed, of course I know this Winifred meeting is huge for you, but we can't just drop everything, you know? We've commitments. I'm the best man for starters. I'm sure she will understand that and we can make some alternative arrangement?" Adam's tone is low but solemn.

"I know." I get up, go back into the kitchen, and pour him a glass. His phone rings out, he immediately puts it on silent and stuffs it into his back pocket. If he thinks I don't see his phone lighting up on silent all the time he's very much mistaken. It pains me he's taken to hiding the fact that Martha calls him constantly, and as far as I'm concerned, Martha's using this wedding as an excuse to call even more; fittings and rings and speeches and whatnot. But yet again, I bite my tongue.

"By the way, how did Freya's qualifier go yesterday, sorry I never even asked?"

His face lights up. "So great: two clear rounds, she's becoming a top-class rider. She can't stop talking about this course she's waiting to hear from. She's dead set on making a career out of course building. The way she was explaining, the last course she rode, the pole sizes, the water jump widths, the parallel bars on the corner, the triple bars, the distances, she's so enthused by it all. I keep trying to change the subject because we'd rather she – I – I mean . . ." His eyes pop. "I mean *I'd* rather she went to regular college to get a degree in something first." He corrects himself for my benefit.

I let the *we* go; of course they are a we when it comes to parenting their daughter. I hand over the wine.

"Lovely, thanks love." He accepts and moves into the living area, folds his six-feet frame onto the couch, bends over to untie the laces on his three-striped runners.

I know I can't get out of attending Martha's wedding, but maybe I can get out of attending the rehearsal dinner? What was it Mam said? Trust the process. Something deep down inside me tells me I have to trust my gut and go meet Winifred tomorrow.

I have to.

But how?

# 12

*"Oh Christmas isn't just a day, it's a frame of mind."*
Kris Kringle, *Miracle on 34th Street*

I DRAIN MY WINE AND REST IT ON MY DRESSER as I slide my feet into my heels under the wide leg of my jeans. Annemarie's still stuck in bumper-to-bumper Christmas traffic. I wish she'd hurry up, I need to talk to her about Winifred; she'll help me, she's great at making clear decisions. Rolling on some clear gloss, I smack my lips and make my way back into the living room, my coat and leather bag over my arm. Adam's watching MTV of all things, with Frances in his arms again, while Mam perches elegantly beside him. Her posture is Pilates perfect. The Top Ten 20 Christmas Crackers roll by at the bottom of the screen as Mariah Carey slides down the snowy mountainside laughing, flashing her pearly whites, dressed as Mrs Claus.

"What is keeping the girl?" Mam asks, manoeuvring herself to the edge of my low couch. "Excuse me, Adam, I need the bathroom again," she over-explains as she goes out.

"Five minutes according to her Google Map location," I reply, putting my glass in the dishwasher.

"You look gorgeous." Adam gives me a wink as he crosses his long legs out in front. "I'll wait up for you so we can chat later. All okay now? You sorted anything in your head about Winifred?" His eyes dip, avoiding mine.

"Hm, not yet. It's just you know how much Máiréad meant to me: I was all she had, a volunteer in a nursing home." I adjust Frances's sleepsuit over his shoulder again. Already I know she will be awake half the night.

"You were much more than that. Now, come on, you were practically a member of staff . . . just, unpaid. I'm sorry I never got to meet her," he adds kindly.

"She knew all about you. Mam!" I call, "Where's your coat?"

*He's assuming I'm just not going to go*, I think. I haven't decided that at all. I remember the night after I first met him, we'd slept together in his single room in Jury's Inn, Christchurch. I'd been in Sir Patrick Dun's the next day hosting a book club. I hadn't an iota of guilt about the sex, but I had a glow. I was walking on air. I was exhilarated. I'd met the man of my dreams. I was in a daze.

*"A man." Máiréad, her hair in pink rollers, had crossed one orthopaedic navy shoe over the other as I handed her a cup of hot tea (teabag still in the cup).*

*"A man." I crossed my eyes and we'd laughed.*

*"Kind?" was all she'd asked me.*

*"I think so, yes," I'd replied, handing her the teacup.*

*She'd sipped, loudly. "Nothing else matters."*

Now the kind man pulls me onto his lap. But I'm not sure that nothing else matters, even though he smells amazing, a mix of my sweet shower-wash and strong, masculine cedarwood aftershave, and turns me on like I didn't think was possible. I know I have Frances to think of but I matter too. My happiness matters. It's so complicated.

"How did I ever live without you? Love you." He can almost read my mind at this stage as he lifts my chin.

"Love you too." I lean my head down to meet his. Again he parts my mouth with his tongue, probes softly and moans under me.

I pull back, smiling at him.

"I wish we had a night together on the couch," he admits with a little sigh.

"Me too." It's true.

"I love this white shirt on you, it's so goddamn sexy." He nuzzles into my neck, slides the collar down, parts the three open top buttons and plants small butterfly kisses along my cleavage.

"Don't . . . my mother's coming back!" I manage a pathetic pant. "I need to . . . I can't, and Annemarie will be here any second."

I move off his knee and plonk beside him.

"I'll be there in a sec!" Mam hollers from the other room. "Just on the phone to your dad!"

"Shuuussh!" Adam panics as Frances wriggles.

And out of the blue the people in my brain stand up, my mind turns over and my mouth opens for me to blurt out: "I have to go tomorrow. To Galway. To see Winifred."

"W-what? You can't be serious?" His eyes pop.

"Deadly." And I am.

"Let me get this straight, you want to drive to Galway tomorrow, a what? Almost three-hour drive to meet this woman and—"

"Winifred," I snap, with a curl of my lip.

"Winifred, I'm sorry, I don't mean to be disrespectful at all—" He raises his hand in a pacifying motion, "—to give her the ring. That means I will have to fly on my own . . ."

"Well, with Frances?" I add.

His face drops. Literally, his mouth flops open. "You expect me to take Frances?"

"Well, yes, I can hardly take her to meet Winifred. I'd follow you both over on the last flight. I'd miss the rehearsal dinner but I'd be there for maybe a nightcap and bedtime?" I clasp my hands together. I don't see how this plan does not work.

"But the dinner tomorrow night will be a late one. A heavy session. You know what Dominic's like?" He shakes his head.

"Daddy says hiiiiiiiiiii!" Mam roars. "His nose is feeling better, and he found the fridge!"

I ignore her, so focused am I on the conversation happening on the couch. "I can book a sitter at the Moritz, like we did in the summer. Or Freya can mind her, she is her half-sister after all, she adores her . . ." I trail off.

"Freya's not gonna be a babysitter, she's tasting her first glass of champagne at the dinner tomorrow night!" He eyes me with concern.

"What? I think that's terrible!" I raise my chin. She is *not* old enough to drink.

"Two seconds," my mother shouts at the top of her lungs now. How far away does she think we are?

"Why? We all did it," he says with a one-shoulder shrug.

I scrunch up my face. "She's only sixteen."

"It's a Cooper family tradition." He shrugs again, clatters his empty glass down on the side table. Frances stirs.

"Well, Frances won't be drinking at sixteen," I tell him firmly.

Nothing comes back.

He ignores me.

I hum. Wait for him. Eventually he says calmly, "You'll miss the whole rehearsal dinner. You need to be there, Lexie. They are expecting you."

"Are they?" I make a face, I can't help myself.

"Yes."

"So?" I can hear how childish that sounds but it's all I can think of.

"So? What will they say? Your meal is paid for. The photographs? You'll be missing from the Coopers pictures."

*But I'm not even a Cooper,* I think.

"Can I let you in on a secret?" My heart starts to pound.

"Sure." He looks worried now.

"I've been dreading this Christmas in the Cotswolds." I wipe my sweaty palms on my jeans.

"What?" His eyes pop again, his mouth hangs open for so long he could catch an entire army of flies. He really is shocked.

*Oh you didn't just tell him that, Lexie,* I shout in my head. It's the glass of white wine. Lady Petrol. This was not supposed to come out tonight. Frances cries and spits the soother, wide awake now.

"Ohhh, I had no idea." He stands up carefully in his bare feet, rocking Frances.

"I mean . . ." I try to backtrack. "I can't wait to see Freya . . . I love her, to bits, she's a sweetheart, but she alone isn't enough to encourage me to be enthusiastic about seeing most of your family . . ." I say haltingly.

"That's . . . really hurtful," Adam says quietly, makes soothing noises for Frances.

"I'm sorry but it's the truth. Obviously your parents are lovely, Heather has been nothing but generous and welcoming to me, but have you noticed how they literally show their faces, have a drink and leave, your mother citing those headaches all the time?"

"She suffers from migraines."

"I know," I say. "You ran all the tests at the hospital to make sure it wasn't anything sinister, I remember."

He studies my face. "What am I to say to this?" I can't believe how dumbfounded he looks – I mean, I'm not asking to miss the actual wedding!

"Tell them the truth." Suddenly my going-out jeans feel way too tight and I want to escape into my leggings. Free my muffin top. I feel damp patches awakening under the linen of my armpits.

"Let's be realistic for a second here, yeah? It's just shit timing, Lexie, you have priorities . . . You have to come home with me tomorrow. Both of you," he states as I feel my temper rise, because he knows how much this means to me.

*Ding.*

*Dong.*

It's Annemarie and the taxi.

Saved by the bell.

# 13

*"There's room for everyone on the nice list."*

Buddy, *Elf*

"Guess what?" I say as I swing the hall door open, my cheeks burning red, my mouth dry.

"Professor Plum in the kitchen with the pipe?" Annemarie answers with a brazen grin.

"Máiréad's-daughter-just-miraculously-messaged-me!" The alliteration sprays out with some spittle into Annemarie's wind-chilled face.

"Ew! Stop spitting on me, woman." She shakes her head like a sea-swimming dog post splash.

"She's in Ireland!" I clench my fists and raise them up.

"No way? That's amazing! Shut the front door!" she cries, stepping inside. Little hailstones are melting into her red coat.

"I know, right?!"

"No, I mean, really, will you shut the front door, it's bloody Baltic out there! The taxi wouldn't wait, absolute asshole and refused to go by my route, hence we ran into awful holiday traffic near Busáras. We have to call another one on the app. Tell me all in the cab!" She peers at me over the pile of immaculately wrapped gifts in her hands, her wild curly red hair, now exempt from her greys, blowing across her freckled face. The collar of her coat is turned up, her black pleather leggings like a second skin clinging to her stick-thin legs. I gaze down in awe at her towering, strappy, open-toe, silver high heels.

"Oh sorry! You look stunning!" I shut my front door behind her with a flick of my heel, the small pane of glass rattling in the frame, and help her with the gifts.

"The new babysitter is lovely but so young, Tom swore he'd be home by four to help her but he was late again. He's stressed out of his mind with work. I didn't even wait to hear his excuse, I was sitting in the taxi, engine running, Ben on my knee, waiting for him as he pulled in."

"How are things?" I ask, putting my hand on her shoulder.

She shrugs. "Same."

"Reeeaaaaaaaady!" Mam hollers.

Annemarie does a double take. "Is Adam on hormones?"

"My mother's here. Surprise." I hunch my shoulders and pout.

"No way! Barbara! Oh my God! Where are you woman? Get out here, Mrs Byrne. Tell me you're hitting the town with us?" Annemarie beams.

"She is. But before we go in, wait, I swear to God I'm—" Frances cries out.

"Oh shit! I woke her? Why is she asleep at six?" Annemarie flicks her wrist and checks her fitness watch, clasping a hand over her mouth. "It is six, I thought we said six o' clock? Out early, home early? New us, remember? Did I get the time wrong?"

"No, she's awake, she's been out of her routine all day today. Adam stuffed the soother in her gob so she nodded off earlier."

"Thought you were weaning her?"

"*I* am," I grumble.

She purses her lips. "Did you tell Adam that?"

"Yes." I eyeball her, lean right into her face and hiss dramatically in her ear. "I really want to give her the ring tomorrow, but he says I can't."

"Am I supposed to know what you're talking about, my precious?" She tries to step back from me.

"That's not the half of it. I'll explain all, it will blow your mind. Let me call another cab."

She leans against the door and I take the remaining gifts from the top of her pile. Black strings dangle beneath velvet red bows and handwritten gift tags. She's so kind and thoughtful.

"Ben bawled when Tom took him as I left." She puts her lower lip over her top.

"He will be fine!" I put my hand on her cold cheek, where it rests momentarily.

"I hope you like your gift. It's as much for me as it is for you, but there ya go. Yes, it's a voucher for that new day spa in Castleknock. Now, come on, get your shit together, call the cab! I'm dying for a night out. I'm spitting feathers! I haven't been out in so long, there is an Annemarie Rafter shaped hole in my armchair." Annemarie curls her long hair behind her ears and shakes her skinny backside.

"I really need your advice. Shit's hit the fan over what I have to tell you!" I open my eyes wide as I tap on my phone's taxi app.

"Okay. We'll talk about it when we get into town," she rushes.

"I don't think I'm going to go to the Cotswolds tomorrow," I mouth the words.

Her face crumples in confusion. "You don't think you're getting a cotton swab tomorrow?"

"I don't think I'm going to go to the Cotswolds tomorrow," I hiss.

"Cos Barbara arrived? Fair enough. You do everything you can for Adam's family, you ask nothing of him for your family, don't go," she whispers back.

I shake my head dramatically. She holds up her hand, raises her voice.

"What is going on? Have you been prinking? You know you can't prink!"

"Shush!" I wave my hands wildly in the air, in front of her face.

"Why are we huddled in the hallway whispering, just ask me my advice here?" She glares at me. "Is it about taking the job at Sir Patrick Dun's?" Confusion reigns down upon her. "Obviously I think you should take the job there, it's madness. If I had my way I'd be a stay-at-home mam, but I've half a mortgage to pay, so I can't!"

"If it wasn't for the free childcare I'd take up that job offer in Sir Patrick Dun's, but I can't, it . . ."

". . . kills me you went to college in New York to train and there is a job waiting for you in there."

"It is what it is. I need childcare and it would take up all of my wages if I took the nursing job." I've been over this with her a million times.

"This country needs its head checked. When will we pay the right people the right money? Nurses? Teachers?"

"Why are we talking about this right now?" I ask.

She gives me a scathing look. "You asked my advice on it?"

"No, no I didn't! I was going to ask—"

"Helloooo? What's going on?" Adam sticks his head into the hallway and we both jump.

"Hi! Merry Christmas, Adam. Sorry if I woke her? She's never usually asleep at teatime." Annemarie oh so subtly gets her dig in and click-clacks in her strappy heels down my hallway towards him. They disappear into the living room.

*"Find her, Lexie . . . Find her for me, won't you love?"* Máiréad's last words fill my head and I swallow a lump, her whiter-than-white face and paper-dry mouth coming to my mind as clear as day. I lean against the bathroom door.

"Ready." My mother steps out of the bathroom now in a lilac trouser suit and I almost fall over.

"Are you tipsy already, dear?" she asks.

"No." I straighten myself up and rest against the hall table.

Her freshly blow-dried hair glints under my draped fairy lights that hang over the bathroom door frame. My phone beeps.

"Taxi's here," I shout and put my phone down.

"You look like you have the weight of the world on your shoulders," Mam says.

"I made a promise to someone, and I want to keep it."

"So keep it. I brought you up to have morals." Mam opens my front door, then calls over her shoulder, "Grab me my coat and let's go, us girls just a wanna have fun!"

*

The Brazen Head is hopping as we emerge from the stifling taxi. It's one of the Twelve Pubs of Christmas favourite haunts and the colourful Santa jumpers are everywhere. Slade sing out through the speakers wishing it could be Christmas every day.

"My shout! What'll we have?" Annemarie rounds the lonely smokers and I follow close behind, taking Mam by the hand.

"It's terribly busy," Mam states the obvious.

"Just have one here, Mam, then we go for dinner. It's a Christmas tradition for me and Annemarie, is that okay?" *Maybe it will be too packed for her,* I suddenly worry.

"No! I love busy, dear!" she tells me in her faux-fur trimmed coat. "Busy is my middle name."

"Three gin and tonics, maybe?" I shout behind her.

"Any chance of a Christmas kiss?" A young guy steps in front of us, his reindeer jumper flashing green and red. He's holding up a bit of a branch he's pulled off a Christmas tree somewhere.

"That's not mistletoe," I say.

"I don't wanna kiss you! I wanna kiss Curly Sue here." He makes a face at me as he intentionally looks me up and down.

"Does he want to kiss *me*?" Mam asks.

"No, Mam."

"Pity I'm married," Annemarie jumps in, grabs for the shamrock brass handle, and flashes her ring.

"So wha'? I don't care. He's not my husband." His eyes twinkle with the alcohol.

"Even so, I can't kiss you, Santa's watching!" But she smiles and winks at him as he roams off in the other direction, nearly taking a young one's eye out waving his branch in the air like a woman detector.

"Bit flirty, madam." I eye her as we step inside the body heat whacking us in the face.

"This place is fabulous!" Mam says, taking it all in.

"Yeah." Annemarie gives me a huge smile, a shimmy of her shoulders.

"Not like you?" I pose the question.

"I'm not like me," she says lightly.

"After you, Mam." I step back to allow her to cross in front of me. Miraculously, I spot a tall table with only one high stool and run for it.

"Follow me!" I shout back at them. It's tucked away beside the Christmas tree and the roaring turf fire, obviously too hot for these youngsters in woolly jumpers.

"Sit up here, Mam." I pull out the stool from under the table. "It's not too high for you, is it?" I ask as she settles herself on it.

"Lexie, I may be in my seventies but I am as fit as a flea. I do Pilates three times a week, I walk for an hour every evening on the beach, I eat a Mediterranean diet. Please don't be ageist." Her nose twitches.

"I-I'm not ageist, I'm being respectful . . ."

"No, you are treating me as a lesser, dear, as though I'm on my last legs," she tells me with a knowing smile.

"I don't mean to . . ."

She waves my apology away. "Don't worry, dear, go get us a large liquid aperitif."

I follow Annemarie to the crowded bar and sidestep my way into the second row of the queue, where I spot her at the edge.

"Up here!" I beckon. I'm taller, so the barman always sees me first; she's cuter, so the barman always serves her first.

Annemarie squeezes her thin frame into a space, grasps the bar top, and I push my way down to stand behind her. I always feel oversized in packed pubs. I struggle my arms out of my coat, drape it over my arm.

"I meant that, I'm not like me right now, I'm sick of being me," she shouts back in my ear. I have to wiggle my finger in it as she's so loud. But before I can answer the barman sees her.

"Go!" he calls as he wipes the wet counter, then throws the dirty tea towel over his shoulder.

"Me?" I nearly fall over and clutch Annamarie for support.

"Sorry, no, she was first."

See?

"Three gins, two tonics and one slimline, please, and take one for yourself! I've never any change for tips these days!" Annemarie's on her tippy toes screeching at the bartender and I have to laugh: it's like old times except it's been so long since we've had a night out on our own.

The tall tumbler glasses with gins and ice and limes are shoved across the bar, followed by the slim tonic bottles. Annemarie taps her card.

"Why would you be sick of being you, by the way? You're fabulous!" I shout as I pour the tonics in and push the empty bottles back across the bar. A sweaty young guy grabs the empties and rattles them with a clatter into a bottle bin underneath the bar.

"Dunno. Lots of reasons. Perimenopause probably doesn't help. So I've been told." She squeezes out and we zigzag our way back towards the table by the fire.

"By the doc?" I ask, handing Mam her drink and balancing my glass carefully on the not-so-steady table.

"By Tom." She sucks the alcohol up over George Michael singing to us so beautifully about that crowded room and his friend's tired eyes.

"How does Tom know about perimenopause?" I ask.

"Lexie, menopause is the most talked-about symptom in the country. Pharmacies can't keep HRT in stock! He listens to the radio when sailing. He knows more than I do about the bloody beast!"

"Menopause?" Mam catches the word and stands as we both drape our coats over her bar stool. She sits back taller than before.

"Would you girls like me to tell you a thing or two about the menopause?" Mam offers, bobbing along to George.

"Go on, Barbara, horrify us with your tales of insomnia, night sweats, weight gain, anxiety, hair loss, hair growth, flaky skin, no libido . . ." Annemarie stops abruptly and her smile starts to fade, so I jump in.

"Oh I have the anxiety alright," I say, sucking on the fresh lime I've plucked from my tumbler.

"Well, girls," Mam begins in a sage voice, "you may be surprised to hear what I've to say. Menopause doesn't have to be this great big black cloud of fear hanging over us in our forties, fifties and sixties. Believe you me, it can bring positive changes to your lives."

"Like what?" Annemarie lifts her glass with a sceptical look on her face.

"Okay, I say the word menopause, what's the first thing that springs to your mind?" Mam points at me.

"All those unwanted symptoms Annemarie's just mentioned!" I cry.

"They are disheartening alright." Mam sits on the stool, holding court. "But where's the media mention of the positive impact? Not all changes are negative. Let's take the dreaded period, for example. The bane of women's lives. Stopped me playing sports, swimming in the summer, crippling pains in school, not to mention the shame I used to feel . . ."

"That's gone now, Mam, the shame part," I tell her.

Mam just raises an eyebrow. "In my day, Marina, the friend I met today, was housebound on the days her bleeding was very heavy. She was actually fired from her job in an accountant's office for missing two days every month when her cramping was so severe she literally couldn't get out of bed. For Marina, entering the menopause was utterly liberating. She even said to me again this afternoon, and she is seventy years old, that she still rejoices at all the white trousers in her wardrobe now!"

Annemarie and myself both laugh at that.

"My PMS has been awful," Annemarie confesses. "I'm due in a few days. My boobs are agony tonight, for example, and I know I'm so irritable."

"At least you don't bow down to the food cravings like I do!" I roll my eyes.

"Menopausal women can enjoy sex without having to worry about a possible pregnancy," Mam continues with a little giggle.

"Mother!" I throw my hands over my eyes.

"Oh how did you get here, Lexie, did the stork drop you at our doorstep? Listen, when I started perimenopause, a good friend who was ten years older than me gave me some great advice." Mam lifts her glass, takes a small sip. "Lovely, thank you, dear," she says to Annemarie, then continues. "She said, don't expect the symptoms of menopause. They can get into your head. So I refused to focus on any of the negatives, same as my mother before me, who by her own admission 'hadn't got time for the menopause'! Ha! But when I began getting hot flashes when I turned forty-five, I focused on the positives of them and tried not to overthink it."

"But so many women go through hell, Barbara," Annemarie points out, quite rightly.

"Of course. Menopause can be a shit show, of that there's little doubt. But once you're through the worst of menopause, you realise that what you've experienced is actually a huge change of life. It's rightly called 'The Change', because it is a change. And that change of life isn't just physical because, post-menopause, in your fifties and in your sixties, that is very often when we begin to lay down the labels that we have had attached to us for most of our adult life."

I'm intrigued. "Such as?"

"Like the label of mother, daughter, or your professional label." She takes another sip, I can see she's really enjoying this conversation. "This change allows us to become someone new, and when we start to think about who we want to become, in this new phase of life, we realise that the person we want to become is very often closely aligned to the person we used to dream of becoming when we were little girls. Do yourselves a favour, read *Wise Up* by Barbara Scully."

"Noted." Annemarie nods thoughtfully.

"If only you had your notebook." I laugh at her, though not unkindly.

"Let's start empowering each other by telling positive stories about older women and the menopause. Yes, women go through hell, and it's fantastic HRT is there to help, but can I very quickly tell you about my journey of self-acceptance? Am I boring you?"

We both shake our heads.

"When I was about the age you both are now, I stopped focusing on all my perceived flaws. I cared less what people thought, slept naked with the windows wide open despite you father's protests of the wind chill. I accepted changing." She nods, looking very happy with herself indeed.

Annemarie drapes her arm around my mother's waist. "That is empowering, Barbara."

"Wow, Mam, you okay?" I stare at her; she's not usually this outspoken.

But she is positively beaming now. "Couldn't be better. Looking at you two does me a world of good. Friends are so important. Cherish each other. Walk each other through the change. Be there for each other. And accept each other as you both change. That's when real friendship is tested. That's my Ted Talk for tonight. Now, have you talked to her, Annemarie, about moving to the Cotswolds?"

She had to go there.

"Mam!" I admonish.

"Kinda but . . ." Annemarie chases her miniature straw with her lips, looking anywhere but at me.

"She's dreading this wedding," Mam tells her.

"I know . . ." She catches her thin black straw, sucks hard as if to give herself time to reply.

"They all hate me there," I tell them honestly.

Mam wags a finger. "Hate is a very strong word, Lexie, a word I dislike enormously."

"A few do hate her, though," Annemarie tells my mother, and I'm so grateful she's sticking up for me.

"It gets harder and harder to play nice with them all. Except his parents, I do like them. Heather and Jeffrey are such lovely people."

Annemarie is distracted, pulling out her ringing phone. "Tom. Again. He let the babysitter go! Men! I wanted him to train her.

Jesus, he can't cope for a few hours. No doubt it will be, 'Where is the remote control?' He can feck off." She stuffs her phone back in her pocket, rolling her eyes. "He can just manage alone. All that effort to get the sitter."

Mam casts a disparaging look at the device. "Another thing I thank my lucky stars for – that those dreaded phones were not a part of my life as a young mother. You really get no peace away from the children."

"Thanks, Mam, I see you didn't fret about me on your nights out with Marina!" I joke.

But Mam laughs. "Drink up, I'm starving. Let's go eat."

"Barbara, I want to hear all about life in the sun and that amazing six-month-long Spanish cooking course Lexie told me all about, up in the hills of Frigiliana, wasn't it? I adore paella, if I could I'd eat it every night for the rest of my life." Annemarie kisses her fingers.

We politely polish off the drinks and I can't say I'm sorry to leave the noise and Christmas chaos of the pub. Outside light snow falls and we all link arms. We stroll around the corner on the Quays in the refreshing cold evening breeze to Little Leond's Napoli, our favourite Italian.

"Aha Lexie Byrne! Benvenuto!" Paschal, the waiter, embraces me. Adam used to find it so amusing that the head waiter knows me so well.

"Paschal! Merry Christmas, ma chara," I greet him warmly.

"Too long, no?" He's smartly dressed as always in his black suit and red dicky bow.

"Yes, busy with work and baby – you know how it is."

"I have six daughters, I know only too well." He shrugs as if to say *what can you do*, but I know he adores his girls. "Look at you?

Glowing," he compliments me, looking me up and down (but not in a creepy way!).

"You're not, are you?" Annemarie hisses.

"Not what?"

"Up the . . . Pregnant!"

"W-what? Again? No!" My hands cover my stomach in the billowing oversized white shirt.

"Paschal said you were glowing, Italian men can sniff out pregnant women quicker than sniffer dogs at an airport . . ." she says.

"It's the shirt." I pull at my waistband, try to tuck in one side. "Unforgiving floaty bastard."

"Oh." She curls her hair behind her ears. "Only Alexa Chung can do a man's white dress shirt, Lexie, we all know that." She looks sad for me.

"You know," Mam says, "we need a name for the pouchy bit under our stomachs after we give birth to normalise it. We all have it, or at least we should. Women are supposed to get softer as we age."

We follow Paschal to the back of the dimly lit room, red and green chequered tablecloths and tall white candles burn brightly, past the white Christmas tree to our window table.

"Hungry, girls?" Mam asks.

"Starvin' Marvin," I tell her as we all sit and grab the soft-backed menus.

"May I take your coats?" Paschal asks.

"I'll just have a main." Mam hands her coat and pulls up her reading glasses on the chain.

"Share a starter?" I ask Annemarie, who has her nose in the menu.

"Sure. Bruschetta? Order some wine?" she says, twisting in her seat to look at the specials board written in chalk above the long, stencilled window.

"Oh, look at that special, creamy prawn linguine. I'm in. Red or white?" I answer as her phone rings again, now propped up on the candlestick holder. "Put it on silent!" I hiss, as Mam peers over her glasses, and she grapples to shut it up.

"I need to be nicer. Make peace with my PMS, Barbara's right. I was so ratty to Tom when he pulled in. I scowled at him in the taxi as I handed over Ben and his potty. Here, say hello, let's see what he can't find!" But she actually giggles, hits speaker and we both huddle across the table, although it seems Mam hasn't heard it ring over the raucous background noise and she's reading every main course on the menu out loud to herself, her glasses barely resting on the tip of her nose.

"Yes, Tom, how can I help you? Have you checked under the couch?" Annemarie says, leaning forward, holding her hair back.

"Annemarie! Jesus Christ Almighty! At last! You need to come home. Now. Right now!" His voice booms out of the phone's speaker.

Her face pales in the flicker of the candlelight. "W-what's happened? I-is it Ben?"

"No . . . um, no, Ben's fine. I have to . . . I have to get to the Rotunda," he yells.

"The Rotunda?" She leans in closer.

We share a quick look. The Rotunda is a maternity hospital.

"Yes . . . Gail's . . . gone . . . Gail's gone into labour." His voice is sharp, broken and frighteningly high pitched.

"Gail's *pregnant*? I didn't even know she had a boyfriend?" Annemarie frowns.

Oh fuck, I think. My palms start to sweat. The truck driver gets me with an upper cut.

"Is all the beef Irish?" Mam, sitting back, is oblivious.

"She . . . She doesn't . . . It's . . . She's having *my* baby." Tom drops a bombshell.

Mam's sweet voice floats over our heads. "I wonder can they do the gnocchi without the spinach, it gives me terrible indigestion?"

My hand jerks with the shock and I send the carafe of water spilling all over the tablecloth and my jeans. It misses the phone. I do a double take, down to the spillage and back to Annemarie.

"Oh dear, don't worry, spills happen." Mam throws down her menu and is up like a flash out of her seat chasing after Paschal.

I can actually see Annemarie swallow. She stares at me in slow motion; it's like someone took a paintbrush and whitewashed her face.

"W-what? Tom, w-what did you say?" It's me who speaks, not her.

"Oh. Lexie? That you?" He heaves loudly.

"Yea. Um, what are you talking about, 'your baby?'" My heart's pounding out of my chest now and Annemarie has moved well past the whiter shade of pale, her hands shaking.

"This – is – oh fffuuccckkkkkk." Tom makes a strangled noise.

"Gail. Gail's pregnant?" Annemarie leans down almost on top of the phone in the middle of the table – thank God we are far enough away from the next table and they are loud, out-since-lunchtime Christmas party co-workers type of revellers, in colourful Christmas paper hats, paying not one bit of attention to us.

I don't know what to do. Do I hand her the phone? Do I leave the table? Do I break Tom's neck?

"This wasn't the way I wanted you to find out, believe you me. It's touch and go. She's four weeks early they say – I tried to tell you but . . . I only just found out myself – I'm so sorry. I'm not in love with her, believe me, Annemarie . . . I love you, so much . . ."

His voice is so high pitched it doesn't even sound like Tom anymore.

A waiter approaches with a cloth, and mops up the table. I'm too stunned to even thank him or get out of the way. Tom's voice comes again.

"Annemarie, I'm sorry but I need you to come home right now."

"No!" she shouts, standing up and knocking over her chair.

"Shush." I put my hand on hers and look around, hoping no one's noticed.

"What's wrong with her?" Mam asks, returning to her seat.

"No! I fucking won't—" Annemarie roars.

"Annemarie Rafter!" My mother looks utterly horrified.

Diners start to look over at us now, and the noise level is dropping around us.

"I have to bring Ben with me then, I have to go, she's eight centimetres . . . Her brothers have been ringing me all night . . . They aren't people I can ignore . . . They are dangerous, they can ruin me!"

Annemarie reaches into the centre of the table and brings a clenched fist down hard on the phone, sending all the silverware flying and wine glasses toppling. Now everyone is staring and a deadly hush descends over the restaurant rapidly.

"YOU FUCKING BASTARD, TOM!" she screams wildly.

I leap up. "Okay! Let's go, Mam, go get your coat from Paschal!" I say, making "go-way" faces at people and watch them turn back to their dinners in loud whispers. I grab my leather bag. "Let's go, we'll go back to mine, come on."

"Does she not like anything on the menu . . . ?" Mam is utterly confused.

"No! I want to go home. I want to get my son," Annemarie declares desperately.

147

"Are we not having dinner?" Mam cross-questions.

I stare urgently at Paschal, who hands us our coats and waves me on by.

"Get me a taxi," Annemarie whispers.

"I'm coming with you," I say.

We walk up Usher's Quay. Buskers strum out carols on acoustic guitars and merry people sway past us.

"I don't know what to say," I say helplessly.

Mam is doing her best to keep up with us. "What on earth has happened?"

"What am I gonna do?" Annemarie heaves.

I shake my head hopelessly. What *are* we going to do? "I don't know."

"Can someone tell me what the bloody hell is going on?" Mam stops and puts her hands on her hips.

"Let's just get you home, Mam, I'll explain later. Adam's there, he'll put you on a pizza." I just want to get my friend home, I've no time to get into the whole Gail thing with Mam.

"I don't like pizza. Can I help?"

"No, not now, but thank you." I link her arm gently, and we cross the Ha'penny Bridge. A row of taxis are lined up across the shimmering dark water and I wave down the driver at the top of the queue. He unlocks the doors for us. I slide into the back seat with Annemarie and Mam gets in the front. I give my address first, then hers. Annemarie is shaking so hard I have to do her seatbelt for her.

"Whatever it is, dear, sleep on it, I promise it will all look better in the morning," Mam gives her useless advice from the front as Dublin city spins by in a blur of red and green lights.

# 14

*"Just once, I'd like a regular, normal Christmas."*
John McClane, *Die Hard*

"**Y**OU'RE COMING IN, RIGHT?" Annemarie unclicks her belt as I take my change from the driver and tip him.

"Nice tip, thanks, ladies. Merry Christmas to yiz," he says, his Christmas pudding hat lopsided on his head.

"If you want me to," I say, nervously. We get out and I look up at her house. Lit up like the happiest house on the street. Her blinking Christmas tree in the window, fairy lights all over the neatly trimmed garden bushes and around the door frame. We crunch up the gravel driveway. A holly wreath sways on a nail on the open door. Annemarie steps in first, and I follow closely. Tom stands in his beanie hat and coat, his car keys jingling in his hand.

"Not now, Lexie." He nods to the door.

"She's staying." Annemarie sounds as cool as a cucumber as she slips off her towering silver strappy heels. "But you're not."

"Honestly, you have to believe me, Amo, it was just that one time, they only told me a week ago, I had no choice in the matter . . ."

"No choice?" Her voice is rising now.

"Ben's asleep, love." He closes the door. I stand a few steps down the narrow hall.

"Don't 'love' me," she spits. "No choice, you say?"

"In the decision . . . to bring my child into the world, no, I was not given a choice."

"So you would have had her abort?"

"P-probably, yes. I love you, Annemarie, I—" he stutters.

"Oh spare me, Tom, please." Annemarie pushes past me and crouches down to pull open a tiny white door under the staircase.

This conversation is so surreal as the house feels so festive, so bright, so happy. It is anything but.

Tom casts a panicked glance her way. "What are you doing? Look, let me just go to the hospital, her brothers are . . . pissed at me, they've been threatening me, to out me – and – and I dunno what they will do to me if I don't show up, I need to explain myself – I need to . . ."

"To zip up your mickey!" Annemarie laughs in scorn, throwing her hand over her mouth, and rummages around in the under-the-stairs cupboard.

"That's a flippant thing to say, you know well how hard things have been between us. I know I'm losing you. I've tried everything to get you to forgive me. I didn't know she was pregnant, Annemarie, I swear on Ben's life. Now she's gonna come after me for maintenance and I . . ."

"Oh don't do that, Tom. Don't." At last she pulls out small suitcase.

"No! Not like that, I mean I want to do the right thing, of course I do! I'm not that guy, you know that! It's a shock for me . . . No matter how hard I try, my whole life is a fucking mess, you – w-where are you going?" The terror in his voice is alarming.

"I'm going to pack my bag while you go welcome your new child into the world. It's not the child's fault. I won't be here when you get back: I'm taking Ben to Lexie's for a few days, then Ben and I will return on Christmas Eve to get ready for Santa, and you better not be here then."

"Talk to her, Lexie, please . . ." He implores, his hands covering his eyes.

"I can't, Tom, it's not my business . . ." I gulp.

"But you're happy to stand there and take it all in?" He turns his anger to me.

"I'm here for Annemarie 'cause she asked me," I tell him calmy.

"Ha! *Now* you're here. Where've you been all year when she's been crying into her wine glass night after night, down here all by herself, our marriage falling apart, unable to forgive me?" He holds his head in his hands.

"How dare you!" she roars at him.

"I'll go up in case Ben wakes." Hand on the banister, I gingerly climb the soft, carpeted stairs, tiny silver Christmas bells that are draped along the banister chiming as I go. Below me, their argument continues.

"Right now I can't stomach you, Tom, get out of my house."

"It's my house too. You can't just throw me out, I have rights."

Tom's phone rings out in the darkened hallway, illuminating his face. "It's them. I have to go." White as a sheet, he leaves and the door shuts with a sad little click behind him.

"Well now . . ." Annemarie says, and I stop on the top step. "It's one thing thinking your marriage might be over – it's another knowing it's one hundred per cent dead in the water." She kicks shut the little door. I walk back down slowly.

"He may be telling the truth? She might not have told him?"

"Maybe." She shakes her head. "Ben will be pleased . . . He's finally going to have a sibling."

"I don't know what to say."

"I've always wanted to be a stepmother."

"Stop," I plead.

The sarcasm fades from her face instantly and her shoulders droop. "Put the kettle on, I need a strong coffee. It's okay if I come back with you tonight, right?"

She stuffs her feet into her runners that sit under the hall table.

"I have Mam there, on the couch, and Adam, I've no—"

"Oh you do, don't worry, I'll go to a hotel."

"Don't wake Ben now, wait until morning," I plead again.

"I can't stay here, Lexie, I need to get away for a few days, I need to clear my head."

"Just till morning. I have a plan for us."

"What plan?"

"Just hear me out," I say as I take her by the elbow and walk her down the hallway into her kitchen.

# 15

*"No one should be alone at Christmas."*

Cindy Lou, *How the Grinch Stole Christmas*

"**W**AKE UP!" I HISS IN ADAM'S WARM EAR. "Please, oh my God, wake up!" I'm physically shivering, my teeth chattering with the cold.

"What the—" He opens one eye, pulls the cotton sheet up under his chin, followed by the heavy duvet.

"You're not going to believe what happened tonight." I unbutton my shirt, wriggle out of my jeans by the light of the streetlamp that shines directly into my first-floor apartment. I slide into the bed under the toasty covers beside him.

"Fu-hu-uk, you're freezing! What time is it?" He turns to face me with sleepy eyes.

"It's after midnight," I whisper.

"I called you. You forgot your phone again, it rang on the hall table. It was Tom calling but I didn't answer it because Barbara arrived back that second making no sense, saying Annemarie lost her mind, then kicked me off the couch halfway through *Die Hard* so she could go to sleep. What on earth happened?"

"I didn't even notice I'd left my phone, I must have put it down after I answered the taxi call. Anyway, doesn't matter, it was all way too dramatic to even begin to try and tell you over the phone. Tom got Groovy Gail pregnant on their one-night stand!" I blurt, hardly believing the words myself.

He sits up. "Nooo."

"Yesss." I sit up too.

"Oh. Shit!"

"Yes. Oh shit!"

We both lie back down. I snuggle into him. My feet are snow wet, icy cold and I'm still shaking, possibly more from the shock than the cold December night.

"He called us in the restaurant and told her. I dropped her home and he was still there, close to tears, saying it was just that one night in early summer and he still loves her but he only found out and he has to do the right thing."

"Shiiiiiit. That's really tough." Adam shakes his head.

"On her," I snap.

"Of course!" Adam pats the duvet close around me, tucking me in. Frances gurgles in her basket beside us.

"Was she okay?" I whisper.

"An angel," he lies. "You should have stayed the night with Annemarie? I'd have managed. I've all the cases at the door."

"I saw that." My heart starts to race; the truck driver has his handle on the door ready to pounce.

"God help them, it's a terrible thing to happen, feel awful for them."

"Things have not been good between them for some time."

"I didn't realise," he says through a stifled yawn.

"She has to get away, Adam, for a few days, sort her head out. I never got to tell you because she literally only told me yesterday how things bad things are, even before this disaster. So I offered her a solution to get out of the house and away from Tom." *Here we go,* I think.

"Stay here while we're away, great idea." He lets out a loud yawn.

"Em, not exactly." *Just say it.* I force the words out. "She's going to come to Galway with me tomorrow. Winifred said she can meet me up to three o' clock. I've made up my mind, I'm going to meet her at the Galmont Hotel. I'll follow you and Frances to the Cotswolds tomorrow night. I'll miss the dinner but be there for a drink at the end of the night like I proposed earlier?" I shut my eyes tight.

"I can't believe you're doing this." He moves his leg off mine. His tone is resigned, not angry; Adam is never angry.

"I have to." I feel so guilty that I'm letting him down, but perhaps I can show him how resilient I can be when the need arises. This is me. I am who I am. This is Lexie Byrne.

"There's no more to be said then. Goodnight, Lexie." He folds his arm under his head.

"Night, Adam." I gather the duvet under my chin and shut my eyes.

A promise is a promise.

# PART 2

# 16

*"I realised that Christmas is the time to be with people you love."*

Billy Mack, *Love Actually*

"LEXIE, YOU UP FRONT, ANNEMARIE IN THE BACK," my mother dictates after deciding to come to Galway also.

"Oh Mrs Byrne, this feels exactly like that hiking trip to Doolin in County Clare you took us to when Lexie first started in Silverside. Remember?" Annemarie straps Ben into his car seat.

Adam stands at the door, Frances in his arms. His lips are pressed into a thin line, but he's otherwise keeping calm enough.

"When you girls had been naughty, as per usual!" Mam says. Bless her, she's spent the morning disinfecting my fridge, keeping busy and out of the way.

"We were in our thirties, Mam!" I half-laugh.

Adam gives us the run-down of our schedules once again, his voice flat and unemotional. "So I've booked you on the ten-fifteen tonight to Birmingham, Lexie, and Barbara you're on the nine-forty to Malaga. I printed off the boarding passes and put them on top of the microwave." He checks his watch; his taxi is on the way.

"Thank you, Adam, I put them in my bag," Mam says, "you're a great lad."

"Can I grab you for a quick word, Lexie?" he asks me, jutting his thumb over his shoulder to indicate indoors, and I follow. We go through to the kitchen, which is a mess with various bowls, glasses and cups still on the table.

"About last night?" he says without looking at me as he settles Frances into her highchair and opens a Petits Filous.

"I know it's really inconvenient, but you know how much this means to me." I lean against the sink, steady my breath as I feel that God damn truck driver get out of his van, ready to punch me in the heart once again. Adam watches me carefully, as though he can see my anxiety creeping up.

Gently, he says, "I do understand you have to see Winifred, so I wanted to say sorry for getting a bit snotty with you last night." He runs his hands through his hair, holds it back between his fingers so his cheekbones are even more pronounced.

I catch my breath. "It's fine." I say.

"I was just disappointed." He tries a corner of a smile.

"I know." I nod.

"I'm just trying to keep everyone happy but all this . . . this trip, with your mum and Annemarie and Ben, are you sure you're up to it, it feels a bit . . . chaotic?" He releases his hair and it flops over one eye.

"What can I do? Mam insisted on coming with us as Dad isn't expecting her back yet anyway and it gives her more time with me. Annemarie needs to get out of that house . . ." I throw my hands out wide.

"Promise me you won't miss the wedding, will you? I need you there to help me; I've so much to do and to organise, speeches and the like, plus Frances – I just need you." As if on cue, Frances starts to cry and flings the yogurt carton off her chair.

I lift her out. "I promise. I've never been away from her for a single night." I feel tears coming now and blink them away rapidly.

"Well." He swallows hard. "Now you'll get to see how I feel . . ."

The car honks in the car park below.

"Okay . . . That was . . . unnecessary." I screw up my face. What a time to be saying something like that!

"I know. Sorry." He scuffs the floor with his foot. "But it's a fact."

"You really wanna go there?" I ask carefully.

"If you do?" He wrings his hands together.

My heart twinges painfully. "I sacrifice a lot!"

"As do I." He keeps his voice calmer than mine, more matter of fact.

"I could be working in my dream job if . . ." Frances pulls my hair, and I wince.

"If what?" he probes, pulling at the feather on his chain.

"If you lived here. With us."

And it's out of my mouth.

"But I have Freya . . ." I can see despair swamping him.

"I know." I shut my eyes tight.

A horn blares again.

"I'd say that's my taxi." He walks up to the window and looks down. "No, but your mother is waving like she's parking an airplane, you better go . . ." He tries to lighten the mood between us.

I kiss my baby, smell her head as the anxiety pulls up and parks the truck in the middle of my brain. "Actually maybe I will just take her with me," I say now with a wobble in my voice, panic brewing.

"Don't be silly, you can't take her. I want to help you, you know I do. Look, we'll talk, okay?"

I nod reluctantly. The idea of parting with Frances is awful now that I actually have to do it, but I know he's right.

"I love you. Give her over, go meet Winifred." He holds out his arms for her.

I wipe my eyes. "Thank you."

"Come to Daddy, we are going to have a great time on the airplane." His phone beeps. "That'll be my taxi now. Listen, maybe you'll have a great time at this wedding and maybe you'll change your mind about moving into Rosehill with me?" The hope in his voice nearly flattens me.

"Like you said. We'll talk . . ." I can't hide my expression.

"What was so terribly bad about the summer anyway? Why did you hate it so much? I tried my best to give you a great holiday. The weather was glorious. Everyone was so welcoming to you?" He moves to the door, picks up his khaki bag and slings it over his broad shoulder.

And he did. He couldn't have been kinder or more attentive and loving to us. He booked me a spa day at the Moritz – robe, slippers, champagne, the lot – and took Frances out all day. The first four nights in Rosehill were actually bliss despite the intrusion of Martha popping in, unannounced, before breakfast two mornings in a row. Making snide comments that went over Adam's head. Adam wouldn't let me lift a finger and the weather *was* glorious. It was all glorious, until we moved to the Moritz Hotel for the last two nights.

"Lexie?" he pushes.

They're in the hallway with his case and her bag. My little family.

*Tell him! Tell him what they said about you! Tell him how they make you feel!* my brain people shout at me through tiny megaphones.

"They . . ." I look at him; he's staring at me, wanting to understand my reluctance to relocate so badly, but I can't do this to him, I can't drive a wedge between him and his sister. I don't give a shit about Martha, but Deb is Adam's little sister and they are very close, so who am I to jeopardise that?

The horn honks again from the car park.

"Nothing. It's fine. I'll see you tonight and we'll talk properly after the wedding." I lean in and kiss his perfect face, then I kiss Frances goodbye. "There is a list in her nappy bag . . . just in case," I say.

"I can—"

"Just in case." Then I chuckle. I know he's more than able.

I lock the door behind us and we each go our separate ways.

## 17

*"You can be a little old for a lot of things. You're never
too old to be afraid."*

Old Man Marley, *Home Alone*

"**M**E AND BARBARA WERE JUST TALKING about that musty hostel we stayed in," Annemarie says as I take my seat in the car, afraid to make eye contact just yet. I can't look across at Frances or Adam in the taxi, or I will burst into tears. I know I've made the right decision but it's still bloody hard. I've also no idea how Annemarie is feeling, or what Gail and Tom had; I haven't asked yet. We're hiding it from my mother, for now.

"That hostel – how can I ever forget." I shiver: a hostel person I am not. All that communal living and shared mugs. Adam's taxi beeps as it does a U-turn and exits through the gates.

"Remember we got lost on the way to Doolin, before the days of Google Maps, and you pulled over to ask a murderous-looking hitchhiker for directions!" Annemarie holds Ben's hand, which makes me physically heave and green with envy, though I know the feeling's irrational. Mam turns the engine over and I twist around in my seat to look at Annemarie.

"Okay?" I mouth.

She nods. She's got black circles under her eyes as she holds up her phone to me, tipping it. "Got your phone?" she says. I cop what she's doing. Pull it out of my pocket. A WhatsApp from Annemarie.

*"Tom never came home."*

I type back. *"Probably for the best. We'll talk later."*

"We'll stop for coffee and cake halfway," Mam says, pulling her seat closer to the wheel, adjusting the rear-view mirror as Annemarie's phone beeps with my message.

"Yep," she says to me, then addresses the whole car. "Barbara, remember the night we met those Canadian lads . . . One of them was the image of Andre Agassi, they bought us cheap beer, and when you came in, Barbara, Andre thought you were our sister! He so had the hots for you!"

"And I put him straight immediately." Mam's still adjusting the seat, so close to the steering wheel that I fear she may cut herself in half.

I twirl Máiréad's engagement ring on my right hand. Close my eyes for a moment and think of her and how happy she would have been to know I've found her beloved daughter. This is the right thing to do; it is.

"Ben all buckled up?" Mam asks as we pull out onto the road.

"Yup." Annemarie gives me a thumbs up. She looks exhausted but incredibly relaxed for someone who got the news she got last night, whistling and looking out the window. Ben sucks on a smoothie pouch while watching his favourite, the old *Bear in the Big Blue House* remastered, hopping off the screen on Annemarie's phone.

"Well isn't this lovely, dear." Mam looks across at me after we've been driving for a while.

I lean my weary head against the window. "I guess."

"A road trip with my daughter and her old best friend." Mam's very cheerful and it feels a bit contagious.

"Hey! Less of the old, Barbara!" Annemarie laughs and sits up between the two seats.

"Why are women so afraid of getting old?" Mam chastises as she trundles my brand new but fifteen-year-old car towards the M50. I only bought the car because I have Frances: I was always happier on public transport, but try transporting a buggy on and off buses in the Irish weather. I will go electric as soon as I can afford it.

"Sure you don't need Google Maps?" I ask.

"It's a straight road once we hit the M50 to Galway."

"I don't care about getting old – I care about being *treated* as old," Annemarie retorts.

"How so?" Mam drives at a careful speed, her hands at a quarter to three.

"I care about being invisible to society—"

Mam tuts. "You mean to men?"

"No . . . Well—" She grunts softly.

"We value ourselves by men's opinions of us far too often. I was a very attractive woman, but I still remember the day I passed a building site at the end of my road and not one builder so much as glanced at me. I was devastated and only fifty."

"Devastated? But surely that was a relief, Mam!" I'm amazed.

"I thought it would have been too. But it wasn't. I was disgusted. I'm just telling you the truth."

"Wolf whistling is intimidating!" I cry.

"I'd never felt that way about it but as I walked to work that day I questioned it for the first time. The bloody CHEEK of

166

them! Manipulating us by giving us attention only when it suited them!" She stops at the lights, pulls up the handbrake. "So I double backed and gave them all a piece of my mind. It was one of the most empowering moments of my life."

"Good for you. I just don't like getting old. I don't like feeling invisible," Annemarie says.

"But invisible to whom?" Mam's using her therapist voice now, her tone calm and neutral as she questions – all those years of watching Oprah when I was at school, she tells me when I pick her up on the "voice".

"Everyone," Annemarie tells us.

"Sexism and ageism will only be defeated when we don't validate ourselves by our looks." I cast a glance and she's doing her Oprah face, eyes wide and lips pursed.

I turn back to the road. "I haven't the energy for this conversation, put on some music."

I hate fighting with Adam. Not that that was a *fight* exactly, but who knows where it would have led to had we both not been in a hurry. He doesn't want to move here, that much seemed very obvious.

"Not yet, let's talk. That's the whole point of this trip." Mam winds down the window.

"Um, no, it's to return the ring," I remind her. "And it's freezing, Mam, can you close that?"

The window squeaks shut again. "Well, I still want to talk about you moving to the UK?" She takes one hand off the steering wheel and pats my knee.

"Okay, so back to ageism!" I divert.

My phone beeps.

It's Winifred.

"*Arrived at the Galmont Hotel. My bus leaves for Cork at 6 p.m. I'm in the foyer. So nervous!*"

"It's Winifred! Her bus leaves at six. You'll have to at least drive to the speed limit, Mam, or I will have to take over." I sound more frantic than I mean to.

"Plenty of time. We'll get there by three. What smells?" Mam sniffs the air.

"Ben. Sorry," Annemarie says. "Can we turn off at the next service station?"

"Sure." Mam winds down her window again, and though it's freezing, I'm now grateful for the fresh smelling winter air.

"By the way, Mam, in case you hadn't noticed, I'm a grown woman. I do know what's best for me." I wish she would back off.

"So you hate his ex-wife . . . That's perfectly normal, honey." Oprahisms.

"I'm trying not to hate her. Like you said last night, hate eats you up. I just have no desire to spend my life with her in it every day. Why would I?"

"But she's getting married tomorrow afternoon?" Annemarie pipes up.

"Oh thanks for that nugget of useless information, buddy!" I turn in my seat, peering at Ben. "Jesus, Ben, what did you eat?" I hold my nose.

"My philosophy on life is to be kind," Mam says placidly, changing lanes towards the exit.

"I *am* kind," I say with force. It's Martha who could do with learning that lesson!

"So am I." Annemarie nods.

"So then why are you both so on edge? Especially you, Annemarie, what the hell happened in the Italian last night, dear?

168

That was some bloody outburst." Oprah has left and Mother has returned.

"Not now, Mam." I glance in the mirror at Annemarie.

"Maybe I can help? I have life experience you know. There's nothing you can throw at me that I haven't already heard." She flicks her eyes up into the rear-view to look back at Annemarie.

"It's alright, Lexie, though I doubt you've heard this, Barbara." Annemarie shifts forward on her seat, holding onto her seatbelt as though for emotional protection, as well as physical. "The dad of you-know-who, here to my left, well, let's just say things haven't been exactly hunky-dory between us and last night he . . . informed me that a woman he was having extra-marital relations with was about to deliver his . . . offspring."

"Oh dear. Oh dear, dear." Mam gasps and turns her head fully now to gape at Annemarie, and the car swerves.

"Mam! Eyes on the road," I shout, my two hands clutching the dashboard.

"Exactly," Annemarie says, apparently unfazed by my mother's erratic driving.

"Service station up ahead." Mam steadies the wheel, exits, detours and we take a sharp roundabout into the forecourt. "That's . . . one I haven't personally heard before." Mam pulls into a parking spot.

"Told you." Annemarie takes her phone from Ben and mercifully mutes the Bear singing goodbye.

"I'll need to hear more, dear, before I can give you my advice?"

"Who wants coffee?" I ask, glad to get out of this moment and stench and stretch my legs.

"I'll have a decaf, dear, and I'll use the restroom too." Mam winds up the windows. The car shudders as she shuts the engine down and pulls the key out of the ignition.

I help Annemarie out with Ben and they head off towards the toilets. I check my phone. A photo from Adam on WhatsApp.

*"Daddy & Frances Fly High."*

It's a gorgeous selfie. They are on the Aer Lingus flight, and she's attached to his strap buckle. My heart lurches. I just need to speak to Winifred and get back to them. Keep my promise. I'll take Mam for dinner before we head back to the airport tonight, offer Annemarie my apartment for the next few days.

"Lexie?" I hear in the distance.

"Huh?"

A man's voice calls my name, and I almost drop my phone when I spin around.

Tom stands in front of me.

"Tom?! What the hell are you doing here?" I can't believe my eyes.

"They were taking the piss." He shoves his hands deep into the pockets of his low-slung combat trousers.

"Who?" I cast around.

"Gail's brothers. She wasn't in labour at all. I need to tell Annemarie, or you can? Gail isn't pregnant Lexie, it was . . . what did they call it now, oh yeah, payback." His face is gaunt and his stubble heavy. Tom is normally clean-shaven; I have never seen him look so dishevelled.

"Oh my God, are you serious?" I gasp with relief. "How did you know we were here?"

"I had Annemarie's location on." He waves his phone. "I know it seems stalky. Is she running away from me? Is she taking Ben away from me? I have to know, Lexie? You have to tell me." He looks so lost I almost, *almost* feel sorry for him.

"It's not for me to say. I don't know Tom. My mother is with us right now, this isn't a good thing to do."

"I love her, Lexie, so much. I don't quite know how to tell you what went wrong but—"

I hold up my hand.

"Let me give you some advice?" I take a step closer to him.

"Please, I'll take anything, I want to save our marriage, I always have." His voice is that of a broken man, and I think he might be about to burst into tears.

"Give her some space, Tom," I say, not unkindly. "Regardless of this news, she needs space."

He nods and looks down at his dirty white Converse.

"I can only imagine what you think of me. I know you've avoided me since. But you don't know the full story . . . It's been really hard, she's been . . . so distant, so removed . . ." He steps one foot on top of the other.

"I know some . . ." I say softly.

"It's not all me . . ." He chokes on the words.

"She said that." I quickly check over my shoulder and edge him around the corner before Annemarie gets back and sees him.

"You think I should go?"

"I really do." And I really mean it, for his sake as much as Annemarie's. They need time apart.

"Okay." His head hanging low, like a beaten puppy, he turns and heads back towards his van I now see parked up by the kerb.

"Tom?" His name leaves my mouth before my brain has even told me what I'm thinking.

He spins around.

"I'll talk to her tonight. I'll tell her about Gail. You just give her space." I hold eye contact with him.

"Kiss Ben for me, will you?" He takes a step back, then pulls a blue square of fabric out of his back pocket. "Give him this if you can: it's his van blankie, he likes to rub it when he's in a car, it soothes him." He holds it out to me.

"I can't, Tom, Annemarie will know I saw you."

He nods pathetically, stuffs it back in his pocket and I watch him slouch away, climb into his van and drive off just as I hear Mam and Annemarie's voices exiting the bathrooms. Like Houdini, I slip inside. Mercifully, there's no queue at the coffee dock so I order three Americanos, one decaf, and when I go to pay I realise I've left my wallet in the car.

"Sorry, one sec, my wallet's in the car." I jog out. Mam and Annemarie are standing by the boot. Ben is cleaning the wheels with a water wipe.

"Keys." Annemarie holds out her hand.

"Yes, please, I need my bag. The coffees are ordered." I hold out my hand, breathless.

"Gimme the keys," Mam says.

"I don't have the keys, you do?" I look down to her empty hands. She looks down to mine. "No, I gave them to you."

"No, you didn't," I tell her.

"Oh no." Annemarie puts both hands on either side of her face and peers in the driver's window. "Keys are in the boot."

"W-what? How?" I shout.

"It's a manual key. I used it to open the boot to get Ben's nappy bag, left them on the back seat and slammed the boot." She closes her eyes and smacks her palms over them. "Oh shit! I'm so stupid!"

Mam steers us into calmer waters, or at least tries to. "Don't worry, dear, no point in crying over lost car keys. Ring the AA."

"I'm not a member." I slam on the brakes of that suggestion.

"Oh dear, dear," Mam says, shaking her head.

I could scream – this is absolutely the last thing I need now. "Someone give me a tenner, quick."

Annemarie opens her purse and hands me a tenner.

"Get someone inside to help us," Mam says, as I dash back inside to the counter to pay and ask the young man behind the till.

"Hi, can anyone help us? We've locked our keys in the car."

"Bill!" he yells.

"Can Bill help?" I check my watch. Winifred is leaving the hotel at six. We need to move it.

"Bill's on lunch." A younger woman, heavily tattooed, comes out from the back, fixing a red and black work laminate around her neck.

"When will he be back?" I plead.

"After lunch," she drawls.

"It's after two," I say, "it's not lunchtime."

She shrugs. "It is for Bill."

"Shit. Can anyone else help us get our keys out?" I practically beg.

"'Fraid not, he's the trained locksmith. Why don't you take your coffees and wait, I'll get to you when Bill gets in."

"Okay thanks. We're parked right outside." I take up the coffees and trudge back out. "We have to wait for some guy called Bill to get back to get the keys," I tell them.

"We could smash the back window?" Annemarie says.

"I'd rather not," I say, "I'm not flush with cash right now, plus I have to get to Galway in the next few hours and back to Dublin airport and we can't drive in this weather with no back glass."

173

"Fair point." Annemarie looks meek.

The clouds gather overhead, darker and darker. Please don't let it start hailing now too . . .

"Let's go inside and wait," I say.

"Problem?" A young guy pulling up hanging tracksuit bottoms asks as he beeps the alarm of the Jeep parked next to us.

"Yes, keys are locked in," I tell him, leaning on the bonnet.

He walks around my car. "I may be able to help. I've an air wedge air pump in the back of my Jeep – hang on."

He opens the door and starts rummaging around. I don't want to get my hopes up, but please let this man have a solution!

"Oh that would be marvellous," Mam says, blowing into her coffee, the plastic lid in her hand, her coat collar turned up against the wind.

"Got it." He holds up the contraption. "It's my good deed to strangers. Máiréad, me mam, is always watching those Hallmark Christmas movies. Pay it forward and all that malarkey." He laughs and slams the Jeep door shut.

We all share a glance at the coincidence of his mother's name, then stand back and watch him get to work. Ben looks enthralled. *Time is ticking,* is all I can think as he tries to slide the air pouch in the closed window. He turns it this way and then that way.

"Ah, I've done it a few times before but on vans, these smaller windows are harder." He hunkers down, looks at the window from all different angles.

"Please don't say we are going to miss Winifred? This is all my fault! I can't cope," Annemarie hisses.

"We'll be okay." I put my arm around her, though I'm less than convinced. The Galway Ring Road is renowned for chock-a-block traffic coming up to teatime.

"Hang on," he says, gritting his teeth in concentration. We all fix our eyes on him; the veins in his neck are bulging. He finally slides the air pouch into the window of my car.

"We're in!" He throws a small victory punch. "Just need to pump this—"

I cross my fingers behind my back as he pumps it up, takes a long metal rod from the ground and then I hear a most glorious sound.

Pop!

The door opens.

"Oh thank you!" Myself and Annemarie squeal at the exact same time.

"More!" Ben shouts, stamping his little Timberland boots.

"Young man, you are our hero," Mam says and hands him a twenty-euro note.

"Anytime. Glad to be of help. Stick that in a Christmas charity box." He gathers up his paraphernalia.

"You don't know how much this means to us. The kindness of strangers is amazing." I want to hug him but better not. "There's a Christmas St Vincent de Paul appeal box inside the door, gimme the twenty, Mam," I say.

"Mam? I thought yiz were all sisters!" he says as Mam giggles like a tipsy teenager and I roll my eyes at her.

Now's not the time for compliments – we're on the clock!

# 18

*"I've found almost everything ever written about love to be true."*

Iris Simpkins, *The Holiday*

"**E**VERYONE. IN," I COMMAND, GATHERING THE COFFEE CUPS and throwing them into a nearby bin.

"Keys." Mam holds out her hand.

I give her an incredulous look. "No chance. We've an hour to get to the Galmont, I'm driving." We pile in, I adjust the seat, the rear-view mirror and navigate my way out of the busy forecourt and back onto the M50. The dial hovers right on the speed limit; I hit the fast lane. No one talks. Ben sings "The Wheels on the Bus" over and over and over with Annemarie heaping praise on his squeaky (read: pitchy) voice every time. Traffic into Galway is bumper-to-bumper and I manoeuvre the car in and out until we break free and finally drive onto Lough Atalia Road, up the hill and left onto the smooth, curved driveway, down to the entrance of the Galmont Hotel.

"We're late," I state the bleedin' obvious.

"Only twenty-five minutes, Lexie." Annemarie grabs the silver bars of my headrest and pops her head through.

"Get out. I'll park the car!" Mam offers.

I stop at the front doors and unclick my belt.

"Go! Run!" Annemarie says.

"Go Lelly! Go! Go fast!" Ben bounces in his car seat.

I jump out, ready to race through the hotel doors.

"We'll park and be straight in after you. I've booked Ben and me in tonight." Annemarie calls out from the back.

"Oh?" I stop in my tracks and turn.

"It's fine – we'll be fine. I got a big family room on a voucher we've had for ages. I'm going to take him swimming. He's brought his armbands."

"I was going to say you can stay in my apartment? It will be free for a few days." It's not like she has any other family she can turn to. Last she heard her dad was in a jazz band in New York and her mother in a folk group in Seattle.

"We'll go home tomorrow, Lexie. I want you-know-who to be in his own bed Christmas Eve; he has his stocking out already, it's not fair on him." She seems determined, so I just nod.

"Okay." Clutching the ring on my hand, I hurry towards the hotel, step into the revolving doors and into the bright open foyer. A towering Christmas tree rises up to the ceiling. I scan the foyer from the check-in desks to the lifts; it's crowded but not full.

"Lexie?"

I spin round, heart thumping.

A woman in a wimple, black slacks with a perfect crease down the middle and an oversized black V-neck jumper in some light-weight wool stands behind me.

"W-winifred?" My voice breaks a little as I take a small step closer to her.

177

"That's me." She gives me a half smile. Her blonde hair slightly escaping from behind her ears, and her glasses are round. It's hard to age her.

"Oh my God! Hi! So sorry I'm late, our keys got locked in the car." I can't take my eyes off her. I wipe my sweating hands, feeling really nervous all of a sudden.

"Shall we?" She points to the corner of the hotel lobby, where two large leather chairs face one another next to a potted rubber tree plant. Two coffee cups sit in the middle on a small, low table.

"Yes, of course." I follow her, my heart pounding as we sit. On first glance she's not dissimilar to Máiréad, though she has lighter hair and a rounder face.

"I'm so excited to finally meet you, I can't tell you," I drop my bag at my feet.

"I know. It's . . . super strange." She smiles at me and links her fingers together.

"It's just amazing," I croak. "I'm sure you have a million questions?" I criss-cross my hands and clutch my heart.

"Of course, I do. I wish we had more time." She checks her wristwatch.

I try to steady my breath. "Where do we start?"

"What was she like? My . . . mother?" Her voice shakes a little.

I reach across and take her hands in mine.

"She was incredible, a brilliant woman. Just so strong and . . . Let me go back to the start? The first time I met her?" I rush, conscious of how much I have to tell her in so little time.

She drops her head and fiddles with her coffee cup. *This must be so hard for her*, I think. I fold my hands back in my lap, worried I've been a bit too familiar too quickly.

"Had you been looking for her long before you got my message?" I ask gently.

"Yes." Her eyes are downcast, and I wonder if she's trying not to cry in front of me.

"Okay. And your father? I always wondered if he was still . . . I'd love to meet—"

"He's dead." Her eyes stay lowered to the floor.

"Jim? Oh, he's not? Oh, no, I'm so sorry. Máiréad . . . your mother, loved him so much. They were so young, so in love, it was terrible what this country did to your mother. How? Where was he? I—"

"My job doesn't allow me much research time," she interrupts me. "In Malawi we aren't exactly set up for speedy WiFi – it's there of course, but very sporadic in the remote community where I work." I notice her foot is resting on a nerve and her leg jumps.

"Of course not. Don't mind me. Your job sounds amazing. Tell me all about it?" I feel like I'm pushing her too hard. I catch the eye of a waitress, raise a finger. "Can I get you another coffee?" She's drained her cup already, maybe because she's nervous too.

She checks her watch again and looks over her shoulder. "People are waiting for me. Maybe a very quick one."

"Oh! I've so much to tell you." I spin round. "Two coffees please," I order.

"Milk and sugar?" asks the waitress.

"Black is fine," Winifred says.

"Same," I say even though I take milk in my coffee.

I slide Máiréad's engagement ring off my finger and put it down in the middle of the table with a clack. She looks at it but doesn't pick it up.

"It's such a pity this is a rushed meet, but I'd dearly love to keep in touch with you? Make another date to talk? To see each other?" I don't want it to be this fast.

"I'd love that. When I can?" She's still looking at the ring but not making any attempt to pick it up. So I pick the ring up, hold it in between my thumb and forefinger. The diamonds glint with the light streaming in from the floor-to-ceiling windows behind us, reflecting delicately on her face.

"Winifred, here is your mother's ring. Jim, your father picked it for her and proposed to her under the Cleary's Clock on O' Connell street. They were waiting for the number three bus to Sandymount Strand to take a walk on the beach. She said it was the greatest moment of her life." I can see Máiréad so clearly now.

"It's very emotional for me, I don't have the words," she says quietly. Her accent is so hard to place, it changes all the time – no doubt from all her travelling with the missions.

I have to find out as much as I can while I'm here; Máiréad will never get the chance, so I must seize it for her. "I understand. Where were you brought up, Winifred? Were you happy?" I lean forward in my chair.

"Lots of different places." She studies the ring. Her heirloom. Her birthright. Distractedly she says, "Yeah, I was happy."

"Can I ask you something? I could only find you by your birth date and location, but your mother gave you a name when you were born, would you like to know what it was?"

"Yes, please?" She seems calm but I can only imagine how she's feeling inside right now.

"Kathleen." I say it loud and proud.

"Kathleen," she repeats.

She's so stoic, it's hard to read her. I begin to fight the tears so hard that my throat feels like it's about to close up. She nods slowly. This is so much harder than I thought; I think I assumed she'd be so joyous, but she seems so on edge.

"Here we go. Two coffees." The waitress sets a large silver pot down with two cups and saucers. "Mince pies, compliments of the hotel."

When we're alone again, I give it one more try with the ring. "Take it." I push the ring further towards her with my index finger and she slowly lifts it.

Her eyes widen, and she starts to cough. "It's so beautiful . . ."

"I know. And very valuable; we had it assessed. I can't believe I'm finally able to reunite you with it." The relief of delivering on my promise to Máiréad is overwhelming. *I did it!* I think.

"I really have to go." She stands suddenly, holding her chest, her face flushed, tears brimming. She clutches the ring tightly in the palm of her hand.

"Oh. Of course, okay." I stand too.

"Thank you." She does a small bow.

"It's just – I still have so much more to talk to you about, so many th—" For some reason I bow back, completely flustered.

She cuts me off. "You have my number?" She adjusts her wimple, eyes looking anywhere but my face. "It's a lot for me to digest." Her voice trails off to a whisper.

"Of course it is," I say. *Christ Lexie, give the woman some breathing room.* I wanted emotion, well, here it is.

"I won't always be contactable but when I am, I will reply to you."

"I hope I haven't come on too strong? I just loved your mother so much." I feel unsatisfied and I wish I didn't. I should be very proud of myself.

"I process emotions slowly. Give me time. I will be back in Europe for Masses in a few months, I'll hope to be in Donegal for Lent. Let's arrange to eat together then and you can tell me more about my mother? Thank you, Lexie. I will treasure the ring. You've made me a very happy woman. Merry Christmas to you and yours." She bows again and blesses herself.

"Merry Christmas to you too—" I really want to call her Kathleen. So badly. But I don't.

Instead, I watch Máiréad's only child cross the lobby and walk out the door.

*

"She's gone, you missed her," I tell them just moments later as Ben trundles towards me.

"Leddy! Swim!" Ben waves his orange armbands in the air.

"Already?" Annemarie's eyes nearly pop out of her head as she grapples the armbands from Ben.

"Not one space in that underground car park! We had to go up and down twenty times!" Mam says. "And don't get me started on the size of the spaces. What do you mean, she's gone? Gone where? You look like you've seen a ghost."

"How was she? Tell me everything," Annemarie talks over Mam, taking Ben's hand.

"She's in shock, I think. It was intense. There was no time. We've arranged to meet in Europe or somewhere, Donegal maybe, in a few months when she's back. We'll have more time then. It was . . . I dunno, awkward, unfortunately." I'm deflated.

I should be elated. I'm not sure what I was expecting, but I did think it would be a bit more than this.

"Did she bawl when she saw the ring?" Annemarie probes for more.

"No," I reply with a sigh.

"Really?" Annemarie stares at me.

Mam pats me on the back. "Well, you did a great thing, dear, you're so kind-hearted. You kept your promise. All's well that ends well. Now, I'm starving, we've a quick turnaround to get back to Dublin airport for our late flights. A chowder and brown bread maybe?" She turns to the same waitress who brought me the coffees earlier. The same coffees that remain untouched. "Excuse me dear, can we get some menus, please?"

"Finished?" She nods to the cups, quizzically. I don't want the coffee, I've a bitter taste in my mouth so I give her the go-ahead to clear them up. Ben charges off around the rubber tree plant pots.

"Slowly," Annemarie calls after him.

I feel let down and I shouldn't. I try to make sense of what just happened. "I mean, I imagine she leads a very sheltered life," I tell them almost absentmindedly, as though my thoughts are coming through, "she is a missionary after all. She was probably very overwhelmed, the poor woman." That was it, I think, she was overcome with emotion. People all react to emotional situations in different ways.

"Of course she was," Annemarie agrees, nodding patiently.

"Well, kick me up the arse and send me flyin' off the Cliffs of Moher! If it isn't Lexie Byrne and Annemarie Rafter! Wha'!?" A Dublin accent beats around us.

I spin around.

"No way!" I jump up as Rachel from Silverside approaches our table, in a tracksuit and sliders, two colourful cocktails with mini umbrellas swimming with fruit in each hand.

"What the hell are yous doin' here?" Rachel puts the drinks down and embraces me warmly. She shakes Annemarie's hand.

"Oh my God! Hi! Oh, long story. Rachel, this is my mother, Barbara." I do the introductions.

"How'rya Barbara, yer the spit of Lexie. Pleased to meet you, hun." Rachel shakes her hand too.

"And you, dear," Mam says with a polite smile.

"Ahhh, so this is the hotel cancellation you guys got! Super nice place," I say as the penny drops and Rachel sucks on her fingers where some liquid has dribbled down the side of the glass.

"It is. Oh Lexie, the spa is heaven on earth, I never want to leave. We went to Shop Street last night to hear a bitta traditional Irish music, got me Guinness and mussels then back here for a night cap. We've met some mad people in the bar, the stories we could tell ya! Great craic though. Proper chillaxin' we are. How's me hole lookin'?"

Rachel bends over and I howl laughing, a great sense of relief washing over me after the meeting with Winifred. I realise only now that I've been holding my breath.

"Still not a fat hole. Must try harder," I wag my finger jokingly as Rachel drags another leather chair across and sits with her legs crossed under her.

"Hiya Ben. You know me, don't ya?" she coos.

"No!" Ben says, as Rachel reaches into her jeans pocket and pulls out a tenner. "Buy him something for Christmas from me and Polly. Speaking of, I better text her, she's waitin' on her cocktail on the terrace. Heated lamps. We can't knock the aul fags." Rachel does an impression of someone dragging deeply on a cigarette and busies herself texting while the waitress returns with menus and we scan them. I try to shake this decidedly underwhelming feeling as I scan the dishes, not really seeing anything. I want to go call Adam. I need to speak to him, see if Frances is okay. I check the time: we need to be out of here in an hour. I'll feel better once I'm reunited with them later tonight.

"There yiz are! What's the craic, lads?" Polly, in a shift dress and oxblood Dr Martens, strolls over, talking as she walks.

I put down the menu and wave.

"I just said goodbye to that lunatic we met up at the bar last night. The scammer?" Polly shakes her head, her plaits swinging.

"Oh. Her." Rachel rolls her eyes, then sticks two fingers in her mouth.

"She was checking out. She did it! She wasn't spoofin' us! She met that poor unfortunate woman and blagged that valuable ring."

Polly adds some choice words, but I hardly hear them. My ears burn. I swallow the bile that's immediately risen into my mouth.

"W-what?" I utter. "What did you say there?" I stare at Polly.

"I'll just have the chowder and brown soda bread, yes, that's a good choice," Mam says to no one in particular, holding her menu up in front of her face. A white noise floats around my head.

"She did not!" Rachel slams her cocktail down now, droplets spilling all over, and Ben goes to put his finger in the spillage.

"No. Do not touch." Annemarie pulls him onto her knee and wipes his finger as he wriggles.

"W-what did you say? About a scammer? A ring? What are you on about?" I lean forward, my heart racing. Annemarie has heard and is gripping my arm.

"Ah, this mad lunatic we met from Dublin. She's a scammer! A scam artist. She goes on this My Hopeful Heritage site, hacks into the DMs and pretends to be someone's long-lost sister, cousin, daughter, whatever, and poses as some reclusive nun living abroad. Gathers up heirlooms and money. Total whack job." Polly twirls her index finger at her temple for good measure.

My stomach flips.

"Oh f—" Annemarie pulls her hand away, covers her mouth just in time.

"Oh no, dear." Mam's heard too. She jumps up, on her tippy-toes, and casts around.

"Wha'?" Rachel looks at me.

My heart is in my throat. I might be sick. "Remember Máiréad Farrell? The old woman from Silverside?" I grapple with what my mind's throwing up.

Rachel nods. "Course I do, total dote."

"Well I just gave that scammer her very valuable engagement ring." My heart nearly bursts with grief.

"No!" Polly exclaims.

Rachel gasps. "Why?"

"Are you ready to order here?" the waitress asks.

"Not just yet, dear," Mam tells her quietly, handing her back her menu.

"Oh my God! She told us all about that ring. A long-lost mother? I had to tear Polly away, she wanted to report her to the police, but then she said she was only messin' with us. She was telling the truth!?" Rachel looks dumbfounded.

"Yes, I'm tellin' ya," Polly says. "She's just flashed the ring at me as I was finishing my smoke outside—" Polly waves her left hand in the air, "—and told me ta-ra suckers!"

"She's gone to Cork." I fight the tears. This can't be happening, *this cannot be happening*. My heart plummets now like a stone off a cliff.

"She is in her hole gone to Cork! I saw her train ticket. She's getting the train back to Dublin now, meeting some rich American from Texas in the Shelbourne at seven o' clock. She's pretendin' to be his long-lost fifteenth cousin once removed. Prays on the Americans tracking their Irish roots. She eats and drinks for free all the time – heirlooms are a bonus, she's a parasite." Polly's face is steaming red.

Rachel jumps up. "Let's go!"

"Where?" I gape at her, feeling completely limp with shock.

"To the train station! We're getting Máiréad's ring back."

"Go!" Mam waves her hand. "Hurry dear!"

"But we have to get back to Dublin. The wedding rehearsal dinner?" I say pathetically.

"Feck Dublin!" Mam shouts. "This is more important right now!"

She's right!

"Hurry up, Lexie." Annemarie waves Ben's armband above her head.

"Oh my God. How am I so stupid?" I howl, grip my head in my hands.

"It's not you. She's an expert at this, hun. She's been doing this YEARS," Rachel tells me. "Now come on! She's picked on the wrong girls this time."

"Dada! Dadaaaaaaaaaaaaaa!" Ben runs from Annemarie.

"Ben! Come back! That's not Dada – that's . . . Tom!" Annemarie's eyes are on stalks.

"Annemarie." Tom swoops Ben up in his arms as he strides into the foyer.

"What are you doing?" She can't believe her eyes, and to be honest neither can I.

I am just about to keel over here. What on Earth is going on?

"Fighting for you . . . both. Hello son!" He squeezes Ben tightly, planting dozens of kisses on his head.

"Swim, Dada, swim!" Ben squeals.

"Hi." Tom feebly waves at us all.

"Go, Lexie!" Annemarie demands.

"Are you okay?" Tom sees my face.

"Hello, Tom, dear, nice to see you again," says Mam but rather than making eye contact with him, she's side-eyeing Annemarie. "Tell you what, safety in numbers. Why don't you all go chase that thief down." Mam walks towards Tom and extends her hands to Ben, still wriggling in his dad's arms. "Ben, I see the biggest ice cream sundaes out there. Will Grammy Barbara buy you one? With extra chocolate sauce?"

"Yes!" Ben almost dives out of Tom's arms and into my Mam's arms.

"Now let's walk." She places him down and takes him firmly by the hand. "We'll be fine."

"What's happening?" Tom pulls off his red beanie, stuffs it in his coat pocket as if ready for action.

"She's right." Annemarie says. "Come on, Tom, follow us, we'll explain on the way."

"Okay," Tom says as the four of us take flight out the revolving door, the fast Galway rain sleeting in our faces as we pelt through the packed streets, narrowly dodging Christmas shoppers.

"Right!" Polly directs. We run up the hill, then down towards Eyre Square and the train station. A Christmas choir is singing for charity outside and volunteers shake buckets in time to the beat of "Santa Claus Is Coming To Town".

Up the concrete steps and out onto the platform. The Galway to Dublin Heuston train is mostly boarded. We run to the small iron gate.

"Tickets please?" the inspector asks as he whistles.

"We don't have tickets! Someone on that train has something belonging to me." I bend over clutch my knees, catching my breath.

He stops whistling. "No ticket, no train."

Surfacing like a pearl diver, I roar, "PLEASE!"

"No can do. More than me job's worth, lovey."

"Can I buy five tickets?" Tom pulls his wallet out of his back pocket. His beanie falls and Annemarie picks it up, hands it back to him.

"I just washed it last week," she says, "it takes ages to dry." They hold eye contact for the briefest moment.

"Machines are inside." The inspector nods as a few latecomers hurry down the long platform, the speed of the wheels on their cases a gauge of how time is pressing!

"Have we time?" I pant.

Agonisingly slowly, he checks his pocket watch.

"The train departs in six minutes."

We all run inside. One ticket machine is out of order and there is a snaking queue of impatient travellers for the other.

"Look! There is a real person behind that desk," I shout, rushing forwards.

"And a real queue!" Annemarie says as I eye up all the excited-looking people heading home for Christmas.

"Excuse me." Rachel scurries to the top of the queue. "It's Christmas and we are in dire need, do not turn us away, we pray?" She clasps her hands prayer-like under her chin.

The older lady looks sweetly at her, calmly adjusting her scarf.

"D'ya think I came down in the last shower! No chance. I need to make that train too!" Her face says it all, she is not for turning.

"Excuse me." A young guy behind her pulls an ear pod from his ear. "Take my place." He steps out of the queue.

"Are you sure?" I ask, heaving for breath now.

"Sure." He moves to the back of the line, saying, "I have four sisters, I can tell you're not messing around."

"God bless you!" Rachel yells.

We get the tickets and run back. The inspector perforates all our tickets and we hop up onto the first carriage. I hold onto the top of each seat as I make my way through the packed carriages. I can't see her anywhere.

"Oh come on! Where are you?" I despair. Then I see her.

Car C. Row G.

She's sitting with another woman, drinking a can of cider and playing cards. Máiréad's much-loved and treasured ring sparkles on her revolting, thieving finger. She is free of the wimple, is not wearing glasses anymore and her blonde hair is tied up in a messy bun.

"There she is!" I turn to my team.

"Wait. Let me go first." Tom pulls his beanie hat back on, almost down to his eyelids. "I'll be your heavy."

I sidestep him and go behind.

"Hurry! We've exactly three minutes to get off this train! I can't miss the flight to Birmingham. I can't go all the way to the next town it stops at or I won't make it." My nerves are shot.

"Yo." Tom stands in front of whoever she is – not Winifred Emit, that's for sure, how did I fall for such a stupid name? What a mug I am.

"Yo yerself," she says, slapping a card down.

Then I step out from behind and her jaw drops.

"Oh, Hello. Lexie. Hi again. This is . . . Bo – Sister Bog." She grapples for words.

"Sister Bog?" I raise an eyebrow.

"The ring. Now." Tom does look threatening in that beanie as he makes his demands, slamming his hand down on the table and flicking the cards away.

"Sir, this is my rightful heirloom." But her birdlike eyes dart in her round face. She's looking to run but no way she can bypass me, Tom, Annemarie, or Polly and Rachel, who are standing with their arms crossed.

"Hiya, hun." Rachel squeezes her head in between me and Tom now.

Polly, on her tippy-toes, pops her head up over Rachel's. "Ya lyin' cow, the game's well and truly up!"

"How about this?" Rachel holds up her phone. "I thought I was taking a photo but it was on video." She presses play.

"Two minutes!" Annemarie warns.

*"Welcome onboard this Irish Rail direct to Dublin. Passengers not wishing to travel must now disembark . . ."*

"Shit! It's direct! Hurry!" Annemarie roars now.

The video plays captured footage. Rachel is taking a selfie her arm at length.

"Say cheese!" Rachel says in the video.

"Cheeeeeeeese!" they all say then Polly, clearly thinking the picture has been taken says, "You better be messing about robbin' that ring off some poor young one or I swear—"

"One minute!" I call out. "I have to get off. Listen to me, you horrible, evil cow. Turn over the ring, now! Then go repent for your sins and do some good in the world!" I seethe, anger well and truly my main emotion now.

A whistle sounds out on the platform.

I grab her hand and tug the ring down. It won't go over her knuckle.

"Watch me fuckin' finger!" she shouts at me.

"Wash your mouth out, sister," I yell at her as passengers around us start to mutter and look on.

She tries to pull it off, but I lean into her and say: "I'll be posting that video of you – to all the hotel managers in the country. And then I'll be going straight to the Guards! This woman is a thief!" I turn to the whole carriage, pointing at her.

Her face is ashen now as all the passengers stare at her and whisper, some taking their own phones out to film.

"Lexie!" I hear another whistle.

"Hold the doors!" Rachels points and Polly runs down the carriage.

"Here. It was a joke, isn't that right, Aaliyah?" the scammer says to the woman opposite.

"A total piss take." Aaliyah nods eagerly, panic swimming in her eyes.

"We were always gonna post it back and let it be a warning to you not to trust people online."

"Shut up. Give me the ring! Now!" I screech like a demented woman.

She reefs it off. I slide it onto my finger and burst into heartfelt tears as the train jolts and starts to move. It's too late! I'll never make my flight now. I should have listened to Adam, I should be in Rosehill Cottage with my baby and my fiancé.

"Hold tight!" Tom shouts and pulls the emergency cord.

An ear-splitting ringing noise howls around us and all passengers cover their ears as the train shudders and screeches.

"Last thing," Tom shouts back to the thieves. "You make any contact with Lexie in the future and you'll have me on your back. Forever. And no one wants me forever, isn't that right, Annemarie?"

"Go!" I scream and we all run to the exit.

# 19

*"But sir, Christmas is a time for giving . . . a time to be with one's family."*

Bob Cratchit, *A Christmas Carol*

M AM AND BEN ARE WATCHING CARTOONS on Annemarie's huge bed when we pile in.

"Got it!" I raise my hand triumphantly, the ring shimmering on my finger as it catches the light.

"I'll call the Guards," Annemarie says kissing Ben on the head, then lifting her phone from her bag and leaving the room.

"What happened?" Mam gasps as I get straight on the hotel Wi-Fi and log onto the My Hopeful Heritage site. I call the number and tell them what has happened.

"We are so sorry," Evan, the manager of the site tells me. "An email went out to everyone last week but unfortunately some ended in spam. Somehow this Winifred Emit person has been able to hack into people's private messages."

I try to control the anger in my voice. "How could you let this happen?"

"The police are involved," he assures me, his voice filled with sorrow.

"I have a video of her."

He heaves a great sigh of relief down the line. "Oh, you do? That is so helpful. Can you come in to see us? It's urgent, we need to stop her."

"I can't! I'm in Galway and I'm due to fly to the Cotswolds tonight, from Dublin. I have to go . . . now!" I'd almost forgotten my rush with all this going on.

"Darling." Mam leans towards me and clamps her hand carefully over my wrist. "You aren't flying anywhere, I've called reservations from up here and booked us a room for tonight. Call Adam, tell him you will be there tomorrow in time for the wedding. He needs to change both our flights to early morning. He has all the details." Mam's tone is strict.

"Oh he's gonna flip." But the shock of everything has disabled my brain somewhat, and I'm grateful she's taking over. Sometimes you just need your mam.

"No he won't, and if he does, don't stand for it dear. This is more important than his ex-wife's bloody wedding." She locks eyes with me and takes the phone, then hands it to Tom, who talks to Evan and discusses how to send him over the video.

I move outside, take the stairs down in a catatonic state and sit on the window ledge, looking over Galway Bay. Just as I am about to press the call button on Adam's name, I hear Annemarie's voice. I spin around; it's coming from the big conference hall to the left. I don't know who she is talking to, probably still the Guards. My finger hovering over the green button, I cock my ear and I hear one name as clear as day.

Gail.

I drop the phone into my pocket and slide in through the double doors.

"What the—" I immediately recognise the woman standing in front of me. Annemarie crooks a finger at me, and I come closer. The woman is bare legged despite the elements, wearing cowboy boots and a short denim dress, her hair braided, holding a large white folder. Her face looks ashen.

"Seems Galway is the place to be this Christmas." Annemarie's look to me is wry. "Not to mention the immaculate conception!" She dissolves into a chaotic, false laugh.

"I've told her it was nothing to do with me," Gail tries to explain to me, "it was a wind-up by my stupid brothers. They have this popular account and wanted to do a TikTok – I left Dublin after the . . . thing with Tom. I live here, I'm the celebrant here for a wedding in the morning." She's shaking in her cowboy boots but stands firm, clutching what I now realise is her celebrant's folder to her chest.

"Jesus, Gail," is all I blurt. I can't believe my eyes.

"Seems Ireland is a very small place," Annemarie says, scowling before clearing her throat.

"I'm sure you hate my guts, but not half as much as I hate myself. There was never anything between myself and Tom. I didn't fancy him, I felt sorry for him, that's all. But that day we'd had a few early drinks . . . he'd needed a shoulder to cry on . . . again, and I'd broken up with Dave . . . well—" She waves her left hand in the air, "—we got back together, we're engaged now."

"Well, whoop-de-do for you," Annemarie throws back at her, shaking her head.

"You were aways so nice to me . . . It was a moment of madness and when I saw you in the foyer earlier with your son, I grabbed my shit and ran. Then I stopped and turned back because I was a coward not to see you face to face before. I ruined your marriage and Ben's family, and I will never forgive myself." Her hands grip the plastic folder so tightly the corners curl.

"Too bad." Annemarie twirls her curls around her thumb like she does when she's uneasy.

I step in, fold my arms and spew the truth. "Look Gail, it was a really horrible thing to do to sleep with someone's husband. There's no apology that's gonna fix that."

"I know. I'll go now and I don't expect forgiveness, but know this . . ." She swallows painfully, so loud I can hear it across the room. "All Tom ever did was talk about you, his Annemarie and Ben, the lights of his life. He'd talk for hours about how much he loved you, but he didn't feel you loved him back anymore. He felt the marriage was breaking down. I tried to tell him to talk to you, and he said every time he did, you'd push him away. He adored you, Annemarie, cried endless tears in that back office over you. Dreaded going home at night because you were so cold to him."

Annemarie is agog. "Is that a fact?" She steps closer to Gail, and if she were a cartoon, fire would be shooting out from her ears. I stand beside her, shoulder to shoulder. Does Gail think she's actually helping with this speech?

"It is. I just wanted you to know that." A page slips from the folder and flutters to the ground. She bends to retrieve it, shoves it back in, but I can see the tremor in her hand.

"Don't you dare tell me anything about my husband." But suddenly Annemarie has gathered herself, her voice steady as she replies to Gail's bent head, although by her side I can hear her breathing is shallow and coming faster. I put my hand on the small of her back.

"I won't get another chance and I owe it to you both. I'm sorry my brothers took the piss and told Tom I was pregnant. I told my sister what happened and, big mouth that she is, she told them! But Tom blocked my number so when I found out about the TikTok prank they have been painstakingly planning, I couldn't warn him. I didn't dare go to the stockroom."

"Are they going to post that?" I ask her directly.

She nods sadly. "Yeah, it's already up."

"Show me." Annemarie's expression has gone from her earlier coldness to undeniable worry and shock.

"It's . . ." Gail stops, pulls her bejewelled phone from her canvas bag and searches up something at speed. Then she takes the few steps towards us. We huddle round her phone; she presses play on a TikTok video. Two guys in their twenties, one tall, one small, but both dressed in dark trousers and hoodies, stand outside the Rotunda hospital with three pink "It's a Girl" balloons. I clock the time at the bottom of the screen – no more than twenty minutes after Tom left us that night he got the call – as we watch Tom round the corner, running, out of breath.

"Tom, is it?" the taller one asks.

I lean in closer to the screen.

"Yes," he answers. Poor Tom looks awful.

"That one-night stand you had with our sister?" The smaller one rolls his fist into his open palm.

"Yes." Tom swallows, looks up to the balloons and back down.

"Even though you're a married man with a baby son yourself, you PIG," the smaller one adds, and snorts over and over.

The taller one throws his hands out wide. "Well, she just had triplets, mate."

Tom just nods, looking like a shell of a man.

"Now snort like the pig you are, mate."

"What?" Tom leans against a brick wall by the hospital entrance, face scrunched up in confusion.

The smaller one moves in. "Snort, piggy, snort!"

"Where is the camera? Who is filming this?" Annemarie asks, desperation oozing from her voice.

"Oh they hide them, probably on a nearby bin, or sometimes Jimmy, my little cousin, sits on his bike nearby and films." Gail grimaces as red creeps up her cheeks, showing her obvious mortification at her brothers' actions.

We all wait as Tom stands up straight and starts to snort like a pig. It's degrading, horrifying, and tears smart in my eyes.

"Louder, piggy! Louder!" The tall one dances on the spot as Tom snorts louder and louder, almost choking on the action as he goes.

"Enough, piggy!" barks the smaller one. "You wanna know their names?"

"It's the least you can do after knocking her up!" The taller one is the aggressive one now, the bad cop. The cruelty on his mocking face is unbearable.

"Yes," Tom croaks, fighting the tears, leaning helplessly against the wall.

"We are half Greek, so they are Greek names."

Tom nods, wrings his hands together and adjusts his beanie. His face is praying for deliverance from this torture.

"Hohw. Wesaya. Gotchya."

They high-five and then fall about laughing, clutching their stomachs, while the camera stays on Tom's petrified face and his breath coming in gulps before they take to their heels and run.

*Public Humiliation* flashes in neon writing across the screen.

"That's horrendous," I stutter. Six hundred and eighty-eight views in an hour.

Annemarie pushes the phone away with her cobalt nail. "So it will go viral and Tom will be a laughing stock, right? This could ruin the sailing and fishing business he's worked so hard to build?"

Gail nods weakly.

"Well, let me tell you a few things, Gail. Firstly, you don't need to tell me that my husband is a good man, I already know that. Secondly, you know nothing about me or my life, so please don't assume you know anything about me. Now, you do want to clear your conscience, don't you?" Annemarie's brow is furrowed.

"Yes. I'm wracked with guilt, I know you're not going to believe this, but it was so unlike me, so out of character. I'd just been dumped by the love of my life because he didn't want to settle down after six years and I was devastated. I'm not making excuses, I—"

"I'm not interested. Just get your despicable brothers to take down that video now, right away, can you do that?"

"I don't know . . ." Her tone is truthful.

Annemarie points to the door. "Go try."

Gail nods and totters off to the double doors in her cowboy boots, her phone pressed to her ear.

"That was nuts!" I say, sitting on the edge of a trestle table. Annemarie paces the table. "Are you okay?"

"I saw her coming towards me, and for a split second I thought she and Tom were here together to tell me they were in love and he wanted a divorce. It all ran through my head. Our life flashed before my eyes, Lexie. But not the bad times, not the miscarriages, the IVF, the sleep deprivation, the anxiety of motherhood, the tension of unwanted sex, no . . ." She stops circling me and perches beside me on the table with a big sigh. "It was all the fun times: the laughs, the little day-to-day things I've been ignoring, how he brings me tea in bed every morning before he leaves for work, how hard he works for me and Ben, what an amazing father he is, his kindness to strangers, his love of dogs but me refusing to get one because they are so much work. I saw him and her in my mind, walking their dog in the park, and I nearly passed out, I thought I was going to faint." Annemarie rocks and I drape an arm around her.

"We need a stiff drink," I say.

"I'm off drink." She turns to look at me.

"Oh." I bite my lip. *Let her talk, Lexie,* I tell myself.

"Oh yeah, sure you know me, a royal fuck-up wherever I can. Whatever's going I'm sure to fall victim to it." She attempts a smile but it wobbles off her face.

"What do you mean?" I probe softly, anxiously meeting her eye.

"Ahh you know. I'm drinking too much. I want to stop, so I am." She shrugs like it's a small thing, but I know how much it took for her to admit that.

"Good," I say, giving her shoulder a reassuring squeeze. *I'm just here to listen,* I think, *not advise.*

"I've been thinking about it for ages. It's been a way to block out everything, opening a bottle most nights, finishing the bottle some nights, headache all day next day. It's not fair on Ben. You must have seen me in the mornings lately?" She curls her lip.

"I had a . . . feeling."

"I knew you did. Look, it never got out of hand but I can easily see how it could. It's so damn easy to blot out the shit day, or the shit evening, or the chaos in your head. Just lie back on the couch and drink the pain away." She laughs mirthlessly.

"You're finding life hard, it's understandable."

"But you don't drink the pain away, that's the thing! You drink the pain away for a few hours. Then you wake with a worse pain, physically and mentally, and you try to drink that away too. You hear yourself every morning, as you down the painkillers, promising yourself that you will not drink tonight. No way will you buy a bottle on the way home from work. And then seven o' clock comes and you are faced with the night ahead and the problems in your marriage, so you pop out to the shops to buy the wine."

"You're not an alcoholic, Annemarie." I tell her this because I know she's not, it's circumstantial. Before Tom, she was the only one who'd happily drink soda water on nights out. Annemarie was always happy to be the designated driver.

"No, but I'm heading that way. I know that. If I don't stop drinking now, for a few months at least, I'm going to go down a slippery slope, I can feel it." She sighs.

"Well isn't it great you're seeing it and doing something about it?"

"For me, it's just breaking the habit." She clicks her tongue off the roof of her mouth, like that settles things – she's really doing it.

I rest my head on her shoulder. "I'm proud of you."

"I wouldn't go that far! I used the wine as an excuse not to go to bed with Tom. Isn't that mad? As an excuse to avoid my husband."

"Not mad . . . sad, maybe?" I offer instead.

"Very sad. But after I called the Guards earlier, I sent an email to a therapist I've been looking up. I want to try again, Lexie – with Tom, I mean. When I saw him here, in Galway, he looked suddenly different to me. Then when I saw . . ." She pauses.

"Groovy Gail!" I nod to the doors.

"Yer one! Exactly. I was sure Tom wanted to divorce me and something flicked in me. He is a good man. I do love him. It's me I don't love."

"Don't say that." I lift my head and focus my eyes on hers. I'm shocked to see she's dead serious.

"It's true, I've always been my own biggest enemy, but it stops now, it stops this Christmas for once and for all." She pushes herself up, dusting her hands off one another.

"I think you're the best person I've ever known," I say, and I mean it.

"So imagine when I'm even better. When I do this work on myself."

"Oh God, you're gonna journal it all, aren't you?" I put my hands over my eyes.

Laughing, she wipes a hand across her eyes. "I sure am! A new notebook for every issue."

"God help me, all those fuzzy top pens I'm going to be subjected to." I roll my eyes in jest.

"I think this moment here with you is my rock bottom. And I'm more than ready for it – in fact I've been waiting for it for such a long time." She gathers her wild curls up in her hands and then drops them, like a weight falling off her.

"Well I'm glad I was here for it." I knock on wood. So glad she saw sense for herself – I always knew she would.

"You're always here for me, and I love you more than I can ever say."

She gulps as Gail strides back in through the double doors, her cowboy boots smacking off the back of her stick thin, bare legs. I can hear the quickening of her breath as she says, "The TikTok is down!" The charms on her phone jingle jangle when she waves the device up in the air.

"Oh that's great, how?" Annemarie asks, wiping her eyes with her sleeve.

She beams. "Let's just say I had some incriminating evidence of my own to hang over them."

"Thank you," Annemarie says. I slip my arm around her waist; I can only imagine how hard it was to say those two words to the woman who slept with her husband.

I have to know something, though. "What was it? This evidence?"

"They used to play dress-up in my mother's clothes as boys and I have lots of videos of them; they didn't like the idea I was going to put them up on my Insta Stories. Especially not Dean – he's the taller brother – I've a video where he's fully made up, bright red lipstick, blue eyeshadow, dressed only in Mam's nursing bra, knickers and stilettos, and Dad's yellow construction safety hat!"

I burst out laughing. "That really would ruin their street cred," I reply. "Seriously, thank you."

"Of course. And again, I really am so, so sorry Annemarie. I truly hate myself." I can see the slight flare of her nostril as she inhales and takes a step back towards the door; she really means it.

"Well, don't. You're forgiven." Annemarie suddenly holds out her hand. "We all make mistakes, none of us are perfect."

Gail steps in again and shakes Annemarie's hand with obvious relief.

"Are you sure?" Her voice wobbles slightly.

Annemarie claps her shoulder. "Just pay it forward?"

"I will. I promise." She nods intently.

"Then this chapter is closed." Annemarie smiles, looks to me for a brief second, still holding Gail's shoulder, then back to her quick as a flash she says, "And by the way, you look so groovy."

*Touché, Annemarie,* I think.

Touché.

# 20

*"If you look for it, I've got a sneaky feeling you'll find that love actually is all around."*

The Prime Minister, *Love Actually*

"I WON'T MAKE THE FLIGHT TONIGHT." I finally get Adam on the phone and I have to come straight out with it. I miss him and Frances so much I've a pain in my gut.

"Oh . . . Are you alright?" I can hear raised voices and riotous laughter over his concerned voice.

"I'm fine." I've forgiven myself for the massive mistake I made. Life's too short to beat yourself up.

"Okay." He sounds relieved.

"But I'm sorry." I gaze outside the window at the group of young girls all dressed in sparkly Christmas dresses, tottering down the hill, all excited for their night out.

"Don't be. I'm more than aware I've made this call to you dozens of times, Lexie, and the rest. You can't make it, you can't make it. Frances is fine, I am fine. Relax. So what happened with Winifred? Are you still out celebrating?" He chuckles.

I fill him in on what's happened. And he's more than sympathetic: he's enraged.

"How dare she take advantage like that! I'd have lost my mind!" he exclaims furiously.

"I really thought I'd found her." But I start to cry again, tears I didn't expect. God, what a *day* this has been.

"And you will. The main thing is you got the ring back and reported her. I'll re-book your flights now for the morning. I'll help you find her, Lexie, I swear. We will find Kathleen." He's moved to somewhere quieter now, and the calm reassurance and love I hear in his voice is the balm I needed for my sore heart.

"I know." I blow my nose. "I just feel so stupid."

"Well, don't. You are a trusting person, don't let the sickos of the world change you. Do not let that horrible person win. Let the police deal with her now."

I roll the tissue into a ball and heave a deep breath. "I will, you're right. You all set for the rehearsal dinner?"

"We are. We've had a hundred pictures taken on the grand staircase already. Frances was an angel. Everyone's been asking for you. Lemme just bring up flights here." His voice fades as he starts *tip-tapping* away on his phone.

"That's nice. Did you put Frances in the good outfit I bought? The little red dress I told you to?" I ask.

"Hmm . . . yeah, look, the wedding's at midday here in the Crucible Hall, so you will have to get the first flight out. I'm scrolling here, one sec. Is that okay by the way?" It's hard to hear him now.

"Of course." I stand up, go out through the revolving door, throw my tissue in the bin and catch my breath as the Galway sleet flies down and the beautiful, giggling girls strut past me. It's freezing but somehow the bitter wind makes me feel a bit better; it's fresh, like a new start. "I'm going to have dinner with Mam and Annemarie and Ben, somewhere nice on Shop Street and get an early night," I shout over the elements.

"That's a great idea." I have to stick my finger in my ear to hear his reply as he mutters. He's only half listening to me as he searches for flights for us. "Right, there's an Aer Lingus flight at 6.50 a.m. into Birmingham – can you grab a cab? I'll get Frances up and ready for her breakfast. It will save us time. You should be back at the hotel in time for a quick shower and to get ready. I brought your case with me as you know, so no need to go back to the apartment, unless you want to?" I feel taken care of in this moment. He has my back.

"Can you book Mam to Malaga around the same time?" I ask.

"Lemme check here." He's walking again.

I can hear Michael Bublé crooning about it beginning to look a lot like Christmas in the background, hear the glasses clinking, people chattering, having festive fun. I'm struck with another thought as the hail pelts down. As always, it seems his life goes on without me. I wish I could fit in over there. I wish it had been different with his family.

"Yeah, there is a 7.10 to Malaga. I'll change both now and pay the difference." The background rumble is getting louder again, overwhelming his voice.

"Thank you," I shout. "I love you, see you in the morning."

"Okay," he shouts back and the line goes dead.

*

Christmas in Galway seems more traditional somehow. Less commercial. Buskers play instrumental versions of hymns. The shoppers stroll, they don't rush. The window displays are more subtle. It feels more spiritual and meaningful somehow. We follow the winding path down to Eyre Square.

"Oh look, the Christmas markets! I've always wanted to see these." Annemarie pulls up Ben's hood and pushes the buggy towards the square that's lit up like a fairground.

"It's so picturesque. Look at all the little circus tents," Mam says, linking arms with me.

"Stalls, Mam. They're called stalls." I giggle.

We have a gorgeous time just browsing, drinking takeaway hot chocolates and buying some Christmas treats for each other.

"Look that way, Lexie," Mam orders me at least three times while she is obviously buying me the rolled gold link bracelet I admired. After an hour or so we are all starving, so we walk back up Shop Street, which is heaving now with Christmas shoppers spilling out from the markets, and long queues form outside all the restaurants; everyone we approach has a waiting list of hours. We turn a corner and I spot a cosy-looking pub.

"One sec." I dart inside. Live music is gifted to me by means of a young girl with an acoustic guitar; she's singing "Fairytale of New York". I approach the barman.

"Don't suppose you do food? I ask, leaning over the bar. My feet are starting to hurt.

He shakes his head. "Only in the summer season."

"Ahh ok." I push myself upright with the palms of my hands and turn to leave.

"I mean I can do you ham, cheese and onion toasties?" he suggests, topping off a pint of Guinness, three spirit optics shining behind him like guiding lights.

"Oh yes, please!" I clap my hands, and rush back outside to rally the troops.

Half an hour later as we sit over empty plates, full to the brim with the most delicious pub doorstep white bread toasties, pots of steaming hot tea, listening to the most angelic voice singing a medley of Christmas hits, my email pings on my phone.

*Dear Lexie,*

*It's Evan from My Hopeful Heritage here. As we are filtering all messages until we are confident we can go live again, I have a message from a Kathleen Murphy. I have checked it out, and I trust it's the real deal. Please also note that two arrests were made last night in connection with fraud on this site. See below:*

*"I am the biological daughter of Máiréad Farrell. I have proof. I saw the message from Lexie Byrne on your site and showed my dad, and he can confirm Máiréad was his fiancée in 1947. Both my birth date and birthplace are also true. However, I was never given up for adoption: my father's family took me from Galway to London, where they raised me as their own while my dad was overseas. My father was never aware I was his natural born child until I returned to Galway fifteen years ago. He was sent overseas for thirty-two years and was told my mother died in childbirth. We would love to meet with Lexie Byrne."*

"Oh no!" My hand flies over my mouth.

"What is it?" Annemarie asks, pouring us all more tea, tapping her foot to the music.

"It's Kathleen. It's really her."

Mam puts her hand on my knee. "Careful . . ."

I read on:

*Call me Lexie, ASAP! I really think this is her.*
*Best wishes,*
*Evan.*

I press dial on the phone number in his email signature, and he answers after the first ring.

"She wants to meet you. Tonight. I told her you were there in Galway," he says in one breathless rush.

"Where?" I make the sign of the bill to the barman.

"Wherever you want." His voice is full of hope.

"I am in the Galmont Hotel tonight." I swallow, my breath coming in tiny pants.

"Hold on." He tap taps then pauses for what seems like hours, and finally says, "She's on her way."

"We have to go," I tell Mam and Annemarie.

They just take one look at my face and pull on their coats.

"This is on me," Annemarie says, "I can't remember the last time I enjoyed a meal as much." She wraps Ben up and the barman hands her the bill.

"Can he?" He holds up a Santa-shaped chocolate lollipop.

"Oh yes, thank you." She beams and she looks genuinely happy for the first time in so long. That's at least one Christmas miracle sorted.

*

As soon as Kathleen walks through the revolving doors of the Galmont Hotel, I know, one hundred per cent she is Máiréad's daughter. Every nerve in my body implodes. She is small in

211

stature, almost sixty years old, with a mane of auburn hair and a kind face. Mother and daughter are the image of one another. It's uncanny. For a moment, I feel embarrassed all over again that I thought Winifred could be her, but I shove that feeling aside; it has no place here now. Next to Kathleen, an old man walks through the side door with the aid of a wooden cane, and I slowly walk towards them.

"I'm Lexie Byrne," I say nervously.

"Can you show me the ring?" the old man asks straight away. He must be Jim, Kathleen's father. His skin almost see-through and his creased eyes fill with uncontrolled tears that drip down his cheeks.

"Dad." Kathleen puts her arm on his shoulder. "Wait a minute, let's hear what Lexie has to say first." Her voice is unusual, a mix of accents, but her mannerisms are acutely Máiréad's.

"Yes, come on, let's sit," I say and we take up the exact same seat we were on with Polly and Rachel yesterday. This time, the meeting will go well, I just know it. I have a warm feeling.

Jim stumbles through the tears with his story. "The Happy Ring House . . . I proposed to her while waiting for the number three bus, we were going to Sandymount Strand to walk on the beach. I thought we could run away. Elope, like Edward and Mrs Simpson. But for years I thought she ran away on me, my Máiréad. My beautiful Máiréad. She looked like Rita Hayworth, did she tell you that? Buses would stop to look at her. Then they said she died in childbirth." He pants.

"You must be Jim?" I smile, hardly believing my luck. All the stories I've heard about this man, this piece of the past, yet he sits here beside me acutely alive now and in the present. I feel closer to Máiréad than ever.

"At your service." He knocks out a surprisingly sturdy salute.

"Was she feisty?" Kathleen wipes her eyes and smiles at me.

I grin, madly. If only she knew . . . "Very!"

"Headstrong?" Kathleen can't keep the huge smile off her face. "Like me dad, eh?"

"Totally." I laugh.

"Happy?" Jim interjects.

"No. Not always," I reply honestly. "But when she spoke of you both, she was the happiest I'd ever seen her."

"Love is pain." Jim weeps uninhibited while his daughter stoically pats his back.

"You wanted to see the ring, Jim?" I offer.

They both nod, and as soon as I've put it on the table, Jim gasps. "She's with us Kathleen, she's finally a part of us again!" Jim places his old, blue-veined hand over the ring and just holds it there, his breathing shallow and fast. Then he says, "Máiréad, Máiréad, oh my poor Máiréad."

I start to cry but they are happy tears. Kathleen follows suit, and we all sit there crying until Jim finally picks up the ring he bought all those years ago for the woman he loved. He holds up the ring to Kathleen, who takes it from his shaky hand and glides it onto her finger. She can't keep her eyes off it.

"Thank you, Lexie. Dad wanted this so badly, as did I. But I have time, he doesn't."

Jim starts to shake, then cough. His old bones rattle.

"Okay, Dad, let's get you some water." Kathleen gets up and hurries to the bar.

I wait for him to catch his breath.

"Thank you for being so good to her," Jim croaks after a pause. "We were in touch with a Kevin, the manager at Sir Patrick

Dun's. We needed to check you were who you said you were as well as that site. I don't trust that aul internet as far as I'd throw it." Jim just has the kindest face. His eyes expose his soul.

"Well you were way savvier than me Jim." I laugh dryly.

"I loved her," he says. "So much." There is so much pain in his voice that it is tearing at my heart and I have to hold back a fresh wave of tears.

"She was lucky to have you," I say tenderly.

He shakes his head with regret. "I let her down."

"No, you didn't, she never blamed you. She felt for you, and never forgave the nuns for taking Kathleen from you both. Know that she never, ever thought or said a bad word about you. You were the love of her life."

Jim's chin wobbles. "My parents, they were very well-to-do, you know – snobs really. They told me the baby was left in an orphanage, and they wanted to do something good, so they adopted her. I can't believe I fell for such a foolish story, but I was away for so many years, I didn't see Kathleen grow up."

"You'd no reason not to believe it," I say.

"Snobs," he says again, nodding slowly and pulling a folded white tissue from up his sleeve. "But I knew," he adds as Kathleen sits with a glass of water and hands it to him. He takes it with shaking hands. "I knew in my heart she was still alive. My Máiréad."

"I believed him," continues Kathleen, "so I moved back to Galway, trained as a paediatric nurse, but I got no answers. I searched for years for my records. I knocked on every door. No one would tell me anything. No records of my mother or my birth at the mother and baby home. Then an anonymous letter arrived, and inside the envelope there was a tiny faded yellow docket, a receipt if you will, for one hundred pounds with FOR

KATHLEEN on it and my date of birth. That's when I knew it was me and I changed my name back." Kathleen clicks open her bag and carefully takes out the well-worn docket, hands it across to me and I study it.

"Oh no way? What did they call you?" I have to ask, handing it back to her.

"Victoria-Anne." Kathleen smirks.

"When she told me I was her dad, not some adopted brother who was away her whole life, in the navy, I couldn't believe it. We couldn't—" Jim tries but can't finish his sentence.

"What did your parents say?" I butt in, I can't help myself. How could these people have done this?

"They had long since passed without ever uttering a word about buying her, can you believe that?" Jim slumps back into the chair.

I cannot bear this poor man beating himself up about this, so to make him feel better I say, "No but they were different times. I suppose in their own terrible, warped way they must have thought they were doing the right thing by you."

Jim coughs again, a deep rattling sound. Kathleen immediately leaps up to help him.

"We have to go, Lexie. Talk about stealing, Evan told us that whole horrid affair last night but I've literally stolen dad from his hospital bed. I work in the same hospital." She makes a face and laughs. Her laugh is exactly like Máiréad's and my stomach flips over.

"You laugh just like your Mam," I tell her as I rise and help him up towards the doors.

"You've made me the happiest man in the world. I will rest easy now." Jim shakes my hand. His paper-thin skin is cold beneath the raised veins on his hands.

"Here's my number." Kathleen hands me a small card. "My daughter, Siobhán, is getting married in the spring and I'd love you to come?" She raises her hand to the taxi that's just pulled up and Christmas revellers spill out, clouded in vape smoke as they dance toward the doors.

"Máiréad's granddaughter's wedding! Wild horses couldn't keep me away!" I beam, pocketing the card in my back pocket.

I wave them goodbye as they get into the taxi. At last, my heart feels full. Two Christmas miracles in the bag!

"I did it, Máiréad." I look up to the Galway night sky and feel at peace now. I gaze at the same stars that Máiréad looked at when she gave birth all alone to her precious daughter here in Galway, almost sixty years ago.

Now for miracle number three: time to sort out my own life.

# PART 3

# 21

*"That's the one good thing about regret:*
*It's never too late. You can always change tomorrow if you want to."*

Claire Phillips, *Scrooged*

SNOW FALLS LIKE CONFETTI. That lovely light feathery snow scatters as I cross the pedestrian walkway to stand in line for a taxi at Birmingham airport.

"Hope they don't cancel the cab service with this weather." A girl comes behind me dragging her bulging wheelie, cream-coloured, furry earmuffs clamped on her head.

"Oh don't say that . . ." I can't even engage with her, I'm so terrified I might not make this wedding. I miss Frances so much my stomach hurts.

"Next." She nudges me as a black cab pulls up and I pile myself into the back seat.

The driver turns round, hugging the seat, and tuts. "Lost yer luggage, did they? Never stop losing luggage in there."

"Oh no, it went on ahead of me, my partner brought it with him . . . I am in a bit of a dash to make a wedding, though." I belt up and hope he gets the hint.

"Oh I love me a good wedding chase, I do! Where to?" He adjusts his mirror and revs the engine.

"The Moritz Hotel, Great Tew?" I read the rest of the address from Google Maps and he inputs it into his phone mounted on his dash.

"You're not the bride, are you?" he jokes.

"No." I laugh, looking down at my engagement ring on my left hand and thinking about my mother's wise words as we parted at the airport this morning. I'd left her at departures with a coffee and a croissant as I was dashing to my gate.

"Before you go." She'd stirred her coffee slowly and looked up at me. "Be there for others, Lexie . . . but never leave yourself behind." Her eyes told me she meant every word.

The car rears forward. "I'll have you there in no time. The roads are clear despite the worsening weather," the driver assures me.

Mam's words are so wise, I acknowledge as I sit back and try to relax. I have been putting everyone else before myself. I concentrate on regulating my breathing; in for three, out for six. When we've been driving a while, I press my nose to the car window; we whizz by green fields that are slowly disappearing under a blanket of untouched white snow. Slow-pacing Gloucestershire cows, clusters of fluffy sheep and ribbons of drystone walls all merge into one as we speed by. It's Christmas postcard stuff.

"Oh dear." The driver tuts again.

"What?" I strain to look out between the Perspex glass separating me from him.

He points through the windscreen. "Straight ahead."

A tractor, belching thick black smoke, is blocking the road with an old man trying to wave traffic by the tiny gap.

"I'm not sure I'll get this taxi past this, love." He sighs, leaning dejectedly on the steering wheel as the cab slows to a crawl.

"Oh don't say that!" I clutch the seatbelt as the farmer waves us next, and inch by painful inch we edge forwards, until the driver has to admit we can't get past. The black smoke continues to sinew up into the cold air.

"Reverse," the farmer yells.

"I can't!" the taxi man yells back through the half open window.

"Oh please try!" I beg him.

And he does. He puts it into reverse, then first, inches a little bit, reverse and first, reverse and first. It's no use, we can't get past. He gets out and talks to the farmer. They walk around the tractor, crouch down and have a look before he hops back in.

"Okay I think we've found a way." He screeches the black cab into reverse again and this time inches it to the right, then to the left, then back to the right, then back to the left, then we bounce right up, onto a mud pile, sway on the side, until HALLELLUJAH! We bypass the tractor.

"Yes!" I yell, hanging onto the high hand rail.

The driver winds down his window the rest of the way and gives a thumbs up to the farmer as my phone rings.

"Hi!" I answer breathlessly.

"Hey. Nearly here?" Adam asks.

"Oh Adam, I'm a bit behind . . ."

"Don't worry, relax, Freya has taken Frances to her room to change her for me—"

"It's the velvet red dress and black shoes, right? I spent half my week's wages on that outfit for her in Tiny Hands on level one." I want to get as many pictures as I can of Frances in that outfit because at the rate she's growing it will be in a charity bag next week!

"Eh, yeah, we got it."

"And a little red hairband is in my case, the zip part."

"I'll tell Freya that too, and I'm just in the reception room having a swift one with Dom . . ."

"Oh, how is he holding up?" I force interest; I'm going to try and be a part of this day as best as I can.

Adam laughs. "He's the furthest thing from a nervous wreck."

The tension begins to melt from my shoulders. "Okay, I should be there in . . ." I lean forward to speak through the Perspex divider. "How long are we now?"

"Fifteen, it's saying," the driver tells me, tapping the map on his phone.

". . . fifteen minutes, I'll meet you in the lobby?"

"Perfect, I love you."

"Love you too." I exhale deeply.

*Come on, Lexie,* I give myself the pep talk, *be grown up and graceful, it's one day and one night – you owe him that much. Remember what your mother also told you, "love is hard to find, harder to keep," so work with it.* As if on cue my phone beeps and it's Annemarie.

"I just left that therapist's Zoom room . . . She got a cancellation!" Her voice is filled with happiness.

"And?" I'm shocked at how different she sounds now.

"Very interesting, can you talk?" Her voice is positively buzzing.

"Very quickly – we're not far from the Moritz and the wedding's in half an hour," I say, feeling a touch guilty for rushing her now when she needs me.

"Ready for this? She thinks I might be *asexual*?" Her tone of relief is crystal clear through the phone.

"What?" I ask, hold the phone tighter.

"Asexuality. It's a real thing, Lexie. I spilled all my truths to her. You know, I was never sex mad, ever, before Tom. It all makes so much sense to me now. I thought I was losing the plot – why didn't I want to rip his clothes off? But I'm not so unusual after all! There are plenty of women and men like me. She made so much sense. It's like someone lifted an elephant off my shoulders!"

"Okay." I take it in – this is not at all what I expected. "That is mad, go on? Tell me more?" We round a familiar road and the snow beats off the windscreen now, the wipers swishing overtime to keep up, but even if I have to walk from here, I'll make the wedding.

"It's the lack of sexual attraction to others, or low, even absent interest or desire for sexual activity. That's me, Lexie! I don't and have never really desired sex! I mean don't get me wrong, I have enjoyed sex, but I don't really think about it that much. Plus, I've been comparing my sex life to yours and that apparently is so wrong." She seems happy. I'm still a little stunned and mute as I search for the right words.

"So what happens now? With Tom I mean? How does this work?" I ask.

"Where do I start! He joined the Zoom along with me – it was couple's therapy, really – I just blurted my truth to the both of them as soon as we were all on the screen. You'd want to have seen his face, Lexie. It was like he finally understood what was happening to us. The therapist was inspiring, honestly, she was saying no relationship should be based solely on sex anyway."

"Of course not," I agree wholeheartedly as we rock along the bumpy Cotswolds roads.

"If we want it to work, and we both do, communication is key. There are a million ways to be intimate, she told us. Tom needs to decide if a sporadic sex life is a deal breaker for him. There are lots of sessions to go, but at least I feel normal now after wondering for years what was wrong with me. Jo – that's the therapist – said she's been inundated with women since Paris Hilton revealed she's asexual in her memoir. Are you still there?"

"Yes! I'm listening. I'm just . . . taking it all in."

"Do not tell Jackie, this is private," she warns me.

"Of course not!" I say. "Circle of trust, always." I'm feeling positive for her and Tom for the first time in a while. If I've learned one thing these last few days, it's that Tom adores Anne-marie and he will do anything that makes her happy. They will figure this all out – together.

"Oh and there's something else she told us. A lot of women who aren't very sexual are only turned on by their brain not their body! It's utterly fascinating, and it makes sense to me!" Her words are tumbling over each other.

"How does that work?" I ask, utterly intrigued. That's not how it works for me, but I'm glad she's learning what makes her tick.

"Okay, quickly, for example if Tom is annoying me at all, I physically can't have sex, my brain won't go there. However, if Tom has done something really nice for me or for someone else – or he's just, I dunno, shown compassion, intelligence . . . that turns me on."

"There she is, the Moritz Hotel. Can you make it out through this blizzard?" the taxi man announces as the engine rumbles to a crawl.

"I'm so sorry, but I gotta go, I'm here," I tell her. I cannot wait to be home and catch up with her – this revelation is huge for her and I'm actually really hopeful this will help her marriage massively.

"Go! Call me later. Tom, myself and Ben are watching *The Muppet Christmas Carol* and ordering Thai food. Send pics? Drink wine! Please yourself!" Her voice disappears as I cut the call, throw my phone back in my leather bag.

"Well I wasn't expecting that . . ." I muse, shaking my head.

As the glittering Moritz Hotel comes into view, I'm immediately triggered, the truck driver hops out once again and anxiety takes over.

It's hard to explain, but arriving back at a place that doesn't hold many good memories (apart from Ben's birth) sets me on edge. This is the Coopers' place. They celebrate every event here: marriages, christenings, birthdays. The snow is coming down heavy now as the taxi man circles for a parking spot near the door. I pull out my makeup compact and fix my face. I just need to slip into the black dress and the tan heels, brush my hair out and all should be fine. I pay the driver and give him a good tip.

"Happy Christmas, may the new year be good to you, me darlin'." With a loud rev, his car skids away through the falling snow.

\*

The luxury hotel smells of Christmas and yes, Christmas does have a smell. An open fire, gingerbread, roasted chestnuts, cinnamon, cloves, wet clothes, damp air – I breathe it all in. I spot Adam immediately, laughing at the end of the grand staircase, and he takes my breath away. I pause by the reception to look at him for just a second. Dressed in a sharp black suit with a black dicky bow and white dress shirt, he looks utterly dashing. I just want to be with him so I can stop craving him.

"Oh, come on," I whisper to myself, then tentatively I walk over. "Hi there!" I do a little fluttery finger wave.

"Ah, there she is!" Adam's face positively lights up. His eyes crinkle at the sides as he takes me in his arms and kisses me. "I've missed you. Frances is literally pining for you." His reaction to seeing me tells me all I need to know. It's not like I don't know he adores me, I do!

"Oh, I can't wait to see her." I kiss him back and hug him tightly.

"Rough trip?" he asks, and immediately I pat my hair down. Those compact mirrors only tell half the story.

"Long story," I say, sighing, "lots to tell you."

"Dom, you remember Lexie, my fiancée." Adam takes a step to the right.

Dom turns to me. He's heavy set, an ex-semi-professional rugby player, with a thick neck and a ginger beard but warm eyes.

"Course I do. Wasn't I the one who brought you and Adam together!" He raises his pint of Guinness in the air.

"Um, no!" But I laugh. Dom was in Dublin with Adam on that St Patrick's night three years ago, but he never introduced us – as I remember he barely spoke to me that night, or the night of Deb's engagement here in the Moritz, and he was away with the rugby club coaching the Under 16s at camp when I was here in early summer. Dominic is a perfectly nice guy but more of a . . . how do I put this, "a man's man". Means no harm.

I check myself and smile brightly. "Congratulations."

"Thanking you, sweetheart!" He bows. "I can't get this man down the aisle again! Once bitten and twice shy, isn't that it?" He waves his pint and guffaws. "I'm hoping this is the last wedding I

226

have to go to for a while!" He laughs even louder, slapping Adam on the back as Adam's phone rings.

He smiles ruefully at me and reaches into his inside jacket pocket for it. "It's your Mrs to be," he tells Dominic, then holds my eye. "Martha needs me for something urgent, more wedding kerfuffle." He rolls his eyes.

"Erm." I raise my finger as he's about to take the staircase, his shiny shoes glinting in the light of the massive crystal chandelier that hangs above us. "What room are we in? I have to go see our daughter. And get ready." I pull at my damp, thick winter coat; I'm desperate to get out of this thing.

"It's 245, second floor. I'll be there in a few." And he takes the stairs two at a time.

"See you in a bit," I say to Dominic as I head towards the lift.

I take the lift to the second floor, and as the gold door slides across I see the room number right in front of me. I knock. Music plays inside.

"Lexie! Hi!" Freya opens the door, standing there in a stunning pink trouser suit with a waistcoat underneath, looking more eighteen than sixteen as she embraces me warmly.

"How are you? You look beautiful! How is my baby?" I almost run to the window where Frances is propped up in her buggy. I stop. Stare at her. She's in a lace black dress, black tights and pumps.

"What is . . . she wearing?" I groan and turn back to Freya.

"Erm, isn't that what you wanted her in?" Freya enquires.

"No. Who bought this outfit for her?" I feel the expensive material between my fingers.

"Erm, either Auntie Deb or my Mum, I'm not sure; she was dressed when I got up to the room. Dad said I was to dress her but they were rooting for a hairband in your case when I arrived. I was desperately waiting for the postman but he never came." She grumbles, oblivious to my thunderous expression.

I try to keep a measured tone in front of Freya. "Oh – that's – very kind of them, there was no need, I'd packed her stuff . . . did the letter come?" I gasp, hopeful.

"No." She grits her perfectly aligned teeth. "Yeah, Dad told me about the stuff you packed Lexie, do you want to change her?" Freya picks up her straightening iron and clamps her hair, steam rising from her long tresses.

*Don't make a fuss, Lexie,* I tell myself as I unclick the straps and swoop Frances into my arms. I inhale her like my life depends on it.

"No, it's fine, honestly." I wave the idea away. "Did you miss Mammy? Did you? Mammy missed you, soooo much!" I raise her over my head. Her little legs kick in the sheer black tights and she reaches to grab hold of my hair.

"We were just doing some sister bonding, she's so adorable." She squirts some product in her hair.

That's when I spot the full flute of champagne on the dressing table in front of Freya. I don't say a word but I'm less than impressed, and I've only been here ten minutes.

"She is." I kiss Frances all over. "Has she eaten?"

"Yes, I gave her some yogurt and rice cakes for breakfast and Mum gave her some blended green beans and tofu."

My antenna rises.

"Did she vomit?" I only half joke.

Freya laughs as she concentrates on the next section of her caramel hair.

"There is a baby bowl ordered for her for after the vows." She picks up the champagne and tilts it carefully at me. "Do you want this?"

228

"No, thank you. How did you like your first sip last night?" I grin at her. I shouldn't judge, it's not my place.

"I didn't." She runs the iron down her hair, making it poker straight. "I didn't want to. Someone has to be the first to break some of the very strange Cooper traditions. You can thank me later, Frances."

"Well, it's not my business, but I'm so happy to hear that. Eighteen is time enough to start drinking, believe me."

"That's exactly what Dad said to everyone at the table last night." *Well now, Adam,* I think, *you did think I was right after all. Good for you for telling them so.*

"Still, Mum brought that glass up earlier in case I changed my mind." But she laughs.

I won't comment on Martha's parenting, so I quickly change the subject.

"Thank you so much for watching Frances by the way." I try to release my hair from her vice-like grip.

"My pleasure. Now, hadn't you better get ready?" she asks me, taking in my get-up.

I check my watch. "Yes! Can you watch her just until I freshen up and slip into my dress, please?" I wish I could just stay in the room with Freya and Frances and order room service, but alas I have the wedding from hell to attend.

"Of course." She waves me towards the bathroom.

"I can't wait to catch up later, I want to hear all about the riding and more about this course building course. Still no sign of the letter yet, so frustrating?" I grimace.

"I know." Her gaze drops. "It's not looking good. I took my final practicals last week. I know the letters went out as I've seen a few people on Snapchat saying they got theirs. We were supposed to get the official letter this week." Her face looks worried.

"Don't worry, Christmas post is notoriously slow, not to mention the havoc the weather can play. You're amazing, I bet you will get a place on the course." But I'm doubtful now too. Of course I'd be sad for her as I know she wants this, but selfishly I was hoping this would help Adam and me.

"My friend Abbey got her letter yesterday and she lives in Great Tew, she got in." I can tell she's trying to keep her expression neutral, but she's chewing anxiously on her lower lip as she continues to straighten her hair.

"Keep the faith," I say, "what's for you won't go past you." I hold my arms open, and she steps in for a strong cuddle. Then I grab the dress that Adam has kindly hung up. In the large bathroom, I breathe slowly as I undress, throw on the shower cap provided by the hotel then jump under the hot jets for five minutes. As I turn off the shower, I hear the room phone ring and Frances cry. Hurriedly, I step into the new heels and dress. With all the panic and running around the last few days it's a little loose when I zip it up. A quick spritz of body spray, a dab of powder, a red lip and I emerge as Freya hangs up the phone.

"Oh, wow! Look at you! That dress is stunning, Lexie."

"Thanks. Last-minute purchase, you know me, not one for fancy outfits. Was that Adam?" I'm still adjusting the dress.

"No, that was Auntie Deb looking for Dad."

"I'll call him," I say, take my phone out of my bag and press redial, but there's no answer.

Freya unplugs her hot iron and swoops her long, straight hair back. "I better go down. I have to greet the guests as they emerge from the Chill Out Bar into the reception room. Half of them are already sloshed: the Great Tew rugby oldies love their pints of ale." She looks at me. "Would you like me to wait for you? Walk down together? Where the heck has Dad got to?"

"No, don't worry, love, he'll be up to get us in a sec," I tell her, shooing her on with my hand.

"Drink that Moët if you like. That first taste last night they all made me have is still on my tongue." She makes a bitter face.

"You make your own decisions." I have to be careful but I am insanely proud of her.

She makes another face. "Or this suit." She scoffs at the floppy cuffs.

"Well, you could wear a black sack, Freya Cooper, and you'd still be a knockout."

"I was here last night too, I was so busy pacing up and down the village main street looking for Lar – that's the postman – I forgot to go in and get myself a change of clothes for tonight. I asked Mum to bring me some for later but I know she won't. She picked this. She'll want me in it in all the hundreds of photos they will take."

A knock at the door.

"Ah there's Dad. I'll see you after the vows, Lexie." She steps into her shoes.

"Can't wait. Be sure to go get your phone – I want to see loads of your pictures on Mr Jangle, all those red rosettes." I pull her into me and hug her tightly again. "I'll be relying on you to sit with me." I wink. She knows only too well the difficulties I've had with her mum. And she's also well aware that Martha has tried to sabotage myself and Adam for three years now. Freya is an astute girl.

"I thought you'd left me—" I pull open the door but it's Deb, Adam's younger sister, and maid of honour today, standing there in a full-length, ruby-red halter neck dress, her hair piled up in an old-fashioned chignon, bare eyes and her trademark matte red lip.

"Lexie? You made it." She makes a smile, then pensively runs her finger under her lip. "Great." Her fake smile grows even bigger.

We don't embrace. Deb has never been warm to me: as she's Martha's best friend, we didn't get off on the right foot.

"We have to take Adam off you again I'm afraid, you must be sick of this big family." She tries to peer around me.

"Not at all," I say with a polite smile. "You look fantastic, love the dress."

She looks me up and down, does not return the compliment, then crooks her head even further around me. "Ads!" she calls. "Come out! She needs you urgently." She's only short of stamping her foot.

"He's not in here," I tell her, feeling self-conscious once again as I shift the cleavage on my dress.

"He is. I can hear someone . . ." she says quickly.

"Hi Aunt Deb. I know, I know, I'm on my way." Freya pushes past us, smelling of grapefruit body spray.

"Go, darling! Rally the troops." Deb clicks her fingers three times.

I step back from Deb. "See? Adam's not here."

Frances starts to cry again now. I can feel my stress levels creeping up and Deb is really not helping right now.

"Shit," she says, pressing her lips together.

"What?"

"We're running late if we don't get Adam up there now . . . I mean, he's the head usher and they all need ushering."

*How ever will folk find their seats without being ushered?* I wonder, but bite my tongue. Frances is fussing increasingly loudly now. "Just a sec." I go and grab Frances, perch her on my hip and return to the door.

"Hello, my little niece, what a dote." Deb actually displays a genuine smile for once. "Well, if he comes back in the next five minutes, send him down immediately or he's in big trouble." She wags a finger and the smile dissolves.

"Sure," I say, gratefully closing the door on her.

I gently release my hair from Frances's hand and put her back in the buggy. She rubs her eyes, tired and cranky. *Same, baby girl,* I think as I gather up my bag.

"Okay, just this once. I bet I only have to look in one of your daddy's pockets and I'll find the pacifier." I give in and root through Adam's jeans pockets in the wardrobe.

"Voila!" I hold up the little green rubber silencer, and a piece of paper falls to the ground. I pick it up. It's folded in half, and I can smell the perfume off it.

*Her* perfume.

# 22

*"Strange, isn't it? Each man's life touches so many other lives.*
*When he isn't around he leaves an awful hole, doesn't he?"*

Clarence, *It's a Wonderful Life*

"DON'T READ IT," I TELL MYSELF. "Put it back." But I don't put it back; instead I put it on the bedside table beside Adam's book, ease the pacifier into Frances's mouth, cover her with her favourite blanket and hastily leave the room with her.

Downstairs there's a big kerfuffle. Hushed whispers and small groups are gathered. Freya stands on the top step of the staircase holding a wicker basket, like Little Pink Riding Hood.

"What's going on?" I call up to her.

She shrugs. "No sign of Mum. No one will tell me anything – it appears that there is some—"

"Sorry all!" Adam emerges from the lift looking more than a little flustered. His usually calm demeanour is nowhere to be seen. "Everything's fine now! Just a bit behind, that's all. The bride is on her way! Now, everybody please, eyes on the staircase."

He walks straight past me and Frances, and begins to usher the people over to the bottom of the staircase like some kind of demented shepherd. I push the buggy over. Already the heels are starting to cut into the back of my ankles. I'll be keeping plasters in my bag for a month after this and no doubt have blood-stained shoes within the hour.

"All okay?" I whisper in his ear. He seems almost shocked to see me, though smells utterly divine, as usual.

"Lexie!" he yelps.

"Yup. All the way from Ireland. Remember me?" I only half take the piss.

"Oh sorry love, I had a bit of a – she was – it was – I had – oh no, is she asleep? Can you wake her? They need her awake for the wedding pictures!" His words tumble out, his eyes are on stalks.

"Relax." I put my hand on his shoulder and he drops it like I just put a hot stone there.

"I am," he pants.

I take a step back. "Okayyyy."

"Wake her," he orders.

I take a moment, blinking at him. His tone surprises me. "No, Adam. She's shattered, she'll cry through the vows and I'll have to take her outside." I stand firm, staring at him in shock.

"Ffffuck." He runs his hands through his hair, which now appears to be gelled flat.

"It's not that big a deal," I defend, astonished and irritated at his franticness now. He's so distracted, I've never seen him like this. "Who dressed her?" I can't help myself; it feels like something's going on here.

He looks around, his head bopping like a hungry ferret. "Huh? Oh, Martha did, I think, or maybe Deb, dunno."

"I bought clothes for her, they were expensive, I took the time to—"

235

"She looks beautiful, Lexie," he cuts across me. He pulls up his jacket sleeve, checks his watch.

Adam's parents appear behind us. "There he is, our handsome son. Where do you want us, darling?"

"Hi, Mum. You and Dad are to the left inside, front row, beside Marie and Robert." He kisses them both distractedly.

"Hello there." I push the buggy forward, plastering a pleasant smile on my face despite this tension.

"Lexie! Hello there, darling. How wonderful that you made it with this snow." Heather, Adam's mother, looks beautiful in a cream two-piece with a pink hat, and pink flower pinned on. She bends over the buggy. "Oh, she's sleeping." She fixes the blanket and lowers her voice. "We had such a great day with our newest grand-daughter yesterday, didn't we, Jeffrey?" She turns to her husband.

"The best. Hello, Lexie, dear. Don't you look fabulous." Jeffrey leans across and shakes my hand, looking dapper in his grey three-piece suit.

"Indeed you do and it's so lovely to see you, dear. How was your fli—"

"Adam says you'll be moving over to us after Christmas – and about time too," Jeffrey interrupts, gently prodding me.

"Hopefully, Dad, I said hopefully." Adam's face flushes and he looks everywhere but at me.

"I'm sure Lexie has a lot to consider, Jeffrey, dear," his mum says, always the one to smooth things over. "It's a very big move for her. See you after, Lexie, we better take our seats. If I know Martha's parents, they will have been seated for the last hour, we can't be seen to be the ones holding things up, you know how anxious Marie gets. I feel a bit of a headache coming on, Jeffrey, I might not be able to stay out too long. Oh! I think I see the blushing bride." Her eyes drift to the top of the stairs.

And there she is.

Martha. With Deb behind her, holding a long, lace train.

"Everyone in!" Adam waves his hands frantically. "Freya, darling, go."

A lone violinist plays the opening of "Here Comes the Bride". Freya walks down the stairs, scattering white petals on the strip of red carpet Martha's had laid.

"Where am I sitting?" I hiss at Adam.

"Shuuuussshhhh." He puts his finger over his lip, gazes up at Martha. I feel anger erupt in my stomach. I do not like to be shushed, but especially in this moment!

"I am whispering," I whisper.

"We are in the second row, on the right." His head jerks to indicate the right spot.

"And the buggy?" I push Frances forward, under his nose.

His face is beaming as Freya and Martha walk towards us all. "Don't they look beautiful?" he says, grinning madly.

"Just stunning, make you wonder why you ever divorced her." He turns to me, eyes wide.

"Oh, no . . . I don't mean . . ."

*Oh God, why did you say that?* I scream internally.

He seems to shake himself awake. ". . . Sorry, yes, the buggy, I made sure we had space along the wall, just don't put it too far up, I need to be mindful of the fire door. Is that okay?" He looks worried again.

"That's fine," I say as Freya passes us now and Adam dashes in front of me, waving people inside. I follow and gasp as I enter the reception room. It's stunning. The four-piece string orchestra starts now and takes over for the violinist on the processional song. People scurry into their seats, silver chairs with huge white bows on the back. Frances starts to stir, so I softly rock the buggy and take my seat at the end of the row. Freya walks slowly up the makeshift aisle now, holding the most magnificent bunch of snowdrops. Adam slips in beside me as Freya passes.

"Sorry, are you okay? It's been mad. You have no idea what Martha was saying to me, what I've had to listen to up in her room, I'll tell you later. She almost didn't—" he hisses as heads turn and people ooh and ahh.

"Shhhuusshh!" I childishly put my finger over my lip but he laughs at me, and nods in recognition of what he just did to me. He squeezes my knee.

I look over my shoulder. I have to admit, Martha is striking. A beautiful woman with the body of someone who works hard at it, every day. The dress is sculpted to her body, like a second skin, and her winter sun holiday has tanned her skin golden. Her dress is a white satin, backless, scoop-neck number, the skirt boasting hundreds of minute pearly buttons that look like they need surgeons' hands to close.

She reaches the top of the ballroom. I see her suddenly shake her head. Deb rubs her back. Then she shakes her head again. The glistening tiara wobbles. Dominic looks at her. His smile widens ridiculously in front of my very eyes as she leans forward to the celebrant and the celebrant slowly hands her the microphone.

"Hello, everyone." The mic crackles.

Adam shifts in his seat, and her eyes flick to him.

Dominic touches Martha's shoulder. "You look amazeballs, babe!" he shouts into the mic over her shoulder. People laugh.

Martha smiles at him, then takes a step forward as the laugher settles.

"As unconventional as this might be, I'd like to take a moment. Before we exchange our vows, I just want to welcome you all here today." She beams around at the small congregation of maybe thirty people.

"What is she doing?" Adam's hands are shaking, I notice now.

"This is a very special moment for me to have all my family and closest friends in this room. We are all a family – the Coopers, the Woodcocks, this community; I couldn't live without you all. Dominic and myself have been friends for years, introduced of course by my ex-husband and best friend in the entire world, Adam Cooper . . . Where is he? Stand up, Adam."

"Oh my good God." I gasp as Adam slowly places his two palms on the edge of the chair and pushes himself up to standing.

He flicks his hands down the crease of his trousers.

"I love you, Adam, so much . . ." Martha can't take her eyes off him.

And it hits me. She wants him to declare his undying love for her, right now, in front of the entire village. The woman is utterly delusional.

"I wish . . ." Adam coughs into his cupped hand, his cheeks are dotted red and beads of sweat form on his forehead. "I wish you both every happiness in the world."

I can't even look across at him, it's all beyond bizarre.

The mic visibly shakes in her hand. I can sense the celebrant doesn't know where to look. I dare not catch Freya's eye.

Dominic just grins and wobbles slightly; from all the early pints, no doubt. "You're the best, man . . . ha! The best man . . ."

Martha steps forward again. "I couldn't stand here today and not say thank you for always being there for me, Adam. You are my rock, my voice of reason, part of my heart . . ." She clutches her heart with her free hand, still looking directly at him and I can't help it, it just happens – I burst out laughing.

239

"Lexie! No! D-don't!" Adam hisses at me through gritted teeth. But now I release a snort.

You know one of those laughs that starts in your nose, rushes down your nostrils and then you explode? It's that. I cannot control it. The church seems to stiffen, I can feel it. Adam looks at me, utter horror on his face. Is he *actually* serious right now? I pinch my nose with my finger and thumb; everyone is staring at me. Tears stream down my face.

"Something funny, Lexie?" Martha asks me from the altar, her voice tight all of a sudden.

"Kind of." I sniff, take my hand from my nose and sit up straight.

"Do you want to share it with us all?" she asks, her pursed mouth a thin line now.

"Probably not the right time, as I think you're about to get married to Dominic, right?" I try to compose myself.

Adam plonks down and whispers in my ear. "Lexie, what the hell are you doing?"

"It's okay, Adam," Martha says now in some sort of baby voice, "don't worry, darling."

My heart races and I think I'm going to throw up.

"I love you," she directs at him, and pauses, standing scarily still. Seconds pass; you can hear a pin drop. I sit rigid. It feels like hours but it is really only a matter of seconds before she turns to Dominic, the microphone still near her mouth. "Let's get married then, shall we?" she spits.

# 23

*"Faith is believing in things when common sense tells you not to."*
Fred Gailey, *Miracle on 34ᵗʰ Street*

THE BEDROOM IS DARKER THAN DARK in the way only hotel rooms can be, with those solid, heavy drapes pulled across. I turn, drag the buggy in backwards and slide the card into the socket. Lights blare.

"Jesus." I release the word in a fast breath. I'm not angry anymore, I'm humiliated and disillusioned, and just want to get out of here! How I got through that reception, I will never know.

Martha actually sat me at the children's table with Frances, with Adam at the top table next to her. His speech made me cringe as he bigged up Martha and I stuck to water just in case. He told us all what a unique woman she was and how lucky he and Freya were to have her in their lives. He gushed over her finest qualities, none of which I've ever witnessed, and told Dominic, on the other side of Martha, that he was the luckiest man in the room. I felt utterly queasy. Quickly I push the buggy back out into the dim hallway, wedge the door open with the heel of my blood-stained tan shoe and run back in to turn on a soft, bedside lamp and switch off the big light.

"What was that about?" Adam asked me after the vows, side-eyeing me while everyone took their seats at the various tables.

Frances was still sleeping as I pushed her around, the dress digging in under my armpits, as I searched for my place name. "Where am I sitting?" I ignored his question, thinking it was better not to tell him what I *really* thought.

"Family photos on the staircase, please!" Deb was using her hands on either side of her mouth.

"What possessed you to laugh like that in the middle of Martha's speech? I mean I know it was . . . weird, but that wasn't the time." He wiped his forehead with the back of his hand. "Everyone is asking me about it."

"Oh, I'm so sorry. Got a fit of the giggles, it happens to me." I gritted my teeth and moved over to the next table, scouring for my name.

"It's okay, I – I get it, I really do – it was just . . . unexpected. You wanna hear what she was saying to me before the wedding ceremony?" He held my elbow and turned me to him.

"In a word. No." I'd reefed my elbow free and stopped at the next table. A low table with a plastic Santa Claus wipeable table covering and four small chairs – not even a high chair for Frances – and that's when I saw my name, spelled incorrectly.

"Adam! Over here!" Martha sashayed towards us again.

Deb then appeared at my side. "Can we borrow your beautiful daughter, Lexie." It wasn't phrased like a question.

"Sure." I bent down, woke my sleeping baby and gently lifted her out. Her warm body curled up, and she immediately started to bawl.

"Hang on, Martha," Adam called back, his voice more impatient now as I kissed her gently and slid the tuft of wet hair off her face.

"Sorry, Frances," I whispered in her little hot ear, "it won't take long, baby."

"Come to Daddy!" Adam held out his hands, and Frances roared louder as I handed her over, then sat back down on the too-low chair. Adam just looked down at me. "Aren't you coming?"

"No. No, I'm not getting into Martha's wedding photo album. I'll just wait here." I poured a glass of blackcurrant juice from the large jug into a Rudolf paper cup, raised it and knocked it back.

"You're almost . . . well . . . ya know, kinda family too, Lexie," Deb said in a forced tone behind him.

I just stared at her.

"Let's go." Adam turned his back and walked away from me, Frances kicking up an absolute storm. My mother's words were ringing in my ears – *Be there for others but never leave yourself behind.* Well, right now I'm so not here for myself; in fact, I feel invisible.

*You're better than this Lexie,* I think resolutely. *Let them all off. You're done.*

"Pack up. Get the hell out of here!" I tell myself now, jogging back to reverse Frances in again and I carefully tip back the buggy. She sleeps soundly as I catch my reflection in the mirror. I just look like a total fish out of water, exhausted and humiliated.

"You're right, Lexie," I say out loud, sighing. "It's all too much and he's never going to be able to leave here, and you shouldn't make him. He belongs here, you do not."

I gather my small makeup bag and pull off my agonising heels, then chuck them both in my case. I struggle with the zip on the side of the dress and finally reef it off over my head, taking my

243

earrings with it. I throw that in on top. I pack up Frances's bits and set out the nappy bag for travelling with, then I check my watch. Five hours to go.

"Okay, you got this," I try to convince myself.

Annemarie's booked me on the first flight out of here at 6 a.m. I check my phone now; bless her, true to her word, she's checked me in and forwarded me the boarding passes. A light knock on the door, so light I think I imagined it. But there it is again. Oh God, it's him and I don't want to see him. I don't want to have this conversation again.

"Lexie," he hisses through the door.

I ignore him, sit on the case and zip it around.

"Please, let me in?" I can hear the pain in his voice, so I go over and gently pull down the handle.

He slips into the room. "You're leaving." It's not even a question, he knows well.

"Yes." I nod.

"Why?"

"Just don't." I'm so defeated I have no fight left in me.

He leans against the bathroom door, the dim light of the room shadowing him. "I thought we were staying another night, it's Christmas Eve tomorrow? Father Christmas comes to the hotel Christmas morning?" He's chancing his arm, he has to be?

"No." I half laugh at the idea. As if this farce needs to go on any longer. "Definitely not staying."

"Look, you know what they are all like by now. They mean no harm. You know all this." He throws his hands out wide as if to say, *what can I do?*

I sit on the bed. There is a lot he *could* do . . . if he wanted to. "I do."

"So?" He walks towards me, his face coming into the lamplight.

"I don't like the person they turn you into. I don't like who you become around them." That's what I've wanted to say for so long.

"They're my family." His eyes pour into me, pleading.

"And I get that, I really do."

He sits beside me. "I don't know that you do."

"One thing confuses me about your—" I know it's so childish but I do finger quotes anyway, "—family."

"What's that?"

"What are we? Me and Frances?"

"You're my family too." He sounds incredulous now.

"But we don't fit in here."

"You do," he insists.

"We *don't.*"

"Of course you do!" He puts his hand on my hot cheek.

"Well she does, but I don't." I gently remove his hand. "And you know what, I don't care anymore. After the summer, I just, urgh." I shiver.

"Don't let Martha come between us, please?" He gets up from the bed and falls to his knees in front of me, taking my hands in his.

I tense my hands in his. "I swear to God, Adam, if I hear her name in that way one more time I will scream, and I'm not a dramatic person, you know that!"

"She's not worth giving your energy to."

"That's a stupid thing to say." I'm trying to control my temper with him but I'm on the edge here.

"Why?"

"Because she just comes between us, all the time. I'm not a fake person, Adam, I can't pretend."

I realise I'm in my bra and knickers. I let go of his hands, stand up and pull my jeans off the back of the chair. I pull them up and throw on my hoody.

"It will be easier if you move over . . . She will finally—"

"I'm never moving here," I tell him firmly.

"Don't . . . Don't say that," he begs.

"I can't live here." I shake my head so dramatically I hurt my neck.

"You will grow to like them all, I promise."

"I won't, and I don't want to. I like my life at home: I love Dublin, I like my job, I love the old folks I take care of at the weekends, I love my friends. I have Annemarie and Ben to think of too. They are my family. This – this isn't going to work." I drop my face into my hands.

There it is at last. My words rain down on top of us like silent missiles.

"I can't leave Freya," he whispers.

I take my hands away and stand up tall.

"I know, and I don't want you to, but I need more and you can't give it."

"I can, Lexie, please, just give it time. If you really won't come here, I will move to Dublin, you know I will, just two more years until she finishes school."

"I'm not so sure you will," I whisper.

"I will!"

"Oh, I know that you would and even believe that you want to, but things will happen here, things that will keep pulling you back. You . . . You belong here and I—"

A knock on the door, a loud thud.

Frances stirs. I shake the buggy.

"Shush!" I flick my head to the door. "I don't think it's going to be me they want, Adam."

"No, I want to talk," he insists.

A louder bang.

"Fine, get the door," I tell him.

When he opens the door, Deb stands there, two goblets of gin in hand.

"You're not staying in this room all night, are you?" Her eyes wide, she has the tone of surprise.

"I – I . . ." He starts as she thrusts a glass into his hand.

She steps in, sees the buggy, and whispers really loudly, "Oh, Lexie, let him come out to play like a good girl?"

And there it is. It starts in my toes and whooshes up through me. A red mist.

"Adam. Sit with Frances," I command.

I stride past them and take Deb ever so gently by the arm.

"What are you doing?" She wriggles free, almost tripping over the ends of her dress.

"A word," I demand.

I shut the door behind me as quietly as I can. I guide her to the purple, suede bench by the lift.

"What are you doing?" she asks again.

"Listen to me, Deb, I don't want to be here anymore than you all want me here. How dare you or that other crazy wagon change my daughter's clothes? Don't worry, we are leaving in a few hours and with the grace of God you won't ever see me again—"

"Crazy wagon!"

And out she steps from behind the huge plant pot. Her goblet empty. Her eyes blazing.

Martha.

Now in her afters outfit, a white jumpsuit with a skinny gold chain belt and towering suede Louboutin stilettos, she wears her hair in a short, sleek, back ponytail.

Her jaw drops. "You broke up?"

"Yeah, he's all yours." For once, I feel strong in the presence of these two women.

"It's for the best, sweetie," she says with a Cheshire cat grin.

"Don't call me sweetie," I tell her calmly.

"I warned you, we are a big family. I did. I warned you right here, in the ladies at Deb's engagement, that Adam belongs here. You didn't listen to me."

I eyeball her. "Do me a favour, though? Let him live his life. He deserves more."

"I don't owe *you* any favours." Her lips purse in a mean little pucker. She looks me up and down like I'm a piece of crap on her designer shoes.

"Let's go, Martha," Deb tries. Her voice is small and, if I'm hearing her properly, a little shaky.

"The little speech you made at the top of the room to Adam was wildly inappropriate, you both have to see that?" I implore, my hands gesticulating madly. "I mean, come on, your husband-to-be is standing less than a foot from you and you're declaring your undying love to your ex-husband. It was beyond bizarre to sit and listen to." I take great pleasure in telling her this.

"Adam is my soulmate," Martha spits, "so tough shit!" She abandons her empty gin goblet on the wooden ledge of the seat; we all watch it wobble. The metaphor is not lost on me, so I pull myself together.

*Steady, Lexie,* I tell myself.

"I would like for us both to be adults here, Martha. You've made it more than difficult for me over the past three years. But even more difficult for Adam. All the times you have sabotaged us getting together, using Freya as a pawn. The guilt you make him feel. Shame on you. You're not a very nice person."

"Just not to you, because you're a family wrecker."

"Your marriage was well over before I met Adam. You'd been divorced for three years, for crying out loud." I give a flick of my wrist.

She steps closer to me. "True. But we had been getting along better than ever that last year, we'd started to go out on Saturday nights as a family, here, to the Chill Out Bar, we were planning on taking a family holiday after Deb's engagement – isn't that true Deb?"

"It is . . . But then just before my party . . ."

"Adam went on that bloody trip! The Great Tew rugby guys asked him along to Dublin and he wasn't going to go, he said no for ages, but bloody Dominic persuaded him and then he met you!"

"Think your marriage to 'bloody Dominic' might be a bit of a sham!" I spit now. She really is a piece of work.

"Don't you dare judge me or my marriage! You know nothing about me, or any of us. You're a blow-in and that's all you'll ever have been!"

"Oh, I know more than you think." I give my most sarcastic grin.

"Like what?" She sneers.

"Be careful of gossiping in that ladies toilet downstairs, you never know who's listening."

Deb turns a worried look to me. "What does that mean?"

"Or who's recording that conversation on their phone," I add, making the sign of a phone by shaking my thumb and little finger extended on my left hand. I don't have any such recording, but Polly gave me the idea when she confronted Winifred, or whoever the hell that woman is, on the train.

"I couldn't care less what you heard today." Martha huffs, and for the first time I notice how pinched her face is. The cheekbones I once envied, so high and pronounced, look now just like sharp angles in her skeleton.

"Oh no, not today. No, in the summer, when I was here, just after we'd had dinner in the hotel, the dinner you both ruined."

They look at one another, faces pale now.

"You may both recall, I excused myself from the table to go check on Frances and the babysitter up in the room. On the way to the lift I needed the loo, so I popped into the ladies. I was in the last toilet cubicle, just about to walk out, when you two came in." I stop. Anger gallops in me at the memory. "I think it was you, Martha, that started the conversation about how heavy I was and how cheap my dress looked? That the bowl of pasta I was eating was grotesque, a bit like Lardy Lexie herself. You both laughed recalling how you told me it was 'comfy' looking."

"Now hang on – that—" Deb tries but I shush her with another flick of my hand.

"Then you, Deb, commented on how my types never lose the baby weight. That I was guaranteed to let myself go. That people who worked in shopping centres weren't educated about food and fitness." I tilt my head at her, open my eyes wide.

She swallows visibly. "I don't recall ever saying that."

"Well, you did. Maybe you aren't getting enough green leafy veg or fatty fish? You should really check out the Harvard Health Guide to help you with that. Walnuts are good too. Take some time to educate yourself on nutrition." I sneer.

"Let's go, Deb, we don't need to listen to her."

Martha takes Deb's arm, but I step in front of them both.

"Get out of our way." Martha tries to step around me while Deb remains still, like a rabbit in headlights.

"You said I was of a lower class. You also said Adam must still be going through this mid-life crisis and that he was freaking out that I'd got pregnant, so he'd had to propose. Allow me to enlighten you, because you never let the truth get in the way of a good story, Martha. We've told you all a million times, I didn't know I was pregnant when Adam proposed."

"Yeah right!" Martha snorts. "No one bought that!"

"I don't give a shit if you believe me or not, but what I do give a shit about, and think is horrific, is that you told Deb in that toilet that once it got close to the wedding date with Dominic, Adam would come running back."

Her face drops now.

"I—"

"You said time was ticking and Adam needed to step up and get rid of me so that you could call off the wedding to Dominic."

"I'm pretty sure it's illegal to record people's private conversations, by the way," she says feebly, but she looks stunned for once, and Deb mortified.

I shrug. "I'll see you in court so."

"I – I love Dominic . . . I just . . ."

"No you don't."

"Look, just go away, will you! You and Frances, go, leave us all alone!" Martha shouts now.

"Martha . . ." Deb tries.

"We're going. But believe you me, Frances will be back. She belongs here, she is Adam's daughter, Heather and Jeffrey's granddaughter, Freya's half-sister and your niece, Deb, so please be kinder to her than you've ever been to me. That's all I ask."

"We love Frances. I love her to pieces," Deb whimpers.

"If she is even Adam's . . ." Martha fires.

Deb turns to her, her face a mask of shock. "Oh, Martha, don't . . . don't say that." Even for Deb, it's gone too far.

"She is Adam's daughter. Was I supposed to supply you with a DNA test, you lunatic?" I shout.

She stomps to the lift. "I'm not interested in talking to you, never was, never will be."

"You're just a mean-spirited person, Martha," I say to her back. "Adam doesn't love you, and he will never get back with you despite you running me out of his life. And I pity the next person he falls in love with, because you will sabotage her too."

She spins around, her face contorted with fury. "You were never good enough for him."

"Is that so?" I stay as calm as I can, and it seems to rile her up even more.

"Look at you! Look at him! I mean, you're just a . . ." She spits venom now and before she can finish we hear a door slam.

"Enough!"

We all spin around. Adam stands in the corridor. He is breathing very heavily, his chin jutting out, his hands bunched into fists.

"I've heard it all. They said all those things about you, Lexie? Why didn't you tell me?" His eyes are dark and searching mine.

"Where's Frances?" I ask.

"Asleep, there." He nods to the buggy that I can't see obviously, outside the bedroom, blocked by the wall.

"Adam. Let me explain?" Martha tiptoes to stand in front of him. Without sparing her a glance, he steps around her, towards me. Deb stands back a few steps, bows her head.

"It's all true," I tell him.

His eyes are heavy with sorrow. "Why didn't you tell me?"

"I didn't want you to fall out with Deb, I knew it would be a huge row and I never wanted that. I told you, I don't want to come between you and your family."

He turns an incredulous look on his sister. "How could you, Deb?"

She looks sheepish, small and close to tears.

"I – I'm sorry, Lexie. Martha is my best friend, you have to understand that. I was just doing what friends do, I was supporting her. Things were great here with us all. Frank and me had left Ireland and moved back to the Cotswolds, then Adam met you and everything went pear-shaped."

"Deb, for fuck's sake, you of all people know how much I love Lexie!" Adam implodes.

"It's not my fault, Ads," she whimpers like a child.

"Please tell me you haven't married Dominic to get back at me?" Adam says to Martha as he pulls at the dicky bow and reefs it off.

Martha gasps as if horrified at the accusation. "Of course not."

"So what was all that about earlier when you summoned me up to your room the second Lexie arrived?"

"I told you . . . It was nerves, wedding jitters."

"And I believed you, but I don't now – now I think it was something very different. You wanted me to tell you I still love you and call off the wedding, to one of my best friends – I mean, I can't even . . ." He runs his hands through his hair, scratching his fingers through the gel. "And what is *this*?" He holds up a little piece of paper, the one that I found in the room earlier that I left on his bedside table. "You read this, Lexie, I assume? It was on the table, I've never seen it before, I swear to God. I just found it now."

253

Martha shifts from one foot to another. "I was so nervous when I wrote it this morning, I forgot I even put it in your pocket."

"My pocket?" He gasps.

"Oh. Yeah. I found that piece of paper alright, Frances's pacifier was wrapped in it, stinking of Martha's signature scent; I didn't even bother to read it. I could guess it wasn't going to make me happy."

"How did you get this in my pocket?" he asks, anger rocking his voice.

"When we were changing Frances today, I slipped it in," she whines.

"You must have read it?" he says to me.

"I honestly didn't read it, Adam," I tell him. "I could smell her perfume off it and I knew it was going to upset me, I just knew." Still now, I'm sure I don't want to know what's in that note.

"Jesus . . ." He tugs at the chain around his neck.

"I didn't mean it." Martha sounds desperate now. "Adam, I just got cold feet for a few minutes. I needed my best friend, I needed you."

"You aren't my best friend, Martha. I'm not even sure I can be your friend anymore. Can you listen to me, for the last time? Can you do that?"

She nods, biting her bottom lip.

"This note says that you will love me forever. This says—" He holds it up a few inches from his face as he's no glasses on, "—'Adam. I will love you forever. It's never too late.' Well, it is." He crumples the little piece of paper in his hand until his knuckles go white. "Like that." He opens his hand to reveal the crushed paper. "Our relationship is over. It's been over for many years. We share our wonderful daughter and I'm giving all of me, *all of me*, do you hear me, to make Freya happy . . . but I don't—"

"S-stop! Stop right there, mister!" Martha stomps her Louboutins, throwing a tantrum worse than Frances has ever done. "You know it's true, we were going to go on a family holiday before you met her! You know we nearly kissed the night of the village Christmas fête."

Adam looks at me, and he just seems utterly worn out.

"It's true I was planning on going to Barcelona with you and Freya, but that was to make memories for Freya, and I was single. And as I recall, Martha, you pulled me under the mistletoe in the barn at the fête and pointed up to it, and I said I'd hoped we'd both find people to kiss under it the next year."

"This is your last chance, Adam, I'm not kidding . . ." Her voice wobbles.

"Don't . . ." Deb puts her arm around her.

"Why did you marry Dominic?" His voice is lacking any warmth or sympathy.

Tears roll down her face. "Because I don't want to be single for the rest of my life!"

We all hear a ding and the lift doors open slowly. Freya steps out, a large white envelope in her hand.

"Oh!" Her eyes widen. "What's this little gathering all about? Mum, are you okay?"

"Hello, darling." In fairness to Martha, she pulls herself together very quickly. "Oh don't mind me, reminiscing about the good old days, you know what Mummy's like after a few bubblies!"

"Why are you changed, Lexie? The band is about to start." The poor girl looks very confused as her gaze ping-pongs between each of us.

"Ah, I have to leave early, love, I was just telling your mum and dad. Bummer." I slap my thigh.

"Ah no, that is such a shame! I hoped we could do some Christmas shopping tomorrow. I saw these earrings I want to buy you but I'd like you to choose the size. Hoops, of course." She smiles at me.

Deb presses the button on the lift. "I believe there is a wedding going on? I better get the bride back!" She jabs again and again, the button rattling beneath her finger.

"Yes, indeed. I've been AWOL long enough." Martha smooths down her jumpsuit, tugs at the gold chain belt and then pulls the collar up. "It's time to get my new life well and truly started. I'm a very lucky woman to have a man like Dominic who adores me. Well, so long Lexie, we look forward to having Frances back with us soon." Martha extends her hand as if nothing has just happened.

"Congratulations to you both again and Merry Christmas, Martha." I take her hand. I will not let this affect Freya. I will not be that person.

"Actually, guys, have you all got another minute?" Freya asks us all hopefully.

"Sure, darling," Adam says, his voice trying to sound normal but his breath still heavy.

"Not here, can we go into your room?" She nods towards the door behind us all.

The lift doors open and we all look at one another.

"Sure, darling, of course," Martha says and walks in front of us with Deb slightly behind. It's the first time I've seen them together where they weren't literally joined at the hip. Maybe Deb is processing all this, I hope.

"Go ahead, give us two minutes, push Frances in, will you?" Adam says to Freya.

They all clear the lobby and Adam takes my hands.

He heaves a deep, exhausted sigh. "You're right. You've always been right, it's totally dysfunctional this Martha situation. I'm worn out trying to please everyone. I love you. I can't tell you how much. I made up my mind. I'm coming with you in the morning. I'm – I'm moving to Dublin. I'm relocating. My mind is made up." He pulls me into his strong arms.

"But what about Freya . . . You can't . . ." I look up at him, I feel so bad.

"I have to or I'll lose you." His dark eyes are intense with meaning.

"It's not that, I would never put that choice out there. It's just I need you to know I won't . . . I can't move over here to live alongside these people, ever."

"I get it now, I really do." He puts his lips on mine, kisses me passionately.

"Eh? Excuse me, lovebirds? Can you come in?" Freya holds the door open with one foot. "I really need to speak to you both as well."

Adam takes my hand and we walk into the room. I stand by the buggy parked under the window. Frances snores, oblivious to her extended family's shenanigans, and she melts my heart. Martha and Deb perch on the end of my bed. The room is a total mess and I couldn't care less.

"So. I have news. I got in!" Freya squeals, waving the white envelope above her head, then whacks her hand over her mouth, eyeing up the buggy.

"What?" Adam asks.

"Ireland, here I come! I got in! I got a place on the course builders course. I move to Ireland in February for two years. I

257

will train five days a week, weekends are my own." She pulls the letter out, hands it to Adam. "It was in the Campbells' letterbox! Of all the times for Lar to make a wrong delivery!" Her cheeks are flushed and her eyes dance.

"Oh wow!" I clap my hands, turn and embrace her, then release her like a scalded cat, realising her mother should be there first. Frances still doesn't stir. Maybe my mother is right after all, maybe the silent tiptoeing around a sleeping baby isn't the way.

"That is incredible! I knew you'd do it! I'm so proud of you." Adam hugs her tightly as I turn my eyes to Martha. She's sobbing quietly into her hands, Deb's arm around her again.

"Congratulations, my darling," Deb says. "We are all so proud of you." And I can tell she really means it.

"Oh Mum, don't cry. It's only for two years, then I'll be back. You know my plan is to build courses in the UK. It's my dream to build that Puissance Wall at the Horse of the Year Show at the NEC in Birmingham one day. You'll be a long time getting rid of me while I save to buy my own yard eventually. I love the Cotswolds, I love our village, but this is a really good school, the best there is!" Freya sounds, as always, so much wiser than her years.

"Knock knock! Where's my trouble and strife? Do I have a wife?" Dominic steps in, jacket discarded, half a pint of Guinness in hand.

"Hey buddy." Adam strides over to him and claps his shoulder.

"What's wrong? What's going on here?" He sees Martha in tears but he immediately looks to Adam. Adam shakes his head, dips his eyes. Dominic is no fool, I suddenly realise, he knows Martha still carries more than a torch for Adam, but he's also Adam's best friend and he knows it's not reciprocated. Dominic is also divorced and I do recall Adam telling me he was a broken man when his wife left him, so maybe it's a two-way thing with these two. Maybe, just maybe, they will help one another get over their exes.

"What's the matter, darling?" He puts his pint on the dressing table, hunkers down in front of Martha.

"Freya's leaving." She pants and tears flow, and flow and flow. Dominic just holds her, turns his head after a few moments, and winks at Freya, giving her a thumbs up.

"Dad, we got this. You go home with Lexie and Frances, if you need to?" Freya says, calmly.

Adam nods.

"I do." And those two words mean more from him right here, right now, than they will at any altar, ever. They are all the commitment I need.

"And we need to get back to our guests," says Dominic. "There's a Take That tribute band we're paying through the nose for waiting for you to start. Grab me some tissues Deb, can you, chuck?"

Subtly Dominic moves Deb away from Martha and pulls her up. Deb goes to the bathroom, returns with rolled-up toilet paper, and Martha blows her nose.

"See you down there, Freya, darling, don't be long – we're having mushroom vol-au-vents soon, your favourite." Martha reaches across and pats her daughter's arm. "I'm so happy for you, and proud, I know how hard you've worked and how much you want this."

"Be right down, Mum." Freya kisses her on the cheek.

Dominic knocks out a salute to us and takes Martha and Deb with him. Just before the heavy door slams behind them, Deb says, "Safe trip, Lexie, I'll be in touch." And then they are gone.

I feel like someone just lifted the witch's house off my chest.

Frances whimpers softly.

Freya pushes the letter back into the envelope. "Listen, I'm relying on you guys coming to see me every weekend you can, right? I hear there is an amazing outlet called Kildare Shopping Village?"

"Oh it's brilliant." Now my tears are falling as I nod madly. I want nothing more than to take this lovely girl to Kildare Shopping Village every weekend!

"By the way, Lexie, I'm not sure if Dad spoke to you, but Grandad Maxwell left me a college fund and the estate says I can dip into it now for this, so it won't cost Mum and Dad a penny." Again her maturity amazes me.

"That's brilliant, and we are both thrilled for you," I gush.

"Settled then." She beams.

"I need to book my flight, hang on!" Adam says, rummaging in his pocket. "From Birmingham?" I nod, check my own phone quickly to give him the time and flight number, and he types at speed on his phone.

Freya steps closer to me as I tilt the buggy back up and lift Frances out.

"You are the best thing to ever happen to him, Lexie," she says quietly, and it's so from the heart that it really hits home.

"And you," I tell her right back.

"*We* are," Freya corrects us both. She kisses Frances on top of her head. "The three of us are, and we love him."

I drape my free hand around her shoulder. "Yes. We do."

"I love my mum, Lexie, so much, but she's never got over Dad and she never will. Between you and me, I give this marriage a year." She shrugs as she runs her finger along Frances's cheek.

"I dunno, love," I say, laying Frances softly on the bed now. "Maybe they can help each other. Maybe they just both need to move on, open a new chapter?" I want her to have hope for her mum's new relationship.

"Maybe. Let's see, shall we? I love my grandparents to bits but do you notice how they dip in briefly to family occasions now?" *She's so insightful,* I think, not for the first time. Nothing gets past this girl.

I nod in agreement. "I said that to your dad only last week."

"It's because Aunt Deb is always stirring things. Deb thrives on drama. Gramps and Gram don't like that. They are, by nature, relaxed, quiet people. I love how chill Dad is when he gets back from Dublin on a Monday, but then I watch him start to stress and he's worn out by the end of the week with everyone pulling at him, Mum especially. He needs to be in Dublin. And now that I'm going to move out, he's finally free." Her enthusiasm is infectious.

"Our apartment is your home too, you know that, right? You don't need to stay in Kildare unless you want to. This is your family too, your dad, me and Frances." I mean every word. And then the parting conversation I'd had with my mother falls lightly into my head once more as I left her at the gate for Malaga only yesterday, which seems like a lifetime ago already. I watch Freya and Adam embrace as I recall.

"Let go of what other people think of you, Lexie. You're just assuming Adam's family don't like you," she'd said to me.

"They don't, I overheard a conversation," I'd told her honestly.

She'd given a stiff sniff to the air. "I see, dear. Well, in that case, another person's opinion of you is their business, not yours."

"Still hurts, though," I'd admitted.

"I know, but if you worry and stress over things that you have no control over, you'll only suffer twice."

I'd let that sink in as I'd glanced up at the board to see my gate open and boarding.

"And remember this, there is always good that comes out of bad." There was a twinkle in her eye as she delivered these parting words.

I'd wrapped her in a long hug. "Goodbye, Mam, I loved spending this time with you."

"And me, dear, so tell me, what will you do?" She'd removed her glasses, eyeballed me.

"I'll be there for others, but I'll never leave myself behind." I'd laughed and waved her goodbye.

I'm proud of myself for standing up to Martha and Deb. I didn't leave myself or my dignity behind. I think my mother would be very proud of me!

Freya jolts me back. "Dad says you guys were looking at houses?"

"We were . . . Just being nosy really, seeing what's out there. Your dad would never have left here . . ."

"It's time, really," she says, determinedly.

"And I never, ever wanted him to leave you, I just needed him to know it wasn't going to work with me moving over here," I tell her, honestly.

"Totally. I could never see you here, Lexie, I told Dad that, you're too much of a city girl."

"I guess, though I'd love a house by the coast one day." I can dream.

"I'd love to come on the nosing next time?"

"Of course, we need to start saving but your input will be invaluable!"

Frances starts to murmur, then cries out.

"Right. I got a seat," says Adam. "It's the regional Aer Lingus, so only two seats together, but I'm across the aisle from you. We better go because check-in is at four-thirty and the roads are very snowy, I want the driver to snail along." Adam gets the cases as I quicky change Frances's nappy, hand her a rice cake and strap her back in the buggy. She sucks on the yogurt topping happily, swinging her chubby legs. I do one final room check and close the door. The four of us wait for the lift in glorious, comfortable silence. As the lift travels down, Adam puts his arm around Freya.

"I'm so proud of you, my girl." The pure love in his voice melts my heart. *Frances, you are also a very lucky little girl,* I think.

"I'm prouder of you, Dad," Freya says and hugs him tightly. We say our goodbyes as the lift doors slide open and she rejoins the wedding party.

In the lobby a drunken crowd sway to the beat of "Have Yourself a Merry Little Christmas". I push Frances to the revolving doors. Outside, the snow glistens a bright white against the dark night and falls softer now as we are hit with the freezing air. *From now on your troubles will be miles away,* someone sings at the top of their voice inside.

"Are you really sure this is what you want?" I ask Adam for the final time.

"I feel like I'm finally starting my life over. Be there for others but never leave yourself behind, as a wise woman once told me." Adam laughs, expelling a long breath that I can physically see on this cold night as I stop abruptly.

I shake my head at his familiar words. "When?" I gasp.

"The night she came home early from your dinner, we had a long chat."

I chuckle. "Well, well, well, Barbara Byrne strikes again. And she's bang on, it is time we both put ourselves first for a change. We are good people, we deserve to be together and to be happy."

The yellow taxi plate light casts a warm glow around us as we gather by the waiting cab.

Adam turns me to him.

"Is it actually love, Lexie Byrne? Do you think we will make it?" His eyes are watering.

"It is and I do," I tell him, more sure of us than I've ever been of anything in my entire life. I rest my forehead against his. We are still for just a moment out here in the cold night air, listening to the fading revellers inside.

"Let's go home," Adam says, wiping his eyes, then kisses me softly.

"Home." I nod with my heart full of love and hope.

# Epilogue

*"The thing about romance is people only get together right at the very end."*

Sam, *Love Actually*

"I CAN'T BELIEVE IT'S OURS!" I draw in a sharp breath, staring up at the SOLD sign planted in the garden of the home we have secured.

Adam drapes his strong arm over my shoulder. "Well, it is."

"Look, Frances. Look at our new home," Freya says as Frances crawls unsteadily around the grass in the hot August sunshine.

"Serio hun, it's totes amazeballs!" Jackie roars at the top of her voice.

"Bloody hell Jackie. My ears!" Annemarie lets go of Tom's hand, clasping her hands over her ears.

"We both work hard," Adam says to me. "You in Sir Patrick Dun's and me at the Beacon Hospital. We've bloody well earned this." He takes a hefty swig from his bottle of water. I know his nerves are slightly shot from this buy and the new mortgage, but we'll be fine.

I gaze up at our three-bed bungalow in Dalkey, on the coast of Dublin. A three-minute walk from the village. My dream location and Adam feels so at home here too. The house is whitewashed with black shutters on the bay windows. It's a beauty and we got it for a steal. A colleague of Adam's wanted a quick sale as they were relocating to Los Angeles and it didn't go to market. Although the repayments are huge, Adam's rental money in Rosehill to four young doctors helps us out no end.

"It's literally her dream. D'ya remember how she used to go on about owning a gaff in Dalkey?" Jackie licks her ice cream cone, twisting the wafer in her hand.

I glance at my watch. "I have to go!"

"I'm coming with you, Tom's taking Ben to the Vico baths for a swim," Annemarie says. "I'm not missing this."

"Can you believe it?" Adam pulls me close. I look into his eyes.

"It took a few weeks to sink in that Kevin found the tapes and that she was coming up, but I'm so excited . . . and emotional." I'm wild with want and excitement. I snatch his face between my hands and kiss him passionately.

"Oh that you are." Adam laughs loudly as he pulls away. "Come on, we'll drop you."

"Meet yiz in the Brazen Head for a few scoops after my play comes down later?" Jackie asks. "I'll go for a dip with Tom and Ben."

*Life works in mysterious ways,* I think as we all cross the road towards the glistening blue sea and pile into Adam's trusty Volvo. Annemarie sits in the back with me and Frances and we make small talk on the drive. At Sir Patrick Dun's, Kathleen is already there, sitting by the fireplace, smartly dressed in a suit jacket and pencil skirt. We embrace tightly as Ciara, one of the assistants, wheels in the tea trolley. I pour us all a cup and Annemarie unwraps the tinfoil from fresh homemade blueberry muffins she baked for us.

"Thank you, Lexie, Annemarie," Kathleen says. I catch the sparkle of her mother's ring on her hand as she takes the cup.

"How's Jim?" I enquire.

"Not bad, tired, but finally content – and I only have you to thank for that." She beams at me.

"You ready?" I say gently, putting my cup down.

"I've been ready since the day I could talk." Her hand doesn't shake, she seems steady and in control of her emotions, unlike me.

I take the DVD from my leather bag, open the box and remove the shiny round disc.

"Are you ready to meet your mother? This is Máiréad Farrell," I say as I slide it into the player and close it.

Kathleen turns rapt eyes to the big screen, holding her chest.

I rest my hands across my massive bump. An unexpected Christmas present, due in two weeks. Conceived the night Adam and myself got home from the Cotswolds to Dublin to start our new lives.

Kevin sticks his head around the door. "All set?"

"Yes!" I say as Kevin, now my boss, pulls the heavy curtains and the room falls dark.

"Thanks for this Kevin, you are all so kind," I tell him, the remote control tight in my hand.

"I'm just so glad I found them and was able to make this DVD, not just for you guys but for all the residents to enjoy. Come on now, put your feet up," he tells me.

"I tell you one thing." I lift my legs up. "Little Johnny Castle in here is doing the merengue." I squirm with the movement inside.

"You're really calling him Johnny?" Kevin asks.

"Of course, I am. Johnny Castle Cooper." As if there was ever a choice.

We all sit back as I hit play, the DVD player shakes, then springs to life. My face fills the screen, then I move off and there she is. Máiréad.

It's the day I got her into Sir Patrick Dun's. A safe place for her to live and be well looked after, at last.

"How can I ever thank you, Lexie?" Máiréad smacks her lips as she pushes her squeaky, gingham shopping trolley down the long corridor.

My eyes start to leak, and my throat closes up. "Oh my . . ."

"Oh Lord above . . ." Kathleen takes in a big gulp of breath.

"You deserve this, Máiréad, you've worked hard all your life," I tell her in the video.

I steal a look at Kathleen, who is sitting forward on her chair, her chin in her hands, positively beaming.

I walk side by side with my old friend on the screen.

"Who's recording?" I ask Kevin, momentarily taking my eye off the image.

"Me," he whispers. "Keep watching."

The camera follows us as I open the door to her bedroom, pushing it wide open so she can get the wheelie in.

Máiréad's eyes light up. "This is . . . my room?"

"All yours." I perch my hands on my hips. The feelings of how happy I was for her in that moment all flood through me again like warm morning sunshine on my face.

She shakes her head. "How can I ever thank you?"

"You can gimmie a hug?" I tell her. Watching myself, my heart is thudding and my fingertips are tingling.

"This is just the best thing I could ever wish for. Look at her. Look at my mammy." And now Kathleen cries, and they are deep, heaving sobs. "S-she had so m-much sadness, so much heartbreak, b-but there was you Lexie Byrne, a k-kind soul who helped her and made her last days f-full of warmth and love." The longing after all these years in Kathleen's voice is borderline unbearable. She can't sniff up anymore so she blows her nose, and a huge, beaming smile covers her face. "You are an angel," she tells me happily.

I'm just about to protest but suddenly I really see myself. I lift my feet and stand up very slowly, hands clutching my lower back. Closer to the screen. I don't see what I might have a few years ago. I remember how those black jeans I'm wearing in the video made me feel big, too tight, and pushed out my muffin top. I remember those runners I'm wearing, how when I tried them on in the shop another woman had the same pair on and I thought they looked so much better on her with her long, slim legs. I move back. I stand behind Kathleen, put my hands on both her shoulders, and she places her hands over mine.

I remember I'd just met Adam and I was terrified it was not going to last. I didn't think that a man like him would fall in love with someone like me. But he did. And I wish now, as I watch a beaming Máiréad pick up the lilac bedspread and feel the quality, I wish that I'd had this confidence years ago. I wish I could see how fantastic those black jeans looked on me, and how cool the three-striped runners were.

And then the video edit jumps and we are in the communal living area with the pool table Adam bought for the centre.

Máiréad is wearing a pink party hat and a "Who's A Birthday Girl Then?" satin sash. I am fussing around her, fixing her wheelchair and running a brush through her remaining few hairs.

"Happy Birthday, Máiréad!" I sing, as Ciara comes through the door with a cream sponge birthday cake topped with flickering candles, and Annemarie carries a beautifully wrapped gift.

"That makes you look old!" Margaret Kilroy says, giddily.

"That's Margaret, she became your mam's best friend in here," I explain to Kathleen.

"Is she still here? Still alive?" Kathleen asks hopefully.

"She's passed too now, I'm afraid," Kevin says softly. "They're winning at bingo, eating sponge cake together up above, no doubt."

"Big blow!" I direct Máiréad in the video as I crouch down beside her and take her hands in mine. She leans over, the light from the candles twinkling in her kind, weathered face. She blows, the smoke rises and the fluorescent light flickers on as we all clap and cheer.

"I made my wish, Lexie," Máiréad informs me.

"Don't tell me," I say, "or it might not come true." I press a finger to my lips.

"Look down, Lexie," Máiréad says so quietly that I get a shiver down my spine. I vividly recall this moment right now. In the video, I look down to the ground, but there is nothing there, and I look over at Annemarie and we smile. But now, in this moment, I look down to Kathleen holding my hands just as the bells ring out for Mass and I know for sure her wish came through and I have a guardian angel.

# Acknowledgements

THANK YOU TO MY wonderful publishers at Black & White Publishing, Campbell Brown, Thomas Ross and all the fantastic team.

Extra special thanks to Ali McBride, Publishing Director, and Clem Flanagan, my hard-working, eagle-eyed, super creative editor. Thank you both, so much, for all the Zoom chats and the dedicated hard work you've put into the Lexie Byrne series – it was much appreciated.

And you, dear reader, most of all, thank you, thank you, thank you.

# Hi, I'm Caroline!

© Leonan Ribeiro

*I'm a bestselling author of ten novels, a screenwriter, lover of wine(s), hot summer days, a very proud mammy to my two amazing girls, Grace and Maggie, and lucky wife to Kevin.*

*I'm a Creative Director at Document Films, where I'm currently in development with TV and film projects.*

*I'm also a regular contributor on TV, radio and magazines.*

*I really hope you enjoy the final instalment of Lexie Byrne. I've loved writing this series, almost as much as I love to hear from you, dear reader, so please do reach out on any of the platforms!*

📷 *@carolinegracecassidy*

🐦 *@CGraceCassidy*

📘 *@authorcarolinegracecassidy*

*Or my linktr.ee/carolinegracecassidy*

# Also by
# Caroline Grace-Cassidy

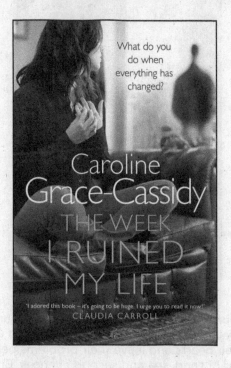

Ali Devlin isn't the type of woman to have an affair...

But as her marriage to her childhood sweetheart Colin turns bitter, she begins to rediscover the woman she once was.

*"I adored this book – it's going to be huge.
I urge you to read it now!"*
**CLAUDIA CARROLL**

Sometimes you just need to put yourself first...

Caroline Grace-Cassidy

THE IMPORTANCE OF BEING ME

"Caroline Grace-Cassidy's writing shines with sparkling wit and warmth. An absolute treat." *Cathy Kelly*

When Courtney is offered a job in beautiful, sun-kissed Cornwall, she and her vivacious best friend Claire follow their hearts and leave their problems behind for a summer of sand, sea and second chances. But when she meets sexy but infuriating builder Tony, Courtney rediscovers her passions for life, for cooking and for love.

*"Caroline Grace-Cassidy's writing shines with sparkling wit and warmth. An absolute treat."*

**CATHY KELLY**

'Hilarious, witty and full of heart. I loved it!'
Carmel Harrington

IRISH TIMES BESTSELLER

## AN IRISH TIMES BESTSELLER

Ava and her trusty bride squad set off on an
unforgettable Irish roadtrip. Along the way there's
ice-cream vans, roguish strangers and a very handsome
Frenchman. Join them for this laugh-out-loud,
feel-good romance with a twist.

*"Hilarious, witty and full of heart. I loved it!"*

**CARMEL HARRINGTON**

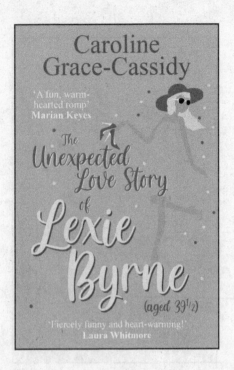

Meet Lexie Byrne. The big 4-0 is looming, but she's perfectly content without a man. How else could she watch movies on repeat and eat crisp sandwiches in bed? Finally free of her love-rat ex, she's never settling again.

Nothing less than 'The One' will do. An irresistible love story . . . delivered with sparkle and wit.

*"A fun, warm-hearted romp."*

**MARIAN KEYES**

*"Fiercely funny and heart-warming."*

**LAURA WHITMORE**